He saved her,
he cared for her,
he loved her.
He was her keeper,
and she was his prisoner.

During a wild rainstorm in a remote, wooded area of the deep South, Wayne Crocker rescues a young woman from her husband's car after it plunges off a bridge. Wayne takes her to his secluded trailer, where his fantasies of having a woman of his own finally become a reality.

Dazed from her near-fatal ordeal, Nancy Barnett awakens as Wayne is stripping her of her wet clothing, and is sure she's being raped. Unable to convince her of his innocence, and propelled by fear, guilt, and passion, Wayne ties her up and imprisons her in his trailer.

———————

Here is a story of longing and suspense . . . and the secrets of a woman held captive by the man who longs to be her

KEEPER

KEEPER

MICHAEL GARRETT

KNIGHTSBRIDGE PUBLISHING COMPANY

NEW YORK

Published in the United States by
Knightsbridge Publishing Company
255 East 49th Street
New York, New York 10017

ISBN: 1-877961-37-X

10 9 8 7 6 5 4 3 2 1
FIRST EDITION

For Jeff Gelb,
the best of friends
whose support and encouragement
made it all possible.
Special thanks also to
Colleen Dimson
for her belief in me.

PROLOGUE

November 1965

The few who met him as he traveled west considered him a bit peculiar. His jumpiness and strong Southern accent attracted attention, as well as the condition of his '60 Chevy Impala. Its bronze finish was covered with a thick blanket of dust, and its back seat, like a mobile footlocker, was piled high with personal belongings — books, records, a guitar, and several pairs of old shoes. The car's Alabama license plate confirmed that the driver was a long way from home.

Debbie Statten of Starkville, Mississippi spoke to him briefly at an all-night café. She scanned his six-foot frame, his brown hair and blue eyes, and estimated his age to be in the early twenties. She was attracted to him despite his shyness and general lack of confidence, the latter obvious from his stance — shoulders drooping, head slightly hanging. She knew he was from Alabama, having glanced at a dusty bumper sticker on his car that said something about Bear Bryant and the Crimson Tide. But this guy who called himself "Bob" didn't fit the typical image of a man of the road. And when she asked what town he was from he hesitated — it was as if he couldn't make up his mind.

When he found the young man asleep at a roadside picnic table, Red Bates of Lubbock, Texas also felt suspicious about the young traveler. Having been a recent victim of vandalism, Bates considered calling the police, but decided against it after hearing the boy's story — he was en route to Tucson to live with his brother, and anyone moving *that* far from home was *bound* to be a bit nervous. But still, Bates had wondered later if he shouldn't have called the law after all.

Other Texans kept a watchful eye on the young man as he passed from town to town. To many, he was obviously running from something, and as long as he *kept on* running, it was fine with them. But others felt sympathy for the boy after a closer look. He seemed withdrawn — nervous and afraid — and certainly not a threat to anyone.

The steering wheel slipped beneath Wayne Crocker's sweaty grasp as New Mexico slid behind him. The miles seemed to pass as slowly as the months and years, as he held to a speed below seventy miles per hour. Crossing into Arizona, he drove in a trance-like state, his face pale, his eyes seldom blinking, red and swollen from lack of sleep.

The faceless towns were like backdrops from cheap cowboy movies, the scrubby southwestern desert stretching endlessly around them. Until now, Wayne had never ventured more than three hundred miles from home, and he hardly noticed or cared about the oppressiveness of the arid countryside he was driving through. His thoughts were centered on Alabama, back home with the people he loved. He hoped to return some day, though heaven only knew if or when or under what circumstances he'd go back.

Soon Tucson lay in the distant past. There was no brother, of course, and he hated traveling under an alias. Neither did he know where in California his final destination might be. He wanted only to put more distance between himself and Alabama.

And somehow maintain his sanity.

Running a hand through his unwashed hair, Wayne glanced at the rearview mirror for what must have been the tenth time during the last half hour. All clear. Still, he cautiously dropped his speed to a steady sixty-five. No need to attract the cops for a mere speeding violation.

He stroked the stubbled growth of his unshaven face and wondered what was happening back home, what his friends and relatives thought of him now. Poor Mom. As if a drunken husband hadn't been enough to complicate her life — now she had a fugitive son to worry about as well. She probably knew by now he had disappeared. But she would never understand. No one would.

Ever.

Wayne tuned the radio to a fading Tucson

station, crackles of interference interrupting the Stones as they wailed "Get Off Of My Cloud". For weeks, it had been his favorite song but now he could hardly enjoy it. The music stopped, and he listened anxiously to an intervening newscast but there was no news from back home. Not that he had really expected to hear anything, having travelled so far from the South. And as a commercial announced that "What's New, Pussycat?" was now playing at the Saguaro Drive-In, Wayne silenced the radio and yawned.

As an orange sunset seared the horizon, his eyelids grew heavy. Wayne's only concern now was to get some sleep.

On the outskirts of Gila Bend, he spotted the Cactus Motel and checked his wallet. Not much cash left — less than fifty dollars. Soon he would be forced to find a temporary job before moving on.

As the Chevy rolled to a stop in the motel's unpaved parking lot, the cloud of dust trailing it, settled on the now motionless vehicle, adding to its unsightly accumulation of dirt. Wayne registered under the alias of "Bob Evans", the name of his childhood Boy Scout leader, and after checking into Room 7, was satisfied that the five dollars it had cost was well worth the long needed rest it would provide.

The room was small and relatively clean, boasting only a double bed, a dresser with a broken mirror, and a portable black-and-white Motorala television set. The aluminum foil covering the chrome TV antenna rods, reminded him of Uncle Ed's blurry set back home. Wayne walked over to the room's only window and gazed at a flickering A & W sign across the highway. He pulled down the shade and retired to the bathroom where he flicked on a dim overhead light, and yawned.

Glancing at a mirror above the sink, Wayne remembered how he'd tried to rid his face of unwanted freckles as a child. He yawned again and drew back a pale yellow shower curtain.

Surrounded by fading seahorses on a worn blue tile, the bathtub was scarred with an assortment of stains and scratches. Testing the flow of warm water from the faucet, Wayne shed his clothes and immersed himself in the tub, reclining as best he could within its confined space. Hoping to experience a few moments of peaceful solitude, he closed his eyes and consciously expelled all thoughts from his mind. A steady drip from the faucet slowly pulled him to sleep, but the blasting horn of a transfer truck outside quickly jarred him back to reality.

After preparing himself for bed, Wayne collapsed across the sagging mattress, lying on his back to examine a maze of cracks across the room's plaster ceiling. The intersecting lines criss-crossed in a weblike pattern and he remembered a silly old horror flick, "The Spider", he had seen with his cousin only a half dozen years before.

Squeaky bedsprings sang in the dimly lit room as Wayne tossed and turned for comfort. How many girls have been laid in this bed? he wondered. They had likely stared at this same ceiling while sweaty studs sprawled all over them and thoughtlessly grinded away.

With eyes closed, Wayne prayed, begging God for forgiveness and pleading that he be given a second chance to start his life anew.

"I don't blame You, Lord, if You feel I'm not worthy," he mumbled, his voice cracking and tears running from his swollen eyes. "I know I only come to You when I need help. But, God, I've lived a decent life till now. And, Lord, I was so lonely, I hardly knew what I was doing."

Memories flooded into Wayne's mind — how, in grammar school, he'd been quiet and withdrawn, his face stinging with embarrassment when a teacher scolded him before his classmates. How he had been voted "Most Likely To Succeed" in the eighth grade. How he had painfuly shied away from girls through high school.

Females.

Why had he been so self-conscious around them? Why had his stomach always twisted into knots at the sight of a pretty girl? Why had he never learned to relax around the opposite sex? Why had the problem only grown worse as the years passed?

Leaning over the mattress, Wayne fetched his crumpled trousers from the floor. Turning on the light, he removed his wallet from the hip pocket, and slid a wrinkled Polaroid snapshot from a hidden compartment inside.

She looked pitiful in the photo, half-naked, unconscious and bruised. But her beauty was not to be denied as she lay there with her breasts exposed, asleep and unaware she was being photographed. Till then, Wayne had been a hero. But only moments after the shutter snapped, the nightmare had begun.

His eyes were locked on the wrinkled photo. She was so vulnerable, so innocent, he realized. Her torment had been far worse than his own.

Nancy. I'm so sorry for what I've done to you. And I'd give anything to take it all back. I only hope you understood before I . . . I . . .

The crunch of gravel from slow moving tires jarred Wayne's thoughts. The police? Quickly he bounded to the window and peeked outside. In the waning light, a tall cowboy was helping a homely, young lady from a pickup truck and escorting her to the room next door. Breathing a sigh of relief, Wayne turned out the lights and returned to bed.

Why did I do it? he wondered. *Why didn't I quit while I was ahead?*

He remembered the freezing river, the panic he'd experienced when she confronted him with a knife, the trail of blood down the hallway.

Screeching bedsprings soon sounded from the adjoining room, accompanied by a steady pounding on the wall. Wayne could tell by the rhythmic clump-clump-clump that the two were making love, their frenzied movement forcing their bed's headboard to strike repeatedly against the wall. He could hear the woman beg for more, gasping with every thrust as even the broken dresser mirror in Wayne's own room began to rattle.

Suddenly the tempo intensified, the bedsprings singing even louder amid a chorus of muffled moans and groans. Lying in his bed, listening to their passionate cries, Wayne felt as if salt had been poured on his own wounded pride. Finally, with the dying ovation of simultaneous release, the noise abated, and silence returned to the Cactus Motel.

The corner of Wayne's pillow was wet from tears. He rolled his head to find a dry spot and tried to sleep, but his mind was racing and unwilling to succumb.

Nancy's image haunted him again, refusing to fade. He remembered the ropes he'd bound her with, the look of fear and confusion on her face as they lay naked on his bed and he explored her flawless body. Wayne longed to hear her voice, yearned for her touch, but the tears returned with such force that he finally had to turn over his soaked pillow to avoid the dampness.

Knowing he did not have the right to feel sorry for himself, Wayne dried his eyes, but it was no use. Badly in need of rest, he tossed and turned but couldn't help thinking of all he'd lost, and all that might have been.

How he yearned to feel the desire of an understanding woman, to have her hold him and draw him inside her — a pleasure in life he had never known.

And yet he had come so close.

So very close.

1

One Week Earlier
Friday
Day One

Sliding a bulky suitcase into the trunk of his 1963 Ford Falcon, Charlie Barnett slammed the lid and glanced disgustedly at his wife, Nancy. As usual, she had packed twice as much as she'd actually need for a weekend trip.

"Is that it?" he snarled.

"I think so," she said, opening the passenger door.

Without a word, Charlie cranked the engine and slowly backed the loaded Falcon from the parking space.

"*Wait!*" she exclaimed. "I forgot my records!"

"Aw, shit!" Charlie groaned. "Didn't I ask if that was everything? *Jesus!*"

Nancy darted from the car and hastily made her way up the stairs and into their apartment. The record albums were stacked neatly on the sofa, right where she'd left them. But now Charlie would complain that she'd been absent-minded again. And he'd also be aggravated that she was taking the records. Just because she happened to like different music was no reason for him to be so irritable. But that was Charlie. His nature seemed to evolve around impatience and narrow-mindedness.

Frantically she raced back to the car, the albums cradled in her arms.

"Okay," she said, catching her breath as she pulled the passenger door closed. "Let's go."

"Did you remember to lock the door?" he asked.

"Oh, no . . . I'm not sure."

"Well, that's great," he said, raising both hands from the steering wheel. "Maybe while we're gone, some asshole will walk through the door and steal your record player. At least then I wouldn't have to listen to this shit anymore."

Angrily, he cranked the ignition and revved the engine.

"I'm sorry," Nancy apologized. "I'll check it."

Upon returning to the door of her modest Columbus, Georgia apartment, Nancy wondered why she had tried to make amends. Everyone forgets at one time or another, especially when travel is involved; there's always so much to do to prepare for a few days away. But, of course, she'd only be gone over the weekend and possibly not even *that* long, if Charlie embarrassed her with his short temper and forced an early departure. Sometimes he was impossible to live with . . .

Sliding back into the passenger seat, she huffed to catch her breath. "Well, it was locked after all," she said laughing. "But sure as the world, if I hadn't checked, some thief would've robbed us blind."

Charlie glanced at the stack of records on her lap. On top was *Beatles '65*. Noticing the movement of his eyes Nancy knew what he was going to say next.

"Why did you have to bring that shit anyway?" he complained. "Can't you live without that stuff for two days?"

Nancy returned an equally perturbed stare.

"Liz just bought a new stereo, and she likes the Beatles," Nancy said. "And besides, nobody will force you to listen. If you don't like it, you can sit in your car and listen to Johnny Cash on the radio."

Charlie backed the car onto the street and headed for the nearby Highway 280 intersection. The tires screeched as he floored the accelerator.

"So what's wrong with Johnny Cash?" he snarled back at her.

"Nothing. Absolutely nothing. And what's wrong with Ringo singing 'Honey Don't' — *that's* country, too."

"Hell, that ain't country," answered Charlie. "That's makin' fun of country."

Taking a sharp right onto Highway 280, Charlie glared silently ahead. With a sigh, Nancy slumped back in her seat. His belligerent behavior was one of the reasons their marriage was dangerously near its end, she feared. She often wondered what had brought them together in the first place. They shared little in common, their personalities often clashed, and their philosophies were vastly different. They had been high school sweethearts, and, of course, physical attraction had played a major role in the development of their relationship. But after three years of "wedded bliss," Nancy had finally realized that sex alone was not enough to keep a marriage together. And in recent weeks, their sex life had diminished altogether. Nancy took a deep breath. Why had life suddenly grown difficult? It would be so nice to be a kid again.

Of course, everyone has problems, she realized, straightening up in her seat. Her cousin Liz back in Selton, Alabama had recently suffered heartbreak of her own. In fact, that was why she and Charlie were visiting Liz, to attempt to cheer her up. But deep inside, Nancy felt that the deterioration of her *own* life took precedence. Who would *she* lean on for moral support?

Within minutes the travelers crossed the state line into Alabama and the Central Time Zone. Charlie wrung a Timex from his left wrist and tossed it atop the albums in Nancy's lap.

"Run this thing back an hour, will you?"

Nancy promptly obeyed and handed the watch back to him.

"Let's try to make this a pleasant trip — *please*?" she asked. Charlie scowled ahead unflinchingly.

"I don't want Liz and her folks to know about our problems," she continued. "Liz has enough troubles of her own. And I think it'll be good for us to get out of town and try harder to get along. We've been fighting too much lately." She hesitated, trying to gauge his reaction, but he appeared as hard as stone. "Please try not to let it show," she begged.

Charlie glared back at her, sullenly keeping his distance. He was still angry, she knew, about sacrificing his precious weekend.

Charlie's selfish attitude had first surfaced during their honeymoon, confirming her father's observation that she hadn't known Charlie long enough to marry him. Now she fervently wished she had heeded her Dad's words. Charlie had argued abusively against this trip, had made an embarrassing display of immature behavior in an attempt to stay at home. But she had insisted, explaining that they needed to be together for Liz's sake, to give the impression that all is not negative in the world of love and romance. She'd been surprised in the end that he'd agreed to come with her.

Now, as she watched him steer the automobile along the narrow highway, Nancy once again wondered how she'd ever chosen Charlie as her mate. Only two short weeks before, she had considered having an affair with Gary Thompson, a former boyfriend. But she had resisted bedding down with him when they had had their illicit liaison. Nevertheless, Nancy had since felt dirty, and had even confessed to her minister. But now her guilt vanished. Charlie's childish tantrum over a simple trip and his perpetually negative attitude had made up her mind for her. She had finally had enough. When they returned to Columbus, she decided, she would see a lawyer.

Flicking cigarette ashes out the window, Charlie stared blankly ahead. Nancy lifted the record albums from her lap and deposited them on the back seat. Well, Charlie had stopped complaining, she thought. Maybe that in itself was a positive sign that he would try to behave himself.

Wayne Crocker motioned the elderly lady away and politely shook his head. "No, Ma'am," he said. "You don't owe me anything."

"Well, at least let me give you something for your trouble," she urged.

"No, Ma'am," he repeated as he stooped to wipe grime from his hands on a clump of dead grass. "I was more than happy to help."

"Well, I certainly do appreciate it," she thanked him again. "Lord only knows what I'd have done if you hadn't come along. My husband is in the hospital, and I don't know who else I could have called except one of those crooked garages. And you know how they take advantage of women."

"Ma'am, they're not all bad. But that spare tire looks awful slick. You'd best replace it, first chance you get."

Wayne slammed the lid of the lady's trunk but it refused to catch. Putting the weight of his whole body behind it, he finally forced the bulky lid shut.

"Well, you have a nice weekend, you hear?" she called as she slid behind the steering wheel of the battered Mercury.

"Same to you, Ma'am," Wayne answered, wiping his hands a second time on a crumpled piece of discarded newspaper. He had just gotten off work at the Pell City Raceway service station when he spotted the woman stranded with a flat tire on Highway 231. Heavy-set with a rasping voice that grated on his nerves, she reminded him of his Aunt Mabel. But Wayne was always happy to lend a helping hand. That was part of living in the rural South — just about anyone qualified as a neighbor, and when a neighbor needed help, it was only natural to offer assistance.

A cloud of exhaust smoke rolled from the Mercury's rusted muffler as the woman cranked the engine. Wayne coughed, shaking his head in amusement as he crawled behind the wheel of his own '60 Chevy Impala. Time to get home and clean up for the weekend. An old friend, Barry Powell, would be visiting tonight to see Wayne's new trailer. Well, it wasn't exactly new — it was actually three years old — but it was new to Wayne.

Its ignition straining, the Chevy finally rumbled to life, but idled roughly, jiggling Wayne's faded high school graduation tassel that hung from the rearview mirror.

Ahead the old woman accelerated and guided her dirty Mercury into the steady flow of traffic. Wayne grinned again and shook his head. The radio was blasting with the Dave Clark Five — he didn't recognize the tune, but could tell he was going to like it. In fact, he was a fan of most British rock groups. Tapping out a steady rhythm on the steering wheel, he gazed ahead and steered the Impala toward home.

God, it was nice to finally have his own place. Total privacy had been a dream for years. But now, with a good job and money to spend, many of the comforts he had always longed for were becoming a reality. And the trailer was the best purchase he'd ever made. It had been repossessed by a finance company from its original owner and Wayne had merely assumed payments. And though it sat empty collecting dust for months at the mobile home lot, Wayne cleaned and shined it both inside and out, until it looked like a flashy demonstrator model for Dixie Mobile Homes. He parked the trailer on his Dad's property, just over the hill from his parents' house. Fortunately, Dad owned 85 acres of prime farmland — more than enough to guarantee solitude. Soon as the trailer loan was paid off, he would offer to buy the land from his Dad. By then, he hoped his Dad would agree to just give it to him. In the meantime, he'd relax and just enjoy his new-found freedom.

Tonight was only the beginning. Barry would be the first guest in his new home, and sooner or later, Wayne would have a girlfriend over. But no need to worry about that now. Tomorrow there'd be college football on television and there were no plans yet for Sunday. Funny . . . his weekends *always* seemed to be open.

Winding his way along the main highway, Wayne turned onto the freshly paved road that skirted the tiny community of Selton. The pavement twisted through sparsely populated Alabama forest, crossed a new bridge over Kelley Creek, and led to still another small unimproved exit to his Dad's property. The crude one-lane road paralleled the barbed-wire boundary of his father's land.

Wayne's trailer rested beneath two tall oaks in shaded seclusion, approximately 500 feet down the private drive. Behind the trailer spread rolling pasture bordered east and west by relatively dense timberland. The trailer itself, blue and white, was a forty foot Clemson with two doors — an opening to the tiny living room area and a separate entrance to a back bedroom.

Wayne brought the Chevy to a stop and as a cloud of dust blew past the car and settled over the trailer, he winced — it was going to be impossible to keep it clean.

Jingling the keys in his right hand, he opened the door and stepped inside the miniscule living room. To the right, filling an entire end of the trailer, was a heavily padded sofa, upholstered in purple corduroy. In a window above was a small ventilation fan. A portable television stood on a small stand directly across from the door, and to the left was a miniature kitchen with a round oak table and two chairs.

Wayne tossed his keys atop the TV set and stepped past the kitchen to the next room. Originally designed as a second bedroom, the space had been cleared for the storage of books, records, and a Philco hi-fi phonograph, though the entire room was barely larger than a standard walk-in closet. The room was a mess, as always.

Next was a small bathroom with hardly enough space to stand between the commode and sink. Beneath a high window was a tiny bathtub. At the far end of the trailer was Wayne's bedroom. He pulled off his shirt, collapsed on the bed, and lay thinking about what was available inside the refrigerator.

As darkness settled over Opelika, Alabama, Charlie Barnett wheeled the Falcon into the crowded parking lot of a Tastee-Freeze fast food restaurant. Nancy confronted him immediately, an air of irritation in her voice.

"Well, I certainly expected a better meal than *this*."

Charlie shut off the ignition and stared her down.

"What else did you expect in this shit-hole town?" he growled. "Besides, who do you think I am, Howard Hughes? We can't afford anything but hamburgers."

Nancy turned away, gazing wearily out the passenger window. Down the road, spectators were gathering outside a football stadium, awaiting tonight's big game. Nancy's thoughts returned to high school, when life was simple. Charlie had been more considerate then — why was he so negative now? Nothing ever pleased him anymore. He rarely took her out to eat, and now a perfect opportunity for a romantic meal was lost. If he would show only the slightest hope of changing, she might delay seeing an attorney. Perhaps a simple separation could save their marriage. But she couldn't salvage the relationship on her own. Charlie would have to do his share.

Charlie handed her a five dollar bill.

"Here," he said. "Get me two burgers, French fries and a—"

"*Are you an invalid?* Why can't *you* get it?" she interrupted loudly.

Charlie shrugged and reached for the ignition.

"No sweat off my back — I'm not hungry anyway," he said. "If you don't want anything, just forget it."

Snatching the money, Nancy got out of the car, slamming the door hard. With a scowl tarnishing her pretty face, she angrily trudged toward a group of Opelika teenagers and took her place in line behind two giggling cheerleaders outside the Tastee-Freeze order window.

Tears blurred her vision. She couldn't stand much more of this. In the beginning, Charlie had been proud of her, but now she realized she had never been anything more than a trophy, just an attractive body he could display in front of his drinking buddies. Nancy was only a status symbol to him, and his feelings for her had been artificial all along. God, how it hurt to recognize the truth. Charlie had never really cared for her, and he certainly didn't love her now.

The two cheerleaders ahead were chattering away, expressing grave concern that tonight's game might be rained out. Nancy reacted with a mood containing both annoyance and jealousy. It had been years since her own worries had been so trivial. Never in her wildest dreams had she imagined herself haunted by a broken marriage. Divorce was still an ugly word here in the Bible Belt. She would be perceived as a tramp if she and Charlie split, and that didn't seem fair at all. Although she hadn't been a virgin on her wedding day, Charlie had been the only man she'd ever allowed to go "all the way." Regardless, people were prejudiced against divorcées, just as she herself had once been. To outsiders, she would be a "spoiled" woman. But there was no point worrying about that now. There was no alternative but to accept her marriage as a failure. She would face public scorn when the proper time came. For the present, she would face reality and get matters under control, start her life anew. Both older and wiser, she would be more careful the next time she chose a husband. And she certainly wouldn't let herself be influenced by others.

Charlie was twisting the radio dial when she returned to the car with an armful of food and soft drinks. He took his own good time to hold the door open for her and offered little help in assisting her inside.

"You picked a hell of a weekend to play goody-goody with your cousin," he complained. "I just heard on the radio we've got a freeze warning up ahead."

The last of the weather forecast could barely be heard, its message distorted by crackles of interference. In the distance, faint flickers of lightning already marred the blackened skies.

Nancy ignored his comment and tossed two hamburgers into his lap. A sprinkle of diced onions fell from the wax paper wrappings and tumbled between his legs. Charlie glared at her, but Nancy failed to notice, her attention glued to the stadium lights that now flared from nearby. Throngs of high school students were pushing through the open gates, most of them clutching umbrellas of various colors and sizes. A light mist had begun to fall but the football fans hardly seemed to care. After all, Nancy mused, tonight was the big night. From the chattering cheerleaders Nancy had learned that the Opelika Tigers' undefeated season was on the line against last year's state champions. Now, her memories returned to her own high school days and how, if she had gone out for cheerleading, she could have met so many more guys and her life could have turned out much differently.

Just as Wayne downed a grilled cheese sandwich and a can of chili, he heard an automobile whine to a stop outside. Barry was on time, as usual. The loud "clump" of a car door rattled the windows of the trailer. Then came a gentle rap at the door.

Hurriedly tugging at the doorknob, Wayne stood face to face with Barry Powell, a harsh cold wind flapping the latter's overcoat.

"Let me in, asshole — my dick's freezin' off!"

Wayne laughed and stepped aside, bowing in comic salute to his friend as he welcomed him inside. "So?" Wayne countered. "You never use it anyway."

"Hey, my sex life is no joke," Barry answered in mock seriousness. Then he burst into laughter, shed his coat and tossed it on the sofa. The two shook hands vigorously.

"Long time, no see," Wayne said. "And you're looking good these days." Barry's appearance had undergone a dramatic change. He'd obviously lost weight, and the transformation was quite impressive. "Are you wearing contact lenses?"

"Yep," answered Barry. "They're a bitch to clean, but I love 'em. At the very least they give me more confidence. So, what have you been up to?"

"Nothing unusual — just workin' and payin' the bills."

Barry glanced at the interior furnishings and nodded.

"Hey, this is nice — real nice. When did you get it?"

"Oh, about three weeks ago. It needs work, though. I've kept myself pretty busy since then."

Following a brief tour of Wayne's new home, the two settled on the sofa.

"So," began Wayne as he brought two icy cans of

Falstaff to life with a rusty opener. "How's your love life?"

Barry took a beer and leaned back, stretching his legs, then relaxing. "Probably about the same as yours," he answered with a grin.

"I wouldn't wish that on anybody!" Wayne laughed. "But you've got no excuse — you're a college man now."

"Shit," Barry groaned. "College is only good for keeping my ass out of Vietnam. Besides, I'm not at the main campus. The extension center is not exactly a source of horny women looking for young studs on the loose."

Barry was in his second year of basic study at the University of Alabama's Birmingham Extension Center. As it was essentially a commuter school, and most students were married and working, campus activities were nil. But soon, Barry would have enough credits to transfer to Tuscaloosa. That's when life would begin all over for him.

"But while we're on the subject," Barry continued, "I suppose I should clue you in on my big date tomorrow night."

"*You?*" Wayne responded in amazement. "A date with a *female*? Complete with tits and *everything*?"

"Her name is Allison Winters and I met her through my cousin. Actually, it's our third date."

Wayne sat in stunned silence. Although only casual acquaintances throughout high school, he and Barry had run into each other at a James Bond film in Talladega, after graduation, and their friendship blossomed thereafter. Both had always been social outcasts, and since becoming close friends, they had leaned on each other on numerous occasions for moral support following disastrous put-downs by callous females. Neither had ever managed a sustained relationship with a woman.

With a touch of envy, Wayne asked, "Why haven't I heard of Allison Winters before?"

Barry took another sip of brew and placed the can lightly on the floor. "Because I only met her a few weeks ago and I haven't seen you since September," he said. "And, besides, it's no big deal."

"*No big deal?*" Wayne roared. "For either of us to have three dates with the same woman is a major happening!"

"I know, I know — sad fact of life, ain't it?" Barry grinned. "But, like I said, she's really nothing special. I enjoy going out with her, but I can't see it developing much further. Honest."

Wayne shook his head, still dumbfounded. Of course, he realized, their luck with women had been bound to improve sometime — he and Barry couldn't remain social recluses forever.

"You and I should get together more often," Barry continued. "But, you know, with football season and all, I haven't missed a game yet. I guess you've heard by now — 'Bama's taking on the 'Huskers in the Orange Bowl."

"Yeah, yeah, I know that already. But what about Allison Winters?"

"Like I said, my cousin Pam introduced us," said Barry. "And before you ask, the answer is no — I haven't made any moves on her . . . yet."

"Do you think she'll put out?"

Barry drained the rest of his beer and chucked the can at an overflowing garbage pail. The metal container clattered noisily to the trailer's tile floor.

"Wayne, ol' buddy, they *all* put out sooner or later," Barry said with a snide expression. "But for guys like you and me, it always seems to be later."

Hoping his jealousy didn't show too much, Wayne shrugged. "At least you've got someone to attempt to screw. All I have is television fantasies."

"Hey, come on," Barry consoled his friend. "Before you know it, you'll be having orgies in this little love nest."

"Yeah, sure," Wayne shrugged again. "I haven't had a date since I moved in. In fact, I've only had three dates this whole year!"

As impossible as it might seem, Wayne's social life had worsened of late. Most of the women he met at the service station drove new GTO's or Mustangs. They were snobs, and looked down their noses at him. After all, what could a grease monkey have to offer? Prior to pumping gas he had worked at a lumber yard, a sod farm, and a temporary construction project, all in virtual isolation from women.

Although deferred from the draft for an asthmatic condition, Wayne was otherwise in excellent health. And he realized deep inside that he really wasn't a bad looking guy. Perhaps he should have gone to college after all, even though he wasn't the academic type. At least then his social opportunities would have improved.

Barry quickly picked up on his friend's depression.

"Your day will come. We both know that," he said.

Wayne hung his head and stared at the floor.

"Come on, man," Barry continued. "If all goes well tomorrow night, I'll ask Allison if she's got a friend you can meet. Maybe we can double date next weekend."

Wayne slowly nodded. Not a bad proposition, he thought. "Where are you taking her?" he asked.

"The Starlite Drive-In in Birmingham," Barry answered. "I think 'Shenandoah' is playing. But who really gives a shit?"

Both chuckled. Wayne snapped his fingers, the evening having passed quickly, and reached to turn on the television set. "Hey, we haven't watched 'UNCLE' together in months," he said as the NBC peacock slowly spread its wings.

Barry's attention was immediately riveted to "The Man From U.N.C.L.E." "Boy," he said, "I'd love to see this in color sometime."

2

Raindrops splattered against the Falcon's windshield as the young Georgia couple passed through Childersburg, only twenty-five miles southwest of Selton. Charlie reached to the dash and twisted the windshield wipers on, gazing ahead at sheets of rain that slashed through the headlight beams. At his side, Nancy cried softly, her sniffles barely audible above the whine of the wipers.

"It's over, you know," he said tersely.

She gave no response.

"Why are we always pissed off at each other?" he asked, reaching with his right hand to pat her lightly on the knee. She stared past him at streaks of lightning to the west. Charlie continued, "We've got to face facts — it's just not working. We're only making each other miserable."

At least they were thinking along the same wavelength, Nancy thought, wiping her eyes. Suddenly, a sharp bolt of lightning sheared the top of a tall pine just ahead. Nancy jumped at the resulting explosion of thunder.

"Can't we at least try to work out our problems?" she sobbed. "What can I do to keep you from getting mad at me all the time?"

"I don't know," he sighed. "We just weren't meant for each other, I guess." Charlie stared ahead impassively.

Nancy watched his face illuminated by the glow of the dashboard lights. How could he cast aside a six-year relationship so coldly, without so much as a single tear? But he was definitely right. Still, it hurt to hear him say so. Nancy sniffled again, trying to hold back another wave of tears. But then she lost control, and covering her face with both hands, felt the warm drops trickle down her wrist.

"Cry on your own time," Charlie complained. "Not while I'm around to hear it."

The silent tears continued to flow, but finally Nancy managed to regain control of herself. "Please try to make it through this weekend without causing a scene," she said, wiping her eyes. "I don't want Liz to see us like this." Trying to force a smile that refused to come, she managed a small laugh which ended up a tearful sob. "Here I am, traveling to another state to console my cousin for her broken heart, and *my* life is more of a disaster than *hers*."

Charlie stared blankly ahead, a grim expression on his face. "If you weren't so fuckin' dependent, such a fuckin' *leech* . . ." he began, but as he ranted on his words faded from Nancy's consciousness.

Her thoughts had returned to Gary Thompson back home in Columbus, and their physical relationship that never quite got off the ground. She remembered how nice it had felt to be held in his arms. Surely there'd be other men who'd be more appreciative of her than Charlie, she thought, turning to stare at him in disgust. Yes, she realized, it was too late to turn back now, in more ways than one.

Napoleon Solo and Illya Kuryakin were heavily involved in another clash with T.H.R.U.S.H. as Wayne and Barry watched intently. Draining a third beer, Barry crumpled the metal can with both hands.

"Hey, you're still nursing your first beer. You're not turning teetotaler on me, are you?"

Wayne blushed and placed his own half-empty can on the floor. "No," he explained, "I don't have any moral hang ups — it's just not my favorite drink, that's all. But I don't mind serving suds to my buddies."

"You don't owe me any explanations," Barry countered as he patted his stomach. "Sometimes I wish I'd never tasted the evil brew."

Their laughter was interrupted by the telephone.

"Aw, shit," groaned Wayne. "I told Mom not to call tonight."

Wayne stumbled to the telephone and, sure enough, it was his mother. Barry held an imaginary telephone receiver to his ear and silently mimicked a jabbering woman. Wayne shot him the finger as his mother's voice droned into his ear.

"Mom, just wait, before you go any further," Wayne snapped. "I told you I'd be busy tonight."

"But it's your father again," her voice wailed. "He came home from work today madder than I've ever seen him. And he was as drunk as a coot, too."

"So, let him sleep it off—"

"He hit me, Wayne. He hit me hard this time," she sobbed. "And just now, he stomped out of here and said he was going fishin'." She sniffled once, twice, awaiting a response, but receiving none from Wayne, finally continued. "The weather's supposed to get nasty and I'm afraid he'll pass out and freeze. He can't do no fishin', Wayne. He's so drunk, he can hardly walk."

"Dammit, Mom — what am I supposed to do?"

"Please go out and find him. It won't take long — you know where he always goes."

"Mom, I'm busy—"

"Wayne, you've got to," she begged. "I won't get any sleep till I know he's safe."

"*Mom*—"

Barry staggered to his feet and grabbed his coat. "Don't let me interfere," he whispered. "I need to hit the sack early tonight, anyhow. Big day ahead tomorrow."

Wayne shrugged and shook his head. "All right, all right," he growled into the receiver. "But I swear, Mom, this is the last time. If I have to move a thousand miles from here, Dad will never screw up my plans again."

"Hurry, son — *please* . . ." her voice faded as he hung up the phone.

"Shit!" Wayne cursed. "I'm sorry, Barry," he said, explaining the problem and asking him if he'd like to come along.

"Nah," said Barry. "I really do need to be going anyway."

Apologizing once more, Wayne shook his head. "I can't believe this is happening again," he said. His Dad had been a source of embarrassment for years, often passing out on the shores of Kelley Creek — but never before in life-threatening weather.

Barry slipped into his overcoat and pushed the door open. Outside a cold wind was howling, whistling through the naked trees, but the rain had yet to fall. "I'll let you know how it turns out tomorrow night," he called back as he raced for his car.

"Good luck at the drive-in!" Wayne shouted above the rising wind.

"Slow down, Charlie — you need to turn off somewhere near here." Nancy peered ahead but the black of night obscured her view. "It's been years since I was here last, and Liz told me the roads have changed."

"Rain and sleet — that's all I need," Charlie complained.

A thin fog blanketed the area, misting over the car windows. The weather was changing rapidly, and driving had become a strain.

"I'm getting cold, Charlie. Can you turn up the heat?"

Charlie frowned, and pushed the heat control a fraction higher.

"*There it is!*" Nancy screeched. "Turn left!"

The spray from a passing truck doused the windshield with a grimy film. Charlie irritably switched the wipers to a higher speed and slowed the car, turning the Falcon left onto a freshly paved road. He noticed that his wife's depression seemed to lift as they neared their destination.

"I wish I could see the countryside," Nancy rambled on. "When I was a kid I traveled these roads everyday. It seems like ages since I lived here."

Loose gravel clicked beneath the bottom of the car as Charlie uttered a tired yawn. Her words droned on, hardly registering in his mind.

". . . and most of these roads were dirt back then, and narrow. When you met a car coming from the opposite direction, you just had to pull over and let the other one pass. It's amazing how everything changes—"

About to interrupt her unending narrative on old-time rural life, Charlie cleared his throat, but a gust of wind suddenly rocked the car, prompting his attention to the steering wheel in order to correct its course. The relentless rain grew heavier, its drops exploding in tiny flashes of white across the hood and windshield. Nancy shuddered. The rain was so intense, it sounded as if a flock of crazed woodpeckers had attacked the car. "Don't you think you should slow down?" she said. "I mean, we can hardly see where we're going."

Charlie's thoughts were now centred on a warm bed. Tired of traveling long before, he was now ready to rest. Nothing seemed more appealing than a comfortable mattress piled high with blankets and quilts.

A rumble of thunder shook the car. Nancy sat stiffly upright, gazing through every flash of lightning at the road ahead.

"Charlie, please slow down. There are some dangerous curves on this road."

The accelerator sank closer to the floor.

Jagged lines of lightning seemed to break the sky in two. Nancy shivered as waves of water washed over the windshield; the wipers were now at their highest speed and unable to clear the view. Terror rose inside her. Her stomach felt queasy, her skin began to burn.

Something was wrong. And Charlie's careless attitude was dangerous.

Suddenly the car bottomed out, swaying on its weakened springs and spraying waves of muddy water from each of its wheels.

He can't see well enough to drive, Nancy realized. And, God, this isn't the right road. It's unpaved and rough and — "Charlie, please," she squealed. "*Stop the car!*"

But even as the words passed her lips, she knew it was too late.

An unimproved road, unsuitable for travel, paralleled the east bank of Kelley Creek for a thousand yards or so, beginning at its intersection with the recently paved County Road 19, known to the locals as Selton Road. Drunks, fishermen, and necking teenagers alike frequented the place, but tonight's threatening weather had canceled most plans. At the terminus of the narrow road, the small parking area, where at all hours one or two cars and trucks might normally be found, was empty. This was the chosen haunt of both loners and lovers, because of its veritable isolation. James Crocker was one of the locals who preferred the area more for its relative seclusion than for its prospects as a "fishin' hole."

And like James, other loners also brought with them a supply of booze to help them escape a fast-changing Southern lifestyle they no longer understood.

As the Impala's headlights pierced the darkness and danced through a thicket of trees, Wayne noted the absence of other cars. Regardless, he stopped the Chevy, cut the ignition, and reached for a flashlight in the glove compartment. His Dad had occasionally been known to park on the opposite shore, but should still be visible across the narrow creek.

A cold, clinging mist hung in the air. Zipping his jacket, Wayne stepped into the night where a bitter wind whipped his jacket and stood his hair on end. Only a fool would venture out on a night like this, Wayne thought. And what better example of that than Dad?

Thank goodness Barry had understood. It had been a shame to interrupt their evening, but the news of Barry's date with Allison Winters had been disturbing and, truthfully, Wayne had been ready for Barry to leave. Though he was proud of Barry's good fortune, his friend's recent success only served as a reminder of his own shortcomings. What was Allison Winters like, and how had Barry managed to attract her? Allison haunted Wayne's thoughts, and for a shameful moment he wished she would break poor Barry's heart. But, no, it was wrong to think such things. Barry deserved the best, just as he, Wayne, did.

Dejected, Wayne reviewed his own social history. Only once had he dated the same girl more than three times and it had still ended in a massive put-down. What could be wrong with him? He wasn't bad looking; of course, neither was he considered handsome. Average, maybe. Still, he had known several less appealing guys who seemed to have no problems attracting girls. Women just seemed so threatening. Over the years he had actually dated a few of the more popular girls, only to be denied a second chance with any of them. It wasn't as if he was overly aggressive — if anything, he was far too shy, and they had obviously sensed his overpowering insecurity.

Of the many girls he courted for only one evening, Susan had been the one he wanted most. She was both attractive and modest, sweet and understanding. He felt unusually comfortable with her that night, dining out at the Pell City Steak House and later catching a movie. And when he took her home and generated enough nerve to kiss her goodnight, he found passion in her lips. A surge of desire ripped through his body, feelings he'd never experienced with such intensity, and for one brief moment, Wayne believed the seemingly endless string of lonely nights were finally about to end. Unfortunately, the very next day Susan's former boyfriend, Harold Gaskins, re-entered her life, and all was lost. She let Wayne down gently, but his ego had suffered another devastating blow.

Now he would be on the sidelines again, watching Barry and Allison. "Spectator in the game of love," that's what he'd jokingly called himself. But, God, how the truth hurt.

How did Allison look? Where did she live? Of course, it really didn't matter. She and Barry were having their *third* date, and that certainly hinted at some type of attraction. What if they were to get serious? Marriage could be a real possibility, and then who could Wayne turn to for moral support? Barry would no longer have time for him.

A cool raindrop broke against Wayne's forehead and rolled down his nose. Ahead lay the dark waters of Kelley Creek. Wayne aimed the flashlight at the flowing water and watched the rain increase, peppering the creek with tiny splashes and battering the kudzu on a nearby embankment.

"Dad?" he yelled. Blasts of wind slammed into his face as he stepped along the shore, and Wayne hugged his jacket closer, feeling a sudden need for warmth. Scanning the shoreline with the flashlight, he saw no one.

"Dad, it's time to go home!"

A blinding bolt of lightning bleached the darkness, its resounding crash of thunder roaring in his ears.

Jesus, Wayne thought. I've got to get out of this!

Ahead loomed the monstrous new bridge where Selton Road had been re-routed. He had almost forgotten its proximity, as the bridge's construction had only recently been completed.

Curtains of rain drenched the area, quickly turning the path along the creek to mush as Wayne raced for shelter beneath the bridge. Already cold and shivering, he leaned against the abutment to shield himself from the wind and catch his breath. Again he swept the flashlight in all directions, but saw nothing. The group of large boulders where his Dad usually rested lay just ahead, but the spot was vacant.

"Dad!" he yelled again, then cut himself short. It was no use. The noise of the elements would mute his call even if his Dad were only ten feet away.

"Shit!" Wayne cursed and stomped the ground. Damn, it was getting cold.

The wind whirled stronger, cutting through his wet clothing and almost knocking him from his feet. The onslaught of bitter cold and lightning was terrifying, as with each blast of wind the smaller trees along the shore doubled over, some snapping in half. It seemed that within seconds the stream had gained strength from the floodwaters fed from the north, and the night had erupted into a tumultuous frenzy.

God, this is tornado weather, Wayne thought, but his fear of the savage winds faded as he stared upstream.

Between intermittent flashes of lightning Wayne saw that the old bridge had been partially dismantled, its midsection now a darkened void. And traveling directly toward it, on a section of old roadway that should have been closed to traffic, he saw the headlights of an automobile.

3

Liz Farrell positioned her hefty body on the living-room sofa of her parents' Selton home and peeked excitedly through the blinds at the heavy rain. Not a car was in sight. Occasionally the house lights flickered, threatening a power failure from high winds and lightning.

Disappointed again, she slumped to the sofa and contemplated the arrival of Nancy. The two had been inseparable throughout childhood until Nancy's family moved to Georgia in 1957. It had been years since the two exchanged month-long summer visits. Liz remembered their confidential conversations — from the time Nancy first admitted an attraction to the opposite sex, to her own confession at age sixteen of having allowed a boy to touch her breasts. They had each been unusually pretty and were quite popular at the local hangouts.

For years Liz had entertained a number of boyfriends, most of whom wanted nothing more from life than to get inside her pants. But Liz's Southern virtue had prevailed in most cases. Only twice before she met John had she allowed boys to go "all the way," and she had grown tired of both lovers soon afterward. But John had been special. With him she had looked forward to marriage and she had given herself freely to him on several occasions.

Then came the uncontrollable weight problem.

Attributable to a glandular malfunction, the condition was unaffected by various diets prescribed by her doctor. And slowly she watched John's attention drawn away by more slender girls. Only two weeks ago he had formally ended their relationship while simultaneously announcing his engagement to Charlotte Cummings. And when Nancy had heard the news only two days ago, she had vowed to return to Selton for a weekend visit to comfort her dear friend and cousin.

Martha Farrell, Liz's mother, entered the room and noted the anxiety on her daughter's face.

"Settle down now," she said. "Nancy'll be here before you know it."

Liz groaned and glanced at the clock on the mantle as she flipped through a copy of *Progressive Farmer* on the coffee table.

"I know," she said. "You just don't realize how happy I'll be to see that girl."

His heart racing, his face frozen with fear, Wayne watched the headlight beams bounce along the rugged terrain, the car's speed never slowing. And through the driving rain, as the car reached the vast abyss of missing bridge, he watched it plummet forward, continuing ahead in mid-air and then slowly arcing downward. It dropped to midstream as if in slow motion, a horrifying sight Wayne couldn't believe he was actually witnessing. A gigantic splash sent mud and grime in every direction, as concentric waves of water rolled from the point of impact and sloshed to both sides of the stream. The automobile floated briefly, then slowly took on water and began to sink as it drifted downstream in his direction.

The eerie glow of headlights shining through the water remained faintly visible, and clouds of steam hissed from beneath the car's partially submerged hood. Then, quietly, the headlights shorted out, and the car was now visible only during recurring flashes of lightning.

For a moment Wayne stood motionless, a sick feeling welling inside his stomach. Never had he witnessed a potentially fatal accident. But then a crash of thunder revived his senses and he raced upstream to meet the sinking vehicle. Twenty feet or so from shore, only the windows and roof of the automobile could now be seen.

Amid the continuing downpour Wayne aimed his flashlight at the car and strained his eyes to see. The passenger side of the automobile now faced him and he could see that the front window was either rolled down or missing entirely. Was there movement inside? He focused his eyes and saw it again. Then, aided by a blinding bolt of lightning, he saw her clearly — a woman, dazed, and struggling to get out.

"Hurry, lady — Get out fast!" he yelled.

She extended a weakened arm outside, past torrents of water that gushed through the open window and forced her back inside. Her fingers curled around the roof of the car and held tightly as she attempted to pull herself out. Wayne kept his flashlight fixed on her obscure image, watching helplessly from the shore as the events unfolded. The current was far too strong for him to swim to her. She would have to escape on her own, and then perhaps he could help her ashore.

Finally, her head and shoulders were outside the car, but the roof was now almost underwater. Suddenly she released her grip and sank back inside. Panic stricken, Wayne waved his arms in exasperation. What could he possibly do? Slowly the automobile dipped below the surface and disappeared. Oblivious to the rain and frigid weather, he shed his jacket and kicked off his shoes. And just as he was about to dive in, the woman's head appeared above the raging current.

"*All right!*" he whooped, a ring of excitement in his voice as he danced along the shore.

But now the helpless woman was being swept downstream. Obviously injured, she could barely keep her head above water.

"Oh, God, don't let her drown," Wayne mumbled as he frantically kept pace with her along the shoreline.

The current was incredibly strong, and her feeble attempts to stay afloat were growing weaker. Within minutes she would be gone.

Mentally gauging the force of the water, Wayne stumbled downstream. It would be foolish to dive in now. He could never get her back to shore, if indeed he ever reached her in the first place. Frantically, he swept the flashlight beam downstream. A large oak tree had toppled into the water only minutes before, the current rushing over and past its partially submerged limbs. The woman was heading directly toward it. If he could somehow make his way along the tree trunk toward midstream, perhaps he could snag her and pull her back to shore.

Wayne raced to the tree and tossed his flashlight to the ground. Blindly, using both hands to feel his way, he groped among the tree's branches, planting his feet firmly step by step along the massive trunk. Occasional spurts of water poured over his feet, tugging coldly at his legs, but he managed to maintain his balance and inch forward. A distant flash of lightning illuminated her approach, her face barely breaking the surface.

Wayne crouched and awaited her arrival, the cold spray of rain and rushing water drenching him. She was almost within reach, only a few feet away. He held tightly to a protruding limb with his right hand and stretched his left arm to its limit in her direction. Then, without warning, she sank.

Wayne's blood froze. How could he come this far and still let her drown? Quickly he lay flat on his stomach and thrust his left arm deep into the frigid water, hoping to somehow snare her as she passed beneath the tree. He could feel and hear his own pulse as the endless seconds passed, the surroundings blotted from his field of perception as he waited. Had he been a fraction of a second too late? Was she already ten or fifteen feet past him?

His arm grew numb from the cold, his fingers stiff and barely able to grasp. But finally he felt something — a tangle of hair perhaps? He swept his arm in circles through the water, gathering more. Yes! Yes, it was her! Gripping the tresses of hair tightly, he pulled until her face appeared above the water. She coughed and gasped for air. Thank God, she was conscious. Steadily, he reached for her shoulders and held her against the tree trunk. His body ached, and his arm was numb, almost immovable from the cold.

Abruptly Wayne felt himself weakening.

His legs felt as if they might break off at the knees as he raised himself to an erect position, with the woman now spread securely over a convenient tree limb. But as he stood too quickly, blood rushed to his head and dizziness washed before his eyes. A shrill whistle sang inside his ears and helplessly he collapsed into the water beside her.

The power went off just as Johnny Carson was warming the audience with a few choice quips about *The Sound of Music*. Tom Farrell was still grumbling when his wife made her way blindly into the kitchen in search of a flashlight.

"You shouldn't complain," she nagged as she passed. "You should've unplugged the set anyway when the lightning first started."

"Humph!" he blurted. "I'm going to bed!"

Liz joined her mother and rummaged through a drawer for candles while her mom looked for the flashlight. When it was finally found, its beam was weak — too dim to be of much help.

"I found a candle," said Liz, reaching across the countertop for matches.

"Here's Tom's lighter," Martha interrupted. She flipped it open and thumbed its ridged wheel, sparking a flame to life. Liz touched the candle wick to the fire and salvaged a lid from an empty mayonnaise jar to serve as a mount. Liz's weak shadow curled across the kitchen curtains as she affixed the candlestick to its temporary perch.

"They should have been here by now," said Liz, walking slowly back to the living room.

"Now, don't you worry about Nancy," Martha said, tagging along behind. "That gal's full of spunk. The weather has been so bad, she probably had to stop over somewhere. I'm sure she's fine."

"I hope so," said Liz.

But a feeling deep inside told her that something could have gone wrong.

The chill of the water stunned Wayne as he plunged into its icy depths. Gathering his senses, he groped for the tree, his fingers digging into a thick section of bark. The woman shifted toward him and grabbed his shoulder, then clung to his neck with one arm, freeing both of Wayne's hands to feel their way along the tree trunk. The growing numbness hardened Wayne's skin as he inched his way toward safety. At times he could barely keep his own head above water as the relentless current tried to wrench his grasp from the tree. The aching cold all but took his breath away, but slowly, determinedly, he continued. Twigs and branches tore at his flesh until at last his feet sank into the mushy floor of the creek.

Silently Wayne summoned a last surge of energy to drag the woman from the water, only to collapse beside her in the mud. The two gasped for air, as stinging rain and sleet pelted their unprotected faces. Wayne reached for her, to determine if she was still conscious, but noticed his fingers were too numb to straighten. He dropped his head back to the soggy ground, his teeth chattering uncontrollably. Exposure would kill them both if he couldn't get them to shelter.

Suddenly the woman began to cry, a moaning, wailing sound as if she were half out of her mind. But at least she was conscious.

The lightning finally moved farther east, leaving in its wake a thick, inky darkness. Wayne rolled over and reached for the woman again. She shivered beneath his touch, and at that same instant Wayne felt a stiffening of his wet clothes. A thin sheet of ice glazed his jacket.

The car. We've got to get to the car.

Even after his eyes had adjusted to darkness, Wayne could barely make out her features beside him. Fighting against the wind which was pinning him to the ground, Wayne clumsily rose to his feet.

When he extended a hand to the woman, to help her to her feet, she, at first returned a vacant stare, then instinctively shifted and raised her right hand to his. Finally, overcoming a lack of traction in the mud, he pulled her erect. She promptly fell against his shoulder and leaned her weight against him.

"We'll b-b-b-be all right," he assured her, though not entirely convinced himself. He was growing weaker by the minute, and their movement was incredibly slow. Each blast of wind sent icy waves of pins and needles through his clothing and into his skin.

Slowly the two trudged down the shore, silently bracing themselves against each other, their steps growing more erratic as they stumbled along a narrow path to the parked vehicle.

A second onslaught of freezing rain began to fall. Wayne leaned the dazed woman against the passenger door as he fished for his keys inside his pocket, the simple task made difficult by stiff fingers that refused to cooperate. Tiny plumes of frozen breath rolled from her lips and dissolved in the wind as Wayne jerked the door open. After positioning her on the front seat, he ran to the driver's side and slid behind the steering wheel.

Shelter from the wind and rain brought instant relief, but the interior of the car was still frigid. Cranking the engine, Wayne held the accelerator at a fast idle to speed its warm-up time. The windshield wipers were slow to start, but finally scraped across a thin layer of ice that covered the windshield. His hand shaking, Wayne reached for the dashboard heater control, but as he forced it toward the WARM position, the thin metal lever broke off in his grasp. Cool air continued to pour from the heater vents, the frozen breaths of himself and the lady frosting the interior of the windshield.

"N-n-no!" he moaned, his teeth clicking wildly.

The woman leaned against him, stunned and unaware of the threat they faced. Wayne pushed her aside and forced the column-mounted gearshift to "reverse". Without heat, and with the windshield obstructed inside and out, it would be impossible to get her to the nearest hospital which was over forty miles away. Wayne's only hope was to get her to his trailer and call an ambulance.

He cranked his window down, leaning his head out to see as he turned the car around. Rolling clouds of smoke boiled from the exhaust pipe as the wind whistled through his hair which had become almost brittle from the ice frozen in it. Carefully he backed the car into an open area, then guided it away from the creek.

The crude side road leading back to the paved road was now a crooked stretch of standing water and icy mud. The wheels of the Impala slid and spun aimlessly, then slowly picked up speed. Though he'd driven on country roads all his life, Wayne still found forging through muddy backroads extremely difficult. Sheets of muddy water sprayed from the wheels as they churned through slush and grime. With his head projected uncomfortably out of the window, Wayne's face became dotted with speckles of ice and mud. Soon the paved road was in sight and the car careened out, throwing loose gravel behind it.

"Ch-Ch-Charlie?" the woman moaned beside him.

"I-I-It's all . . . right . . ." Wayne said, leaning back inside to touch her shoulder.

The windshield visibility was nil, and though his ears felt as if they'd break off at any moment, Wayne was forced to keep his head outside in order to see. The blast of arctic air was almost paralyzing, as flecks of frozen rain and snow stung his cheeks. Ahead, through the glare of the headlights, he noticed icicles forming along the telephone lines.

Just a short distance to go. I think we'll make it.

"Ch-Ch-Charlie — I'm c-c-cold," the woman mumbled incoherently at his side.

She appeared delirious. Wayne forced himself to remain calm, choosing not to respond and, instead, keeping a keen eye on the road ahead. He pressed the accelerator harder, spinning the tires over thin patches of ice, and soon turned off on the narrow chert-topped drive that led to his trailer.

4

"Lizzie, why don't you come to bed?" her mother called from the darkened hallway.

"I'm too nervous to sleep," Liz answered. "Something must've happened."

Next Liz heard the scratchy padding of bedroom slippers in the hall.

"She's bound to be all right," Martha tried to comfort her daughter. "I'm sure they must've stopped somewhere for the night. They're adults — they know better than to drive through a storm like this."

Liz reached for the telephone; its dial tone buzzed into her ear. "The telephone is still working," she said. "They would've called if they had stopped."

A chill lingered in the air despite a smoldering flame in the fireplace. Martha wrapped her housecoat tighter. Her expression revealed that she, too, was concerned about the travelers, but Liz knew her mother wouldn't let on. Shivering, the two women hugged tightly.

"Honey, telephone lines are down all over the place," Martha said. "Even though ours is still workin', the phones are probably dead between here and wherever Nancy is staying. According to the radio, the police are closin' highways left and right, so Nancy and Charlie probably had no choice but to stop."

Liz stirred quietly on the sofa, snuggling beneath a handmade quilt.

"Soon as the ice melts in the morning, they'll come drivin' up, just you wait and see," Martha continued. "You might as well give up on 'em tonight and come to bed."

The candle was burning low, the living room growing colder. It was well past midnight and Liz realized her vigil was accomplishing nothing. Reluctantly, she rose from the sofa and draped the quilt about herself as she trudged down the hallway, her mother at her side.

"I suppose you're right," said Liz with a sigh. "But I'll never get a wink of sleep."

A mixture of fuel odors stank inside the trailer as the temperature began to rise. The flame of the kerosene heater was at its peak, and Wayne had turned on all four burners of the butane stove for additional warmth. Already windows throughout the small trailer were beginning to sweat from the collision of warm air against cold. The woman lay asleep on the sofa, covered from neck to toe with a woolen blanket.

Wayne sat beside the telephone, flexing his fingers to dial. Following a frantic search through the kitchen for the small rural telephone directory, he realized that he could merely call the operator. Wayne glanced again at the pitiful woman, shivering in her sleep beneath the covers. Just as he reached for the receiver, an abrupt ring of the telephone jarred him, the loud jangling noise harsh against his thawing ears. Quickly he snatched the receiver.

"Hello?"

"Wayne? When did you get back?"

It was his mother again. Till now his original mission had been completely forgotten.

"I didn't find him, Mom. But you won't believe what—"

"He's in jail again, Wayne, and you've got to get him out."

"Mom, I can't. There's something I've got to—"

"He's down at Columbiana. Got picked up Driving Under the Influence. I couldn't make much sense of him. But he needs you, Wayne."

"Mom, do you have any idea how dangerous it is outside? Dad's safer in jail. And besides, I can't drive on these icy roads. It's *impossible*."

"Wayne, he needs us—"

"He's a drunk ol' fart and he deserves to be in jail!" Wayne fumed.

"*Wayne Alton Crocker!*" she scolded. "He has his faults, just like me and you, but he's still your father. Am I going to have to ask *Jack* to bail him out?"

Wayne tried to calm himself. "Mom, listen. Jack won't go. The roads are icy. *Nobody* can go to Columbiana in this kind of weather."

Wayne knew she'd never give up, and he could almost anticipate her next words. But he'd have to hang up. He stared again at the sofa. Precious seconds were being wasted. The lady needed help.

"I'll call you back," he snapped, then pushed the switchhook and dialed "0". Static sounded from the earpiece as he waited for the connection. Finally he pressed the switchhook for another attempt, but now there was silence on the line.

The telephone was dead.

The steel bars of the Shelby County Jail were cold to the touch of James Crocker. His head ached and his stomach cramped as if Jack Daniels himself had crawled down his throat and was now in the process of kicking his way out. Crocker's head throbbed in relentless waves; his face was covered with beads of sweat. No one had come to bail him out, and his anger and impatience were compounding by the minute. Finally he stumbled backward and collapsed on the cell's lone ragged cot. The mattress smelled of perspiration and urine, but James hardly noticed. His only hope was to get out of this miserable place as soon as possible, and his boy Wayne should have been here long before now.

"*You tell that boy of mine,*" he yelled to no one in particular. "*You tell him I'll skin his ass if he ain't here in the next five minutes!*"

James paused to massage his temples — his head pulsed like a bass drum. "Goddamn piss-ant," he mumbled, running an unsteady hand through his unkempt hair. Around him loomed a maze of empty cells — a slow night for the fuzz, he thought. Below their quota. Clad only in khaki work pants and a dirty T-shirt, he noticed goosebumps breaking out across his arms.

"Shit, it's cold in here," he said to himself. "*Hey, Sheriff — Where's my coat?*"

Only a hiss from the radiator broke the silence.

"*Hey, turn up the goddamn heat!*" he yelled. "*And you tell that piss-ant boy of mine to get his ass over here.*"

James lurched toward the cell door and shook the bars in disgust.

"*You tell him now, you hear?*"

Clothed in dry jeans, flannel shirt, two pairs of long underwear, and a heavy overcoat, Wayne faced the bitter wind outside the trailer. The cold was so brutal, his fingers were freezing inside his gloves. Icicles weighted down nearby tree limbs low to the ground. Wayne stared ahead, his feet crunching over a sheet of ice as he walked. But despite the protective clothing he wore, his lips began to quiver, his ears began to sting — the weather was unbearable.

He had hoped to drive the injured woman the short distance to his parents' home, but he now knew it would be impossible. A thick layer of ice covered his car, and its doors couldn't be opened without first melting the ice. And, besides, if the car were to slide into a ditch, which was quite possible, the two of them could freeze before getting back to shelter. It was hopeless — like it or not, they were stuck.

The lights from inside the trailer dimmed, then returned to full brilliance. In the surrounding woods the ice-laden limbs of trees crashed to the ground. Suddenly the lights winked out for good, and the spark of broken power lines glowed faintly through the darkness near the main road. Wayne watched the lights fade through the windows, his fingers and arms stiffening again. Cautiously he fought the wind and trudged back to the warmth of the trailer.

Blessed heat welcomed Wayne as he opened the door, but the darkness and silence inside were eerie. Even the ever-present hum of the refrigerator was noticeably absent. Wayne removed his gloves, blew into his palms and flexed his fingers, then groped his way to the kitchen counter and wrestled a six-cell lantern from an assortment of junk beneath the sink. The lantern's beam was harsh, but strong. Swallowing hard, he returned to the sofa and stared at the woman's sleeping form. My God, what a gorgeous face! Through all the excitement, he'd failed to notice how attractive she was. And she appeared to be about his own age.

Wayne pulled up a chair and sat next to her. Tangled strands of her brown hair lay matted against the corduroy sofa. Long errant locks with bits of leaves and twigs lay plastered against her forehead. An ugly bruise marred her left eyebrow and traces of mascara ran from both eyes, though most of her makeup had been washed away in the river. But even in her disheveled condition, she was irresistible.

Was she safe now? he wondered. Was there anything he could do for her? As long as she was resting, he would try not to disturb her. Wayne pointed the flashlight away so its harsh beam wouldn't awaken her, and watched her chest rise and fall through the indirect yellow glow. She looked like a sleeping angel.

He touched her cheek and felt the coolness of her flesh. She should be warm by now, he knew. Carefully he lifted the blanket. Wet clothing clung tightly to her skin, and her blue print dress was hiked high around her thighs. The lower half of her mud-splotched panty girdle was visible, and one of her stockings was twisted around an ankle while the other remained firmly in place, secured by a single garter. But even that stocking was torn by a line of runners and her unadorned leg was etched with a swirl of minor scratches.

The flashlight shook in Wayne's grasp, and his hand grew sweaty as he examined her further.

Her dress was torn at her left shoulder and a dark bruise marked her tender skin. Wayne swallowed hard and wiped his brow. Visually tracing the length of her body, he admired her flawless figure, imagining her in formal attire, her hair perfectly in place, her body accented by a sheer evening gown . . .

With a startled gasp he settled back in his chair. He was getting an erection. God, how could he? This woman was so helpless, so . . . *fragile*. He thought about tomorrow, about how he would find help for her and how she would thank him.

The girl shuddered briefly, her eyes remaining firmly shut. Wayne reached to spread the blanket back over her, then stopped at midpoint. Her clothes were soaking wet. No wonder she couldn't get warm. Should he wake her? He nudged her lightly and watched her head shift slightly without awakening. He shook her harder, until her eyes opened groggily, then closed again.

She could catch pneumonia, Wayne told himself, watching her purple lips quivering in the dim light and remembering the cool touch of her skin.

Should I take off her clothes?

He could feel the nerves under his skin tingle at the possibility.

A drop of perspiration rolled down Wayne's cheek. He turned off the stove burners and lowered the thermostat on the kerosene heater. For a moment he reconsidered. What if she should awaken? He flashed the lantern beam in her face. She was sleeping undisturbed. Wayne's skin crawled with anticipation. He shifted from the discomfort of his untimely arousal and considered his next move.

He decided to proceed.

Quietly he returned to the sofa and gently pulled the blanket to her feet. As before, she was lying on her back, both arms to her sides. Again the rise and fall of her chest elicited waves of desire. Wayne reached for the hem of her dress, gripped its soggy fabric, and tugged it lightly toward her head. Now the sleek curves of her hips came into view, her undergarments stained from muddy water. She wore a full-length slip which was also hiked around her waist, thin layers of mud oozing from its compacted folds. Gently, he tugged the dress and slip together, catching his first glimpse of the smooth, creamy skin of her stomach. And though the breathy movement of her navel was engrossing, it couldn't begin to match the sight of her exposed bra after he'd pulled her dress and slip to a tight bundle around her neck.

Anxiety quickened his pulse. How could he remove her clothing without jarring her injured left arm?

Beads of sweat collected again on Wayne's forehead. Carefully he took her right hand and stretched her arm out and above her head, then bent the arm at the elbow to slip it through the sleeve of her garment. Her skin felt encouragingly warmer. With her right arm free, he slipped the ring of clothing over her head and gently slid it down the length of her left arm. When it was done, he breathed a sigh of relief.

Standing above her, Wayne marveled at her figure, his shadow cast by the lantern light bending across her body and stalking the wall behind her.

She was like no woman he had ever seen.

And yet, he felt ashamed to be aroused by the sight of her vulnerable form. But he couldn't concern himself about that now. Having gone this far, it was too late to turn back. And besides, his actions were entirely justifiable. He would remove the rest of her clothing without lingering and quickly wrap her in a warm, dry blanket.

Wayne slipped his hands beneath her back and fumbled clumsily with the clasp of her bra. The loosened elastic straps contracted in his grasp, and he felt his member growing uncontrollably more erect. The color of her skin looked healthier by the minute, he told himself. Dropping the right strap over her shoulder, Wayne repeated the earlier process so he could remove the bra without disturbing her bruised arm.

The sight of her breasts was almost more than he could stand. Her thick pink nipples stood erect above their soft milky mounds, so much more appealing than those within the pages of a men's magazine. He wanted to caress them and lick them, and it took all his self-control to keep his hands away.

No, he thought, *I mustn't dawdle*.

Bending over her horizontal figure, he tested her girdle — snug, but not excessively tight. There was an ugly bruise above her right knee.

Wayne's swollen penis strained hard against his fly. He squeezed between the wall and the end of the sofa at her feet, then leaned over her knees to grasp the elastic band of the girdle at her hips. He then rolled the panty girdle down an inch or two at a time, stopping frequently to make sure that he wasn't pinching her or pulling her pubic hair. At first he panicked when her head lolled from left to right — what on earth would he say? — but, thankfully, she never awakened.

Wayne closed his eyes and replayed the gentle roll of her breasts as she turned in her sleep. It had been the single most erotic scene he'd ever witnessed, more powerful than anything he'd ever imagined. He paused for a deep breath, then continued, easily slipping off her remaining garments without disturbing her sleep. Her soiled girdle and panties dangled from his fingertips, and Wayne found himself standing mesmerized by the most beautiful woman he had ever seen.

And she was completely nude.

Swallowing hard, Wayne surveyed her body. The triangle of her dark pubic hair sent a surge of desire through his erect penis. Wayne tensed at the sudden buildup of sexual excitement, then lurched with the unexpected release as he ejaculated from the mere sight of her. He gasped to regain his breath and closed his eyes. His heartbeat raced. His mind began to wander . . .

He imagined himself walking a country road, hand in hand with this beautiful woman. The vision continued until the two stopped beneath a massive oak. They gazed into each other's eyes and embraced. Their passion was heated, but not sexual in nature. The feeling was one of warmth and caring, and soared beyond the boundaries of physical love . . .

Calmly he opened his eyes. Perhaps one day he might find such a love. But now he felt only shame for thinking of this poor woman in sexual terms, knowing of the ordeal she'd been through and her helpless condition.

Wayne covered her again and tucked the blanket snugly at both sides, then sat at the kitchen table far from the fading beam of the flashlight. The batteries were slowly weakening. His heart still pounded wildly, his mouth felt parched and dry. Wayne fumbled at the sink for a drink of water, but only a slow trickle dripped from the tap — the water lines were already freezing.

He glanced again at the sofa, at the gentle swell of the blanket as she breathed. *Stop it*, he warned himself. *Don't even think about it. You're still a hero and let's keep it that way.*

Wayne's eyes wandered down the darkened hallway. Inside the middle closet was a Polaroid Swinger camera his parents had given him last Christmas. And if he remembered correctly, it contained film with at least two or three exposures remaining. He was almost certain that, inside the camera's plastic case, was an unopened package of flash cubes.

No. I shouldn't take advantage of her that way.

He rolled his eyes from the feet of her bundled form to her exposed face, her lips so inviting. Would a flashbulb awaken her? he wondered.

With the lantern in his right hand, Wayne twirled its beam directly at her eyes, then flicked it quickly away. Her eyelids twitched but her eyes remained shut.

It's not right. It's an invasion of privacy.

He paused to collect his thoughts.

But she'll never know. It'll be perfectly harmless. And the photos will be fantastic! Besides, I saved her life. She'd be at the bottom of Kelley Creek if it weren't for me. I won't even touch her — and she'll never know.

Quietly he stepped to the closet and opened its squeaky door. He knew exactly where to reach in the darkness, high on the top shelf. With the simulated alligator case in hand, Wayne tip-toed back to the kitchen table and carefully removed the flash cubes and camera. The shadows from the lantern light exaggerating his every move as he nervously peeled away the cellophane wrapper from the flash cubes and plugged one into the socket on top of the camera.

She'll never know.

He stepped to her side and gently pulled the blanket to her waist.

Wayne stood six feet away and framed the sofa in the viewfinder. Fighting his own nervousness, he held his breath to steady the camera and slowly applied pressure to the shutter release.

Nothing happened.

The camera batteries were either weak or dead. Did he have spare batteries? No . . . but wait. He remembered a trick he'd learned from Barry. Wayne pulled the flash cube from its mount and licked the wire elements at the base of the cube, then repositioned the cube in its socket. Quickly he re-aimed and pressed the shutter release.

FLASH!

The lady didn't budge, and continued to sleep undisturbed.

Wayne jerked the paper tab from its opening at the camera's end and pulled the developing print from the camera. Anxiously he counted ten seconds, then peeled away the black covering and gazed at the small black-and-white print.

It was good. Damn, it was *excellent*! The delicate outline of her right breast was clearly visible.

He wanted another shot, this one a close-up of her face and breasts. Readying the camera again, he snapped the shutter. Again the flash didn't bother her. He timed the exposure and peeled away the backing — God, it was perfect!

Caught up in the excitement, Wayne considered another revealing angle, knowing his time was limited. This next picture would be the best yet, a full frontal shot. He pulled the blanket to her feet, then stood atop a nearby chair to look down on her.

Framing the scene, he nervously snapped the shutter and ripped the paper tab from the slot.

The camera jammed.

Frantically, he tried to remove the print, but found it hopelessly stuck. Silently he cursed this foul twist of luck. If there were any exposures left, they would be spoiled when he opened the camera to remove the blockage. And, of course, the shot he'd just taken was already ruined. There was no more film in the closet.

Guardedly, he stopped himself as he was about to slam the camera against the wall in disgust. A once-in-a-lifetime opportunity had vanished before his very eyes. But at least he already had two good photos. The wet prints were lying curled on the table at his side. Retrieving them for another look, Wayne fished a black cylinder of protective coating from the camera case and spread an even layer of transparent gloss over the prints with the applicator. Then, leaving the snapshots to dry, Wayne returned to his guest.

He held the blanket high above her, then paused for one last look. Her legs rested firmly together, shielding any further view. Curiously, he dropped the blanket to a soft bundle, leaned over and touched his nose to her soft bush of pubic hair. Slowly, he inhaled her musky scent.

He remembered poring over men's magazines, but all were quite adept at concealing female genitals. And once a visiting cousin from Chicago tried to describe the lips and folds of the vulva, but try as he could, Wayne couldn't visualize anything that seemed remotely inviting. Then, in high school, an earthy P.E. coach gathered a select group of boys in confidence and sketched a crude drawing of a woman's privates. Still Wayne couldn't relate to it. But now here was a perfect example, alive and beautiful, right inside his home. And though he knew he should spread the blanket over her and keep a respectable distance, he wanted desperately to see just a little more, close up.

Wayne leaned over for another sniff, taking care not to touch her — it wasn't what he expected, but was quite inviting. Raising his head, he redirected the lantern beam to eliminate harsh shadows from the cleft of her legs. The light glistened in tiny sparkles across her wiry pubic hair.

Fighting the urge, Wayne dropped the blanket over her chest and paced nervously to a nearby window to peek outside. He envisioned the warm, moist tissue between her legs and imagined how it might feel. His penis was already hard again and throbbing.

Sweating profusely, he stooped at the sofa, peeled the blanket away, and directed a shaky index finger toward her soft tuft of pubic hair.

A swirl of thoughts collided inside Nancy's mind. Consciousness flirted, but seemed to retreat somewhere short of awareness. Visions of cold, dark water subdued her memory. What exactly had happened? Had it been a dream? Vaguely she remembered riding in someone's car. There was a stranger at the wheel, a man of about her own age. And the cold . . . The bitter cold had nipped her skin. Her teeth chattered unmercifully.

Now it was warm. Almost too warm.

Her body pulsing with waves of pain, Nancy opened her eyes to a blurry, obscure scene. She perceived an eerie darkness, broken only by the misdirected beam of what appeared to be a flashlight or a lantern. Was she inside a cave? No, it was too warm and comfortable. And dry. Her eyes slowly adjusted to the dim surroundings. She was in a room. Very small. There was a television set and, further away, a table and chairs. And movement. Something tickled just below her navel. She tried to lift her head for a better view, her head still groggy, but fell limply back to rest on what seemed to be a sofa. The tickling continued. Upon focusing her vision, her mind suddenly cleared and she realized in one blood-freezing instant that she was naked, and there was a man bent over her waist—

Oh, my God! He's touching me! He's . . . he's. . .

Nancy's heart raced. A rising scream stopped short before escaping her throat. Suddenly her body convulsed and she emitted a low, guttural groan —

The man's head jerked in obvious surprise. Clumsily he tumbled off-balance to the floor, knocking the light from a nearby table. She had startled him, and he appeared as afraid as she — but what might he do next?

Recoiling in horror, she again tried to scream, but choked on her own tongue. Pain seared her joints as she instinctively curled to a protective fetal position. He was backing away now, putting more distance between them. And he was gagging, retching uncontrollably in the floor.

"Oh, dear God!" she wailed, tears streaming from her eyes.

The man was on his knees now, facing her with

vomit drooling from his chin. The beam of light from the floor bathed his forehead with satanic shadows. Nancy cringed. She tried to get up from the sofa, to run for her life, but never made it to her feet. She tensed, felt her pulse quicken, and with a loud ringing in her ears, fainted to a peaceful return to unconsciousness.

Wayne staggered to the toilet and threw up until his stomach ached. Never had he experienced such a burning rush of guilt and fear. She had caught him at the most embarrassing moment, just as he had lost control, on the verge of going much too far. Thank goodness she had stopped him in time. How could he have considered such a thing?

Standing, he wiped a dribble of vomit from his chin with a wet washcloth, then leaned over the sink for a sip of fresh water from the near-frozen faucet. Only a faint taste of puke remained in his mouth.

How can I explain this? What the hell can I tell her?

Wayne gazed at the mirror above the sink, but his reflection was lost in the darkness. His skin tingled with shame, and his pulse was still racing. When he explained, she would understand. After all, he had done her no real harm. He had saved her life.

She would understand.

But the fear in her eyes had hinted otherwise.

Wayne suddenly felt weak and exhausted. Pulling two quilts from his bed and grabbing a sleeping bag from the closet, he stumbled back to the living room.

She was resting soundly again.

He spread the bag over the floor beside the sofa, and quietly crawled beneath the quilts. His body pleaded for rest, but yet his mind wandered. Was Mom all right? He hated to think of her alone in that big empty house during this brutal weather. And Dad — what could be done about his drunken binges? In recent months the problem had gotten worse. How could Mom stand it?

Wayne rolled to his side, his muscles tense and sore from the night's unusual exertion. How could he have been so stupid as to intrude on the lady's privacy? He must have scared her half to death! She'd be angry, of course, and it would certainly put a damper on his heroic feat. But he would prove his sincerity.

He would apologize profusely, and as soon as the roads were clear in the morning, he would rush her to a hospital.

She would understand.

5

Saturday
Day Two

Waking early with excitement in his eyes, nine-year-old Nat Mason inhaled the sweet morning air of the Deep South. Daylight had finally come and Nat was anxious to peek outside. Before going to bed, Ma and Pa said conditions were right for snow, regardless of what the weatherman thought. And for a nine-year-old Negro boy who had never seen snow, the event would, indeed, be monumental. Snow seldom accumulated in this region and when the last had fallen two years earlier, Nat and his family had been further south in Andalusia where Pa was preaching at a revival. Snow was much more of a rarity down there.

Nat kicked out from under covers and dropped his bare feet to the cold floor. Clad only in long-johns, he shivered and rubbed his arms. The air was frigid, as always, in this back section of the house, far from the warmth of the fireplace in the living room. Quietly, he tip-toed to the window for a look outside. Not a trace of snow, but instead a thin coat of ice, sparkling like fine jewelry, blanketed the vegetation. The trees were like the glass trinkets his Ma scolded him for touching at a Sylacauga arts-and-crafts show. It was a crystal fantasy land. But the star-like reflections were fading fast, the ground already soggy from the meltdown. And in spite of the beauty, Nat was disappointed. After all, who ever heard of building an *ice* man?

With a sigh, Nat turned to the floor where his ragged denim coveralls lay in a crumpled heap. Might as well go outside anyway. It had rained hard the night before and Kelley Creek would be high. No telling what he might find along its shores. Last time the creek rose he found two slick tires and an old washing machine his Pa sold for scrap. There was always something. So quickly Nat slipped into the coveralls and pushed his feet into tennis shoes with worn-out toes.

Sneaking through the house, he quietly opened the front door and gently pushed the screened door forward. The scratchy sound of its overhead spring grated his nerves, but he doubted his Pa had been awakened. Outside, the air was brisk, but not as cold as he'd expected.

Skipping down the front steps, Nat raced for the nearby shore of Kelley Creek. Sure enough, the water was intriguingly high — higher, in fact, than he'd ever seen it. The dark muddy water flowed peacefully downstream, circling tree trunks that grew within the floodplain.

First, he'd need a good stick, the crucial tool of all young Alabama explorers. Luckily a nice prospect protruded from a pile of scrub his Pa had recently cleared away. Skinning the limb of its branches, Nat tested its firmness by prodding it into the soft mud along the shore. It seemed perfect.

Fully equipped, he paced the shoreline, a task more difficult now with the water level penetrating thick stands of pines on both shores. But that made it all the more exciting.

Nat gazed across the stream, now more than twice its normal width. It seemed strange to consider that the trails he usually hiked were now under water. Were fishes swimming along his favorite path? Nat chuckled aloud, then stopped in his tracks as something caught his eye. At the water's edge, tiny waves lapped along the shore. And just ahead, bobbing in the water, half submerged, was a plastic box. It was white and shiny and on top there was a black plastic handle.

Nat scurried forward and hooked the stick through the handle. Examining the object more closely, he knew immediately it was a woman's purse. WOW! He hoped there was something good inside! Quickly he pulled it open. There was a hair brush, makeup, and thick, soggy cotton pads whose use he couldn't imagine. And at the bottom was a small change purse that held six damp dollars! Nat pocketed the money and chucked the purse and its contents into the nearby brush. With a broad smile, he ran back to the front porch of the house. The sun was beaming directly across the deck's rotted planks to the side of an old washing machine where he spread the money to dry.

Six dollars was more than he'd ever owned — what a lucky break! And with this sudden turn of good fortune, Nat wondered what other treasures might be found along the creek. Anxiously, he bounded away, knowing the cash was out of sight of his mother if she came to the front door. Skipper, his mutt, would keep thieves away.

Maybe later Pa would drive him to Pell City for some shopping.

The chill of dawn settled over Nancy as sleep slowly ended. Blinking for clear vision, her eyes traced the beams of diffused sunlight that penetrated a nearby window. Through a crack in the corduroy curtains she saw tiny icicles outside with droplets of water swelling and falling from their pointed ends. Turning her attention inside, she gazed down the length of the corridor, immediately recognizing the interior of a mobile home. But how had she come to be here? And where was Charlie?

And why was she lying nude beneath a blanket?

Suddenly her throat seemed thicker, her breathing difficult. Had it been more than just a nightmare, being molested by a strange man in the dark? It had been so horrible, so gross. And yet . . . it had seemed so real.

I'm inside someone's home.

Guardedly she lowered her gaze to the floor.

He was there. The man. Asleep on the floor. Blocking her exit.

A jumble of thoughts rushed through her mind. What had this man done to her? *And what had he done to Charlie —?*

Tensing her muscles in order to rise, she felt a sharp pain race through her stiffened joints.

Oh, my God — I've been beaten. And heaven only knows what else!

She recalled that horrible moment when she awoke to find a man hovering over her waist and could hear and feel his heavy breath again.

Panic-stricken, Nancy strained again, hoping to somehow get to her feet, but it was impossible. She was much too sore. Nervously she settled back on the sofa.

How can I protect myself?

Shifting her eyes, she searched for a makeshift weapon. If a heavy, solid object were within reach, perhaps she could knock her captor unconscious. Leaning her head as far back as possible, she looked behind the upper end of the sofa. There, on a dusty end table, was a small trophy. Reaching back with her right arm, she grabbed it and brought it back to her chest for closer inspection.

Atop a marble base stood a ten-inch bowler. An inscription read "Selton Strikers, Third Place". Selton . . . She and Charlie had been driving to Selton to see Liz. But she couldn't remember if they'd ever arrived.

Fumbling with the tiny statue, Nancy turned it end over end and gripped the figurine tightly in her right hand, testing the feel of its heavy base against her hip. Yes, with a forceful swing, it could inflict some damage.

But could she actually *strike* this man? Looking down again, she saw that he was still asleep. His face was young and vaguely familiar. Where had she seen him before? She was almost certain he was the man she had surprised during the night. But had she not seen him prior to that? And something about the icicles outside the trailer nagged at her memory as well. Was it because of the chilled, icy feeling she had when she awoke? Again, she remembered traveling with Charlie. They had had a stressful, heart-to-heart discussion, and then came a terrible storm and . . . then what? It was as if at that point her memory had been shredded to a hundred pieces. Thinking about it gave her a headache. But the facts could no longer be ignored — despite his meek and innocent appearance, this man had brought her to his home and removed her clothes. He had obviously beaten her, and she had awakened just in time to prevent him from, from — but what could he have already done prior to her awakening?

Yes. She could strike him in his sleep. A sense of survival demanded that she fend for herself, and without risk. There was no guarantee he wouldn't kill her yet. And she might not get another chance.

Cautiously, Nancy studied the scene. She would need to shift her weight for an unobstructed swing. But when she tried desperately to slide into position, it was no use — it hurt too much. At best she could deliver only a glancing blow with enough force to perhaps daze him. Possibly then she could struggle past him to the telephone before he could stop her. Maybe not. She had nothing to lose.

Apprehensively, Nancy raised the trophy above the man's head, his face reminding her again of the filthy feeling of violation that surged through her body at his touch.

Closing her eyes, she brought the marble base down hard against his forehead.

The dream was progressing nicely.

Rising flames filled Wayne's subconscious. A suburban home was engulfed in fire. In a second

story window stood a beautiful young woman, much
like the one he'd actually saved from drowning.
Courageously, he rushed through the scorching
heat, staying low to avoid the deadly smoke as he
bounded upstairs. The poor girl was about to succumb just as he entered the room. Quickly he
gathered her weak body into his arms and carried
her to safety. Instant recognition followed. He was a
celebrity. People who had previously snubbed him
now greeted him with warmth and respect. Total
strangers vigorously shook his hand. Mom was
especially proud, and Dad had a great story to tell
his drinking buddies.

And the women —

Those who had overlooked him before now saw
him in a different light. Wayne Crocker had become
somebody. His life's destiny, it seemed, had been to
save a life. He decided to redirect his future efforts
to the safety and protection of others. Would he
become a policeman? A firefighter? Or perhaps join
a rescue squad —?

Pain.

Intense, piercing pain.

Wayne's temples throbbed. His head felt as if it
had been split in half.

Then a bulky weight tumbled across his chest with
a scrambling, frantic motion. He was no longer
dreaming. Shrieking screams tormented his ears.

It was her! The woman! But what was she doing?
Why was she reacting this way, scratching and tear-
ing at his face? Her fingernails were long and sharp,
leaving trails of raw, burning flesh in his cheeks.
What the hell was happening?

Instinctively he grabbed her. Though her energy

was waning fast, her screams increased in pitch as he squeezed her arm hard. Her erratic shrieks pierced his eardrums and echoed inside his aching head.

"Wait!" he snarled.

Her right hand clawed the floor, stretching and reaching for the small telephone table near the television. She ignored his command, groaning and twisting away.

"Stop it!" he shouted again, and gave her arm a tight wrench.

She recoiled immediately and wailed in pain. Her bruised and swollen arm felt pitiful in his grasp. He hadn't meant to harm her, but the look in her eyes was frightening. It was a look combining helplessness with terror. How could she feel that way toward him?

Lying with her breasts squashed against the cold floor, she trembled and shook with fear. Promptly he released her to demonstrate his innocent intentions. Then he leaned toward her.

"*Don't touch me!*" she cried.

The two lay paralyzed on the floor, sizing each other up.

Two pulses pounded together.

Two bodies shook with fear.

Two adversaries plotted their next moves.

"I won't hurt you," Wayne said calmly as a trickle of blood rolled down his forehead and dripped from his nose. "Please let me explai—"

Without warning she kicked him in the groin.

"*Charlie!*" she yelled between uncontrollable sobs. "*Help me, somebody. Please . . .*"

Clutching his testicles, Wayne curled his body to ward off further blows. Purple flashes invaded his vision, a shrill whistling sound screamed in his ears as he tried to avoid blacking out. Gagging, he rolled to his side away from her.

She was like a cornered tigress, ready to kill if he couldn't reason with her first. Was she crazy? Didn't she realize she owed her life to him?

A loud clang interrupted Wayne's thoughts. Turning his head, he saw that she had pulled the telephone from its stand and was frantically depressing the switchhook for a dial tone. Finally realizing that the line was dead, she flung the receiver at his disabled form and crawled further toward the kitchen.

Wayne's mind wavered between consciousness and a deep, dark void. In a few incredible moments he had turned from hero to villain to victim. A crash of silverware told him she had pulled a kitchen drawer to the floor. Even if he managed to overcome her, she would report him to the police. She obviously believed him a kidnapper, and he could spend the rest of his life in prison if a jury doubted his story. The glory was gone, and with it, the recognition and acceptance. Now his life would be worse than ever.

Shakily, Wayne wiped away tears and blood that blurred his vision. She was lying on her stomach, facing him ten feet or so away. Shining from her forehead was an ugly bruise and both her breasts lay flattened against the floor.

Slowly, menacingly, she raised her head. Her expression reflected both fear and madness. She grimaced with pain, but took a deep breath, and inched toward him.

In her right hand she held tightly to a butcher knife.

Martha Farrell stood waiting at the door as Tom and Liz returned from their search for a telephone in working order. The sun was shining brightly, the temperature rising, and all traces of the previous night's miserable weather were almost gone.

To the sound of car doors slamming shut and the crackle of hens pecking about in the yard, Martha surveyed the expressions of her husband and daughter. Tears were rolling down Lizzie's cheeks. The news was obviously bad — but just how bad was it?

"Went all the way to Vincent before we could find a decent phone," Tom began, scraping clumps of mud from his shoes on the front steps. "Saw men from the phone company and the power company along the way. They say ours ought to be hooked up again sometime this afternoon."

"Wipe those shoes in the grass!" Martha scolded him as Liz approached and hugged her tightly.

"I called Aunt Helen in Columbus," Liz said. "She was worried sick about Nancy. She tried to call us all night, but couldn't get through since the phone was out. She broke down when I told her Nancy never got here."

"Now, wait a minute," Tom broke in. "You've got to listen to reason." He stepped to Liz's side and placed a hand comfortingly on her right shoulder. "The telephone lines are down all over the place. They probably couldn't call. You know what the sheriff said."

"Yeah, I know," Liz answered with a grimace, looking back at her mother. "The sheriff says we've got to give Nancy and Charlie time to get in touch with us before he can do anything. He says they can't be considered 'missing' just yet. But what if they're dying in a ditch somewhere —?"

"Now, hold your horses," Tom interrupted again, more impatiently this time. "Don't go flyin' off the handle. The sheriff would know if they've been involved in a serious accident. And like he said, the fact that he didn't know of any bad wrecks is in our favor."

Liz settled into the front porch swing and gently began to rock. The morning sun felt warm against her skin. It seemed hard to believe that the night before had been a veritable deep freeze. She glanced at her father who was now rounding the side of the house, on his way to feed the chickens. How could he be so optimistic? Of course, it's just an act for my sake, she thought. She could tell by the expressions of both her Mom and Dad that they, too, were worried.

His bloody face wavered before her unsteady vision.

Trembling, and oblivious to her own nakedness, Nancy inched her way toward him.

"G-G-Get away from the d-d-door," she muttered as she slowly approached, the knife gleaming ominously in her hand.

Wayne sat motionless, only now beginning to regain his faculties. Holding an open palm toward her to motion her away, Wayne slid backwards across the cold floor and rested against the sofa.

Pain ripped through Nancy's body. A surge of adrenalin had enabled her to act, but now the weakness of her limbs had returned. Did she have the strength to continue? Surrender now could mean certain death. But what would she do if she escaped? Was she physically capable of seeking help? Or would she just crawl away to die a slow, agonizing death? Her head throbbing, her right leg resisting all efforts to walk, she hesitated at the door to rest. Glancing back, she saw her clothes folded neatly on the back of the sofa. But it would be impossible to dress without giving her captor a chance to retaliate.

"G-G-Give me the blanket," she said, pointing the shiny blade at him.

Wayne bundled the blanket and tossed it to her feet.

Her right hand reached for the doorknob. Slowly she twisted and forced the door ajar.

"Stay back!" she warned, pushing the door further open.

Wayne's mind raced over the possibilities. *She's hurt. She could injure herself further, not to mention the damage she could do to me if she tells.*

He eased closer and extended an arm to her. "Let me help," he said. "I'll take you anywhere you—"

"No!" she barked and slashed the knife in his direction in a wild, erratic arc. "Stay away from me!"

Wayne dodged the blade and reconsidered. The pain from his head and groin was worsening, and he was further inhibited by the soreness of his muscles from last night's ordeal. If he were at full strength, he could easily out-maneuver her, throw her into the car and rush her to a hospital. But in this weakened state, he'd have to be careful. She could actually kill him.

Wayne studied her slow, calculated movement. He'd have to surprise her, catch her off-guard. He would overpower her and force her to listen. They'd reach an understanding, then he'd take her away.

Her legs were hanging out of the doorway as she struggled to shift her weight outside to the front steps, the blanket wrapped tightly around her body.

I can't let her do this.

Wayne reached for one of the quilts tangled atop the crumpled sleeping bag. Distracted by intense pain, Nancy missed his movement.

She'll tell. She'll tell everybody.

Her attention finally fixed outside, Wayne sprung forward and tossed the quilt over her crippled form, at the same time groping for the knife in her right hand. The girl panicked, dropped the knife, and screamed at the top of her lungs, her voice carrying past the leafless oaks and echoing along the rolling hills that surrounded the trailer. Through tear-streaked vision Wayne grappled with her, losing his balance as he covered her mouth with his left hand. The two tumbled down the steps to the ground outside. Now she was biting and gnawing at his hand.

"Stop it!" he growled, wincing at the pain in his own limbs. Rapping her sharply on the head with his knuckles, Wayne frantically surveyed the area. There was no one in sight. But could anyone have heard her scream? He held his breath and listened. A crow cawed at the rustle of wind through dead leaves and the girl's breath huffed loudly from beneath the quilt. Most likely, no one had heard. In one swift motion Wayne gathered her struggling body into his arms and lifted her to the doorway, then pushed her inside with a forceful thrust.

Impatience warmed his blood. What could he do now? Couldn't she remember how he'd saved her life? If not, it was understandable why she had reacted this way. He rested a moment to catch his breath. How the hell did he get himself into such a miserable predicament? Maybe he shouldn't have gotten involved in the first place. He could've let her drown and gone about his business. After all, his own father could've been in danger. But, no, this lady needed him. She'd fought valiantly for her life, and whatever trouble and red tape he got himself into, it was worth it. A human life was at stake. He'd get himself out of this dilemma . . . somehow.

Wayne removed the blanket and examined the woman's face. Her eyes bulged with terror, and tears were streaming down her cheeks. She was wild, intent on destroying him. But he'd make her understand. And he wouldn't trust her for a minute until she did. Somehow, she truly believed she had been kidnapped. He would have to calm her down and help her remember.

Suddenly her screams returned, deafening him with their piercing tone. The sound reverberated inside his throbbing head.

"Shut up!" he commanded, shaking her shoulders hard.

Nancy cringed beneath the quilt.

Collapsing to the floor, she wept uncontrollably, as visions of life's most pleasant moments flashed into her mind. Gone forever were the Sunday dinners with her parents, her music, her pets. And Charlie — strangely enough, in this dire moment even the bitter arguments with her husband evoked soothing memories. These and so many other precious scenes would forever lay behind her.

But then came a faint sound of hope.

She lifted the quilt from her head to listen more attentively. Her captor's face, frozen with fear, showed that he had heard it, too—

The whine of an engine.

An approaching vehicle.

Panic-striken, Wayne leaped to his feet and peeked out of a window. His father's pickup truck was ambling up the driveway. What could he possibly want? Under no circumstances could his father be allowed inside. And the woman — she would have to be silenced. There was no time to explain.

Wayne flung the quilt away and reached for her clothing on the sofa. "I'm sorry," he apologized, sadness in his eyes. He stuffed a portion of her dress inside her mouth and tied its sleeves around her head to keep her quiet. Then, arresting her struggling limbs, he rolled her to her stomach and tied her hands behind her back with a bra strap, securing both legs with a coiled section of her slip. He hoped the makeshift bindings would hold her long enough for him to turn his father away.

Wayne stood and covered her incapacitated form with the blanket, quilts, and sleeping bag, then tried desperately to regain his composure, to appear normal despite his true condition, as he opened the door and stepped outside.

An empty Schlitz bottle sailed through the air and shattered against the side of the trailer, shards of brown glass barely missing Wayne's head. James Crocker had already exited from his battered pickup truck and was now staggering angrily toward his son.

"You little bastard," James slurred. "Caused me

to stay all night in the pokey. I'll whup your ass — that's what I'll do."

Wayne trudged forward to head his father off when, to his surprise, James took a hard swing at him. Wayne ducked just in time, as the follow-through of the swing caused his drunken father to stumble.

"Go home and sleep it off," Wayne begged as he dodged another wayward blow, and then wrestled and pinned him to the ground, quickly turning his face away from his father's fetid breath.

"Lemme use your phone," James begged. "Ours is dead. I gotta make a call."

Wayne groaned, but held his father's arms firmly to the ground.

"My phone's dead, too," he answered.

"Now, don't try to hand me that bullshit—"

"I said my goddamn phone is *dead*! Now leave me alone, will you?"

James stared past his son's shoulder at the clear blue sky. Having just been on the biggest bender in his life, James hardly knew what day it was.

"All right, lemme up," James drawled, releasing the tension in his arms. "You don't 'preciate me. You never did. I'll get out of your goddamn way."

Wayne eased off and helped his father to his feet. James brushed at the cakes of mud on his knees, then plowed directly into Wayne, knocking him hard to the ground. James stumbled toward the door of the trailer.

"I'll use the goddamn phone whenever I feel like it," he mumbled beneath his breath.

Staring in horror, Wayne quickly scrambled to his

feet. Wavering, James was reaching for the door-knob as Wayne raced madly toward him. Wayne tackled him hard and the two went sprawling to the side of the trailer, rolling and tumbling in the mud.

"I said for you to *leave me alone!*" Wayne growled between gritted teeth. He grasped the collar of his father's shirt and shook it hard. "Can't you under-stand? I don't owe you nothin'!"

"Lemme up," James begged. "Lemme up and I'll go."

Out the corner of an eye Wayne saw the doorknob turn. It was only a slight movement, but enough to send cold shivers down his spine. She's up, he thought.

Quickly he grabbed his father under both arms and pulled him to his feet, directing him away from the trailer and back to his truck.

"I'm sorry, Dad — I'd be glad to let you use the phone if it was working. But there's nothin' I can do. Besides, I wish you'd go home and see about Mom."

"Shit, I'll tend to you later," James slurred. Wayne opened the truck's door and helped James behind the wheel. "I'm gonna teach you some respect!"

"Okay, okay," Wayne obliged.

James turned the ignition and the truck coughed to life. With a sly grin he noticed the blood on Wayne's face, mistakenly assuming he had inflicted the wound himself. Nodding toward the gash in Wayne's forehead, James snarled, "That ought to teach you enough for now. So fuck off."

Whipping the steering wheel into a sharp turn, James stomped heavily on the accelerator, and drove off, too much in a huff to hear the faint squeal for help from inside the trailer. Wayne met the woman at the door and shook her hard, storming at her as she fainted and fell to the floor.

6

Because Sheriff Chester Arnold laughed easily and often, those who knew him least considered the lawman soft, and wondered if he took his responsibilities seriously enough. But in reality, Chester Arnold was a firm believer in justice and tirelessly devoted his efforts to the safety and security of all Shelby County residents. And when the time came to exert pressure, he knew exactly when, where, and how far to push.

Returning an empty porcelain cup to its saucer on the coffee table, the sheriff glanced at the Farrells, who had welcomed him into their living room. As he'd been in the vicinity, the sheriff had, as a courtesy, stopped by their home, fully expecting to learn that their missing relatives had long since safely arrived. And though there had been no further word of them, he was still not terribly concerned. First, he knew Tom Farrell well enough to detect that Tom was not nearly as worried as the two women, whom he felt were merely overreacting. And then, the sheriff was sure that the Barnetts had most likely been unavoidably detained in last night's violent weather. So for the present, the sheriff decided to comfort the ladies as best he could and then possibly do some preliminary checking back at the office before issuing a missing persons report.

Fumbling his broad-brimmed hat in both hands, the sheriff spoke calmly and reassuringly to Liz.

"I can understand your concern," he consoled her, "but let's not worry too much just yet. These things sometimes have a way of clearing up all by themselves."

"But the weather—"

"I'd be a whole lot more concerned if the weather had been normal," the sheriff interrupted. "Everyone involved in serious accidents has been identified, and I can assure you, your kinfolks' names haven't crossed my desk."

Liz sat silently as the sheriff slowly rose from the sofa with a tired grunt and headed for the door.

"These ice storms just tend to shut everything down around here, as you well know," he said. "It takes a while for everything to get back to normal."

With a gruff chuckle, the sheriff pulled the door open and stepped outside. Tom Farrell followed, closed the door behind himself, and faced the sheriff alone on the porch.

"Ain't it just like women to carry on like that?" Tom said. "They just about drove me crazy."

The sheriff tapped his hat on and smiled.

"Well, Tom, I know what you mean," he said.

"But it's gettin' awful close to lunchtime now, and if your niece and nephew ain't heard from soon, I'll begin to get a little jumpy about it myself."

Sheriff Arnold took a deep breath as he descended the steps. Fresh country air — there was nothing like it. The sound of Tom's cattle mooing in the pasture and the cackle of hens around the yard brought back his own youthful memories. He had grown up just a few miles away, but now, he thought, the area was changing faster than anyone could imagine.

"Haven't seen you around these parts lately, Chester," Tom interrupted the lawman's reminiscences.

"No, I've been keeping pretty busy," the sheriff answered, gazing ahead at the freshly paved road skirting Tom Farrell's property. "In fact, today was my first time to cross the new Kelley Creek Bridge."

Tom spat over the porch railing and wiped his mouth on a flannel sleeve.

"Just crossed it the first time myself yesterday," Tom answered. "Those construction boys were haulin' ass to finish up afore the weather broke loose."

Odd, thought the sheriff. Something about that scene had bothered him the moment he crossed the bridge. Something didn't seem right about it, and he couldn't quite put his finger on the reason.

"Glad we got rid of that awful curve," the sheriff commented. "When I was a kid, three out-of-towners from Birmingham died when they smashed into the railing."

"I remember it myself," Tom answered. "A tricky road it was — even for folks who traveled it every day."

The old road. That's what it had been. Something about the old road.

"Well, I'd best be gettin' back to the office before they accuse me of goofin' off on the job," the sheriff chuckled, slipping behind the wheel of his patrol car. "Let me know when you hear something," he called out to Tom.

"You do the same," Tom answered.

The V-8 Ford engine rumbled to a stop and quietly ticked as the sheriff cut the ignition. Exiting, and slamming the door in disgust, he glared past the re-routed roadway. Not a single barricade blocked entry to the old road.

"Goddamn lazy bastards," he mumbled as he paced toward the mud-splotched former passage. Pushed far to the left, a simple sawhorse-style barrier leaned against the brush, a blinking yellow caution light still flashing faintly.

Vandals, he thought. Some wise-ass teenager decided to route traffic down a dead-end road. Shit! As if there wasn't enough to worry about already!

The sheriff dragged the crude barrier back to the center of the road, loose gravel crackling beneath his shoes. *Maybe* it wasn't the road crew's fault after all.

Turning back toward the car, he reconsidered. Hell, this road needs a better barricade than that, he thought, staring at the flimsy sawhorse which looked oddly foreboding. His curiosity hooked, Sheriff Arnold walked briskly past the barrier and around the sharp bend of the old chert-based road. Treetops at both sides of the forgotten artery merged overhead, blotting out the sun with an eerie artificial darkness. *Damn, just driving past here, you'd never know how spooky this place really is.*

Crows cawed at the gentle breeze and fluttered away as the intruder violated their terrain. Stepping past a large mudhole, the sheriff gazed ahead at a bizarre, frightening sight: The old bridge stood partially dismantled, without a single barrier to its entry.

"Holy Jesus!" he whispered, feeling his heart plunge to his knees.

At a slowed pace, he stepped forward hypnotically. A sudden movement in the nearby brush startled him, and instinctively he drew his weapon, sighing with relief as a doe and her fawn leaped away into the forest.

Nearing the bridge he stared ahead at the missing center span. How could a construction firm be so negligent? Nausea grew inside his stomach.

They're down there.

Stepping to the edge, he calmly looked down. Nothing. Dark chocolate-colored water flowed quietly in a peaceful setting. The line on the far shore indicated that the creek was receding. All was well. Expelling a burst of breath in relief, the sheriff pivoted, then froze.

Something caught his eye. A light spot. In the water. Just below the surface, a short distance downstream. Something . . . white.

Liz Farrell's shaky voice echoed in his mind, a wavering tone of alarm carrying clearly over the telephone just this very morning. "Sheriff Arnold, they're driving a *white* '63 Ford Falcon. I don't know the tag number — but it's a Georgia license plate."

The mystery's over, he thought sadly. He envisioned cold muddy water washing over their trapped corpses, floating against the roof of the sunken vehicle.

Sheriff Arnold wiped beads of sweat from his forehead. Although he'd seen his share of grisly automobile accidents, he could feel his stomach muscles tighten, vomit rising to his throat. These victims were close relatives of his friends.

With a hacking cough, he regained his composure. Running back to the patrol car, the sheriff summoned help on the radio and seized the wooden barrier as evidence.

Someone would pay for this.

Nat Mason returned from a second trip to the creek all but empty-handed, his only additional find an ordinary looking hub cap. And though it was of negligible value, Nat thought it might replace a worn-out shoe box as a container for his collection of tiny plastic dinosaurs. Knowing Pa would be awake by now, he had been forced to cut this second treasure hunt short. A self-avowed Baptist minister, Pa held strong convictions about returning lost valuables to their rightful owners, and though a pang of guilt stirred within young Nat, six dollars was just too much to resist. It would have to be kept a secret.

The six bills were almost dry. Nat wadded them into a crumpled ball and stuffed them into his pocket — Skipper guarded them well. With tail wagging, the dog padded forward, his claws clicking lightly on the wooden planks of the porch.

"Good boy," Nat praised him, sprawling beside the dog and stroking the animal's back. "I'm gonna buy you a new chew-toy."

The aroma of sizzling bacon drifted through the air — breakfast! And here it was almost lunchtime already. Pa had been away late last night, returning from a Dothan job interview. Ma had been terribly worried about him driving alone in that awful weather, but in the wee hours of morning he finally arrived safe and sound. That's when the lively conversation of his parents had awoken young Nat. Drawn also by the warmth of the fireplace, Nat had stepped through the chilly hall to the living room, rubbing sleep from his eyes, only to be promptly escorted back to bed by Pa.

"It just might snow tonight, son," Pa had said as he tucked his youngest child beneath a layer of quilts. "It's just ice and sleet so far, but if the Good Lord wants it, it'll snow."

Nat had fallen asleep dreaming of snowball fights, of building his first snowman, of sliding down embankments on strips of cardboard.

"Nat, get in here!" his mother yelled from behind the screened door. "I've been callin' you all mornin'!"

Jumping quickly to his feet and beaming from ear to ear, Nat bounded inside. Money was better than snow, he'd decided.

He couldn't get her to stop crying.

She was hysterical, shaking her head in a wild frenzy each time he spoke, as if even the sound of his voice inflicted pain.

Wayne watched spellbound as she raved. This has gotten way out of control, he thought.

He waited until she was finally exhausted before he made any attempt to approach her. She reminded him of a kitten, helpless and frightened, cowering in a corner at the onslaught of a vicious dog. Knowing she perceived him as a sex offender, he felt ashamed. He would have to be especially careful now. Avoid rushing her.

Give her time.

Give her space.

Tightly wrapped in a cocoon of woolen blanket, she sniffled and wiped her tears on the fuzzy nap.

"Please . . ." she finally spoke. "I need to go . . . to the . . . bathroom."

"Can't we talk first?" he asked.

She lowered her head, then pleaded, "*Please?*"

Wayne shrugged and motioned down the hall.

After a moment she struggled to rise, pain arcing across her stiffened joints. Then she slumped back to the floor.

"I can't . . . walk."

"Let me help you," he offered, then quickly added, "I promise I won't hurt you."

Cautiously he awaited a response, then interpreted her silence as consent. Bouncing to his feet, Wayne approached her, but she gasped at the sudden movement, and he quickly retreated.

"Sorry," he apologized, progressing more slowly this time. "Honest, I'll help you, and leave you alone. Then we can talk." As his hands searched for a firm hold on her shoulders, Nancy held her breath, wincing at the slightest pressure.

"My shoulder . . . hurts."

Dropping his hands to her waist, Wayne awkwardly helped her to her feet, whereupon she immediately leaned her weight against him. Her head bobbing helplessly against his chest, she inched toward the bathroom. Through the kitchen. Past the messy adjoining room where records and books lay scattered across the floor.

At the bathroom he lowered the toilet seat and gently eased her down to the cold plastic rim.

"I'll be right outside if you need me," he said, and slid the door shut.

As Nancy steadied herself against the sink in front of her, the blanket tumbled softly to the floor. Her breath still heaving and tears trickling down her cheeks, she trembled as her muscles relaxed and she relieved herself.

What on earth is happening to me? And where is Charlie?

Her captor was impossible to evaluate. At one moment he appeared a perfect gentleman, the next, a maniac who might bind and gag her. Obviously he was a mental case. But how should she proceed? Go along with his whims and fancies? Gain his confidence and escape at the first opportunity? But what if he should decide to kill her soon? What then?

Her stiffened right leg, outstretched at an uncomfortable angle, ached relentlessly. Gazing about the tiny room, her eyes settled on the small medicine chest above the sink.

Drugs. Suicide. Before he molests me again.

Struggling to her feet, she winced as the pain intensified. Fully realizing she might not be thinking rationally, Nancy unlatched the mirrored door and quietly pulled it open. The cabinet was cluttered with toiletries — Vitalis hair tonic, Bayer aspirin, Alka Seltzer — but no prescription drugs. On a bottom shelf was a tube of Pepsodent toothpaste, a can of shaving cream, a safety razor — and a package of Gillette double-edged blades. Fumbling nervously, she removed a blade from its wrapper. A tiny sparkle of light glimmered from its scalpel-sharp edges. With the blade gripped tightly between her thumb and forefinger, she returned to the toilet seat.

Nancy placed her left hand in her lap, palm open wide toward her, the exposed wrist milky white and vulnerable below her leather watchband. One quick slash and it would be over. A shaking right hand lowered the blade to rest on the tender flesh of her inner arm. Pressing ever so lightly, the tip of the blade pricked the skin, a tiny ball of blood bubbling forth. A streak of crimson curled around her arm and dripped to her leg. And then she reconsidered — why me? *Why not him?*

The blade could be concealed under the blanket. And as the man helped her back to the living room, as soon as his attention was diverted, she could whisk out the blade and drive it into his neck. But she'd have to be careful. With only the one opportunity, she would have to break a vein or artery for it to work. And if she failed, he would likely be enraged and kill her. But what did she have to lose?

Nothing.

Absolutely nothing.

Nancy retrieved the blanket from the floor and bundled it tightly around her. Staring ahead at the sliding door, she took a deep breath and called to him, "I'm . . . finished."

And she thought — *and so are you*.

His stomach growling with hunger pangs, Wayne sat on the floor outside the bathroom, placing loose record albums into their appropriate sleeves. As he had missed breakfast altogether, he was starving and knew his guest must be hungry, too.

Was she suffering from shock or temporary amnesia? Or had the accident inflicted some kind of brain damage? Obviously she'd been dealt a nasty blow. He rubbed the ugly gash on his own forehead where she'd hit him earlier, realizing it needed dressing. Then he turned his attention back to the girl. She needed medical attention. *She could be disabled for life — all because I kept her from a hospital.*

But his own future was also at stake. Sure, he had taken liberties with her. There was no denying that. But exactly what had he actually done? He'd touched her stomach and that was all. If she failed to be sympathetic, what could he be charged with? Kipnapping? But he'd had no motive, and considering the weather conditions and communications blackout, anyone would agree he made the right decision to take her to his trailer. But wouldn't his actions, once he'd gotten her there, be judged more harshly? Taking off her clothes to prevent pneumonia? Hmmmmmm. On the surface, sexual intent might be assumed. If she had been thirty or forty years older, his actions might not be questioned at all. But because she was young and attractive, the judgment might be that sexual motives had been his main concern. That could be tough to overcome.

Rape? Assault? Hell, he'd barely touched her!

Maybe invasion of privacy. That one he couldn't deny. He scratched his head, realizing that his most serious offense hadn't been criminal in nature, but was, instead, the negligence he had shown by not getting her the proper medical attention. But if he could convince her of his innocence, she would likely show her gratitude by refusing to press charges. God, how he hoped that would be the case. If she would just calm down and be reasonable . . .

Absorbed in his thoughts, Wayne missed the faint rustle of movement in the bathroom. She called for help again, and anxiously he sprang to his feet. Sliding the door open, his eyes met hers, but she promptly looked away.

Leaning over her bundled form, he again reached for her waist. "Tell me if I hurt you," he said calmly.

They shuffled inch by inch toward the living room, Nancy dragging the dead weight of her injured leg behind her. *He seems so tender,* she thought, *so concerned. Maybe I should allow more time—*

But at that instant, as the two squeezed through the narrow kitchen doorway, her eyes rested on the dinner table. Photos. Two of them. She was aghast — bare-breasted snapshots of herself! It was disgusting! Revolting!

Wayne sensed something amiss. Gazing around her shoulders, he traced her line of vision to the table. *Oh, my God — the pictures! I forgot the damn pictures!*

Quickly he released her and held up his shaking hands. She leaned against the table, her mouth open aghast.

"*P-P-P-Please!*" he begged. "Let me explain! It's not at all what it seems—"

"No!" she moaned, tears again streaming from her eyes. "What have you done to me?"

Now tears flowed from Wayne's eyes, as well. This was trouble, real trouble. Never had he experienced fear and guilt like this. Reflexively he took a nervous step toward her.

"Please, you've got to understand," he sobbed, reaching out to her.

"Don't *touch* me!" she growled, still brandishing the razor blade out of sight. This can't be happening, she thought. Again her vision wavered, and she felt as if she might faint.

Wayne saw that she was sinking toward the floor and reached to catch her. And as darkness began to cloud her mind, she gathered all her strength to draw the blade from beneath the blanket and slash at him mercilessly. Once. Twice.

Her crumpled form collapsed to the floor. The razor blade hit the tile with a light tinkle and bounced beneath the stove.

A trail of blood followed Wayne as he stumbled to the bathroom sink.

A midday swarm of activity centered around the accident site at Kelley Creek. Sheriff Arnold cordoned off the section of old roadway leading to the dismantled bridge and began an intense investigation while the sunken vehicle was removed from the water. Volunteers from surrounding areas gathered along the shore as news of the accident spread, and a somber mood prevailed — it was such a tragic waste of human life.

Tom Farrell arrived just as the battered car was pulled to the muddy shore. Sheriff Arnold had been watching for him and, amid the flashing red emergency lights, ran to meet him.

"Tom, I just can't tell you how sorry I am," the sheriff said, placing an arm around his friend's shoulder.

Tom silently shook his head and stared into the distance.

"Chester, I wasn't real close to these folks," Tom began, his voice cracking. "I mean, Nancy was my niece and all, but since Martha's sister moved to Georgia, I just ain't seen much of 'em. But you know," he hesitated, wrinkling his lips, "I'd feel pretty damn bad no matter who it was on the bottom of that creek. It just ain't fair. Ain't a damn bit fair."

"How is Liz taking it?" the sheriff asked.

"Oh . . ." Tom began, followed by an expulsion of breath. "I'm afraid the poor girl's on the verge of a nervous breakdown. Lately things just ain't been goin' her way."

"And Martha?"

"Well, she's awful worried about her sister gettin' here safely from Columbus. They're all pretty tore up, as you can understand."

"Sheriff!" Deputy Granger called from the dripping wreckage. "There's only one of 'em in here. Looks like we'll have to drag for the woman."

Sheriff Arnold turned back to Tom. "Maybe you shouldn't look," he said.

Tom shuffled his feet in the moist soil of the pathway. Why look? What good would it do? Only bring nightmares for God knows how long. Besides, why had he even come here in the first place? There was certainly nothing he could do.

"I suppose you're right," Tom said. "I hadn't given it much thought afore I got here. But it's all just now beginnin' to sink in."

The sheriff watched teardrops form in his friend's eyes and patted him softly on the back. Tom sniffled and pocketed both hands.

"Think I'll get on back to the house. See how Martha and Liz are holdin' up," Tom said.

The sheriff led Tom away from the rescue site. Out the corner of an eye he saw three men wrestle a bloated corpse from the Falcon. As if it weren't enough that the young woman had also died, now her loved ones must endure a long and painful search for her remains. How could anyone comfort the family, whose thoughts would naturally be of Nancy's lifeless body being swept downstream, scraped against rocks and trees, possibly even devoured by wildlife? If her corpse wasn't recovered soon, it might never be found.

"I think that's a smart move," the sheriff said. "We'll have to drag for the girl, Tom, and you're in no shape to help. Besides, we've got more volunteers than we can shake a stick at."

"I don't know what to tell 'em back home. The missing body will only upset 'em more—"

"Then don't tell 'em anything," the sheriff interrupted. "If we're lucky, we'll find her real soon. No need to worry anybody just yet. And besides, Tom, it won't be a pretty sight. I really think you should go home."

"Yeah," said Tom, stepping back to his car. "Yeah."

The violent weather had all but obliterated any trace of the doomed Falcon's tiremarks on the condemned road. Walking the forgotten artery again, the sheriff tried to reconstruct what the experience had been like. The Barnetts had been strangers to the area. True, Nancy had lived here years before, but she was just a kid at the time and would be totally unfamiliar with the recent highway changes. The old road was in horrid disrepair — gaping potholes and deepened ruts riddled its surface. Shouldn't the driver have noticed such a marked deterioration? But, of course, the travelers were tired, and the rain was falling in such torrents, the car couldn't have been moving very fast. It was a short stretch of roadway. The weather had likely distracted the driver, and after a few seconds, it would have been too late.

In his mind's eye, the sheriff could visualize it all, as if he had ridden in the back seat, watching the Barnetts from behind. The husband would have been bent over the steering wheel, straining his eyes to see through sheets of rain. The wife was probably staring ahead to help him. Or maybe she was busy wiping fog from the windshield that the defroster failed to clear. Suddenly the car took a nose dive. Neither had likely had the slightest notion of what was happening. The man's head smashed into the steering wheel on impact; the woman hit the windshield. Had they not been rendered unconscious or disabled by the collision, they might well have escaped. But the current had been cold and swift. Even the most able-bodied swimmer might have met his match in the treacherous water.

Having circled the old roadway and shore while absorbed in thought, Sheriff Arnold found himself standing once again at the mangled wreckage among a crowd of onlookers.

"Sheriff?"

"Not now, Zeke," the sheriff interrupted. "Let me go over this again while it's fresh on my mind."

Sheriff Arnold slowly skirted the twisted mass of metal. The entire body was crumpled and warped, as if the car had rolled off Satan's assembly line. While the front grill and hood sustained the most damage, not a single square inch of the vehicle had escaped harm. A layer of mud and debris covered the interior upholstery and dashboard. On the floor a tiny minnow was flopping about, taking its last breath.

The surrounding confusion was getting out of hand. Reporters had already sniffed out the story and Deputy Granger was trying to move them away to a safe distance.

"Jesse," Sheriff Arnold approached his deputy. "Get the camera and take plenty of pictures. Of the car, of the road, the creek and the bridge."

Looking up, the sheriff noticed a television crew setting up. Quickly he headed them off and politely turned them away.

"Now, I know you boys are just doin' your job," he began. "And I'm just tryin' to do mine. But I can't let you folks interfere with this investigation."

"But sheriff—"

"Now I mean it," he snapped. "If you'll just hold your horses a few minutes, I'll be glad to answer your questions. Right now I've got work to do," he said sternly.

Returning to Deputy Granger, the sheriff whispered, "Jesse, I especially want shots of the front passenger side of the interior. Notice the window is rolled down? The girl could've escaped. No doubt she drowned — her head must have been banged up pretty bad. But don't mention it to the press. I want to keep the news down as much as possible."

The reporters scattered among the crowd, grasping for every available fact, and flashbulbs popped continuously. Disgusted, Sheriff Arnold shook his head.

"If you folks don't get the hell away from here and stop interferin' with this investigation, I'll take every one of you in for obstructin' justice!"

With scowls of protest, the intruders backed away. Three men in a canoe streaked through the water applying nets, hooks and other dragging apparatus while a number of volunteers scoured both shorelines.

Deputy Granger was busy snapping photos. He leaned over the right fender for a closeup of the cracked windshield on the passenger side. It reminded him of a glass spiderweb. No doubt the girl's head had struck it hard, but if she'd managed to open the car window, apparently not hard enough to knock her completely unconscious.

Across the creek, John Gibbs, a local high school boy, scampered downstream ahead of the search party. A glory hound, John hoped to find the dead girl all on his own. Along the way he noted an assortment of empty cans and bottles that normally lined the shore. Excitement surged through John's veins. Being first to explore this section of the creek was giving him the greatest thrill of his young life. And finally his persistence paid off. Poking among the branches of a large tree that had toppled into the water, he found a woman's shoe. And at the massive uprooted trunk near the water's edge, half buried in the mud, was an Eveready flashlight.

7

Blood dribbled down Wayne's chin and splattered into the bowl of the bathroom sink. His cheek and neck below the left ear stung something awful, but fortunately the flow of blood was slowing. He'd been lucky. The deepest cut, about an inch and a half in length, had missed his left eye and damaged only his cheek. The neck wound had barely broken the skin. In the mirror his pale, horror-stricken face stared back at him. Coupled with the gash inflicted earlier on his forehead, he looked like an accident victim himself.

Wayne placed a wet wash cloth over the wounds to absorb the last traces of blood, then jumped nervously as the power suddenly kicked on, and the refrigerator resumed its monotone hum. A feeling of horror wrenched his guts. Reasoning with her now would take a great deal of time. And patience. Her hidden ferocity was understandable, since she perceived herself in grave danger. But how could he convince her otherwise? She wouldn't give him a chance.

Hurrying back to the kitchen, Wayne cradled the woman's unconscious body and carried her to the sofa. He could feel the stiffness of her leg and tried not to disturb it. Then, having carefully spread the blanket back over her, he returned to the kitchen and opened the refrigerator. He was famished! She was bound to be hungry, too, and would likely be more receptive on a full stomach. In minutes, four ground-beef patties were sizzling on the stove.

By the time she awakened, the hamburgers were ready, the table neatly set for two. The photos had been hidden in the bedroom.

"Hungry?" he asked at the twitch of her eyebrows.

She stared at him blankly, her face expressionless.

"You don't have to be afraid," he said. "In fact, I'm the only one who's been attacked." He forced a weak smile, then winced as he stroked the gash on his cheek. Her stare continued unbroken, yielding no indication of her current state of mind.

Wayne took a big bite and held a burger up for her to see. "Join me?" he mumbled between swallows, then waited with longing to hear her voice.

She lifted her wrinkled nose and inhaled the delicious aroma, instantly recognizing her own hunger. For a moment, the anticipation of a satisfying meal erased all fears.

"Will you . . . bring it . . . to me?"

"Sure," Wayne answered. "By the way, my name is Wayne. And you seem to have a misunderstanding about how we met."

Wayne brought a plate with two burgers to her side. "Can you sit up?" he asked.

The girl struggled to her elbows, then surrendered to the sofa.

"Wait a minute. Try this," Wayne said. He fetched a chair from the table and placed it in front of the sofa. "Maybe if you prop your leg in the chair, you'll be able to sit."

Groping clumsily, he raised her to a comfortable position. With the plate in her lap, she ate voraciously.

"So, what would you like to drink? I've got beer, Pepsi, orange jui—"

"Water . . . will be fine."

Moments later he returned with two tall glasses clinking with ice cubes. Carefully he leaned her glass against her hip to avoid spillage. She quickly downed half its contents. Between bites of hamburger, she stopped to pull the blanket, which kept slipping down to reveal the cleavage of her breasts, tightly around her neck. Wayne diverted his attention and swallowed hard. She was so beautiful, and he was so bashful, that it was difficult to find the right words.

"I've never seen you around here. What's your name?" he asked.

Her face was hard as stone, her eyes unblinking.

"Nancy . . . Barnett."

It was then that Wayne noticed her wedding band. Funny, he thought, how he had missed it till now.

"You're married, I see. Where do you live?"

Nancy's eyes sprang open.

"Where's Charlie? *What have you done to him?*"

Wayne sat speechless. *Oh, my God — she wasn't*

alone. And she suspects me of doing harm to her family. It's worse than I thought.

"You were in an accident — don't you remember?"

She lifted her right hand and ran her fingertips across the knot on her forehead. Now that he mentioned it, she vaguely remembered the car jolting against something cold. But that was all.

It had been a difficult trip. Charlie had been unusually irritable, she recalled, and . . . she had felt apprehension, because his temper could always change so quickly. He was driving too carelessly. She was scared, and sat nervously at his side. The next thing she recalled, she was lying nude on a sofa. And this strange man was hovering over her privates. God, it was horrible!

Her calm disappeared, as trembling, and with renewed tears, she brought both hands to her mouth.

"Where's Charlie? Where am I?"

"Don't get upset — *please* don't get upset!" Wayne begged. The situation was slipping out of control. "You were in an accident. I pulled you from the creek. You would've drowned — but I didn't see anyone else." He looked worried. "Were there any . . . children?" he added.

Her face brightened.

"He'll come for me," she said. "Charlie will find me. And you'll be sorry—"

"Hold on," Wayne interrupted. "You're not in any danger. I brought you here for your own protection. You're free to go anytime."

Wayne watched her closely, the fear in her eyes haunting him with guilt. Should he admit wrongdoing in examining her body? Maybe if he could be up-front with her, she would be more likely to believe him. But to confess such a thing for a timid person like himself was unthinkable. A lump swelled in his throat. He wanted to say the right words, but couldn't.

"Please believe me," he mumbled. "I wouldn't hurt you for anything. I risked my own life for you."

Nancy gazed at him questioningly. Did he take her for a fool? Why was she here rather than a hospital or at Liz's house? Why was she naked? And why had he taken those pictures of her?

"Look . . . please let me go," she said between sobs. "I promise I won't go to the police. Honest. Just tell me . . . you haven't . . . hurt Charlie."

He was getting nowhere. How could he get through to her?

"I haven't hurt anybody," he groaned. "I only want to get you to a doctor, if you'll just let me explain." He stopped and took a drink of water. How should he say it? No matter how it was phrased, if she couldn't remember, his story would sound outrageous. But he had to try. "The roads were icy after I pulled you from the water. The heater in my car was broke and there was nothing else I could do. I had to bring you here."

"Sure!" she snapped, with an angry nod toward the table where the photos had been. "It was awfully convenient for the pictures."

Wayne blushed and shifted uneasily.

"I'm awfully sorry about that," he confessed tearily. "I don't know what came over me. You were so . . . so . . . But I hardly touched you — honest!"

She glanced at her knotted clothing on the floor

that she'd been bound with. Wayne was quick to notice.

"I was afraid," he defended himself. "Don't you see? At that time you didn't know the truth. I couldn't let anyone see you until after we'd talked."

Nancy regarded him carefully. He appeared meek and harmless, but often murderers were the boy-next-door type. He was probably mentally ill.

She would have to be careful.

Nancy closed her eyes, slowly shook her head, then looked him in the face. To be safe, she'd play along and take him up on his offer to release her.

"I appreciate what you've done for me," she said half-heartedly.

"Oh, thank God," Wayne moaned. "You don't know how relieved I am to hear that! And I was happy to help you. Really, I was."

Nancy forced a smile. Could his story be true? It was difficult to be objective, sitting nude beneath a blanket before a strange man. "Can I have my clothes, please?"

"Of course," he smiled. "I hope we can get to know each other better." Then Wayne cringed with embarrassment. I hope she didn't take that the wrong way, he thought. She still seemed awfully suspicious and, of course, she had a right to be.

Wayne retrieved her clothing from the floor where it lay scattered. Bundling it at her side, he retreated and smiled again.

"I'll wait in the next room while you dress. And please, try not to hold this against me. I'll take you to a hospital and soon this will all be over."

Nancy fumbled with her bra. It was damp . . . and discolored with mud. Dropping the blanket to the floor, she examined her body. Splotches of dried mud covered her skin atop a series of minor cuts and scratches. Undoubtedly, there *had* been an accident. Could this man have forced their car off the road? Perhaps she and Charlie had unknowingly been followed. She remembered feeling as if she were being watched at the Opelika Tastee-Freeze. He could have stalked their car, waiting for an opportunity to strike. But whatever the case, this man Wayne, if that was his real name, couldn't be trusted. She remembered all too clearly how he had bound and gagged her. His raging voice replayed endlessly in her mind. No, his actions implied guilt. How could she afford to believe otherwise? Her only hope was to call his bluff and await a chance to escape.

Nancy inspected herself further. Her left arm and shoulder were badly bruised and swollen, as was her right leg above the knee. There was a large bump on her forehead, and she ached all over. Never had the simple act of dressing been so difficult. Slowly, carefully, she slipped into her clothing, feeling a renewed sense of security once she was dressed.

Finally, harboring the faintest of hope that he might be true to his word, she called to him. If nothing else, what happened now would be a test of his credibility. Her muscles ached, her mind reeled. What could possibly happen next?

When Wayne entered the room, she was running a hand through her tangled hair.

"My hair is a mess," she said. "Have you seen my purse?"

"Nooo," he drawled. "It was probably lost in the accident."

He watched her fumble nervously with her tangled hair. Wayne reached for his back pocket and stepped toward her. "I have a comb you can—"

"Don't worry about it," she interrupted, avoiding his eyes. "Can we go now?"

"Of course," he answered, turning to the television set for his keys. It was a subconscious habit — every time he walked through the front door, he automatically tossed his keychain on the top of the TV set. But now they were gone. "Have you seen my keys?" he asked.

I should've guessed, she thought. Missing keys. Her heart sank at the disappointment.

He looked on the floor around and behind the television stand. No keys. Then he rechecked his pockets in the jacket he wore last night. Still no keys. *Maybe in all the confusion, I left them in the ignition.* Pivoting toward the door, Wayne twisted the doorknob and stepped halfway outside before realizing that he had needed the keys to unlock the door. They *had* to be inside.

Nancy watched the door attentively. Here was possibly one last chance to draw attention to herself, though she knew she hadn't the strength to fight him off again. But she had to try. Quickly she lunged for the door, knocking Wayne off-balance to the ground outside.

"Somebody *help* me," she screeched. "Pleeeaase!"

Panicking, Wayne lunged on top of her. Fear and anger boosted his adrenaline, and his heart was pounding against his chest.

"No!" he growled. "You've got to believe me!" He shook her harder and harder, oblivious to the pain he was inflicting.

Nancy closed her eyes in silent prayer. *God, please send someone for me soon — or let me die quickly.*

Dragging operations continued into the night, the infrequent flashlight and lantern beams of the searchers bouncing along both shores of Kelley Creek. Deputy Jesse Granger had been given the unpopular assignment of guarding the accident site until completion of the investigation. In an out-of-the-way clearing he built a small fire and warmed his hands, welcoming conversation with any volunteers who passed his way. Deputy Granger truly detested this part of his job, for strangely enough, the mood on the site was more depressing than when he had worked on his only homicide earlier in his brief career.

The hoot of an owl startled the lawman, as did the sporadic movement of wildlife in the nearby brush. When would this nightmare be over? He remembered a boating accident in south Alabama a few years back when dragging operations had continued for well over a month before finally disbanding. Of course, this would likely be the only night requiring guard duty, but he still dreaded the imminent demands on his time. This was a sensitive case, and would remain on the minds of the region's citizens for weeks, taking him away from the duties he enjoyed most — like sniffing out moonshiners in the backcountry. Deputy Granger stretched and yawned, then stepped over to his patrol car. The annoying squawk of police calls was a necessary nuisance he tried in vain to ignore. Beneath the front seat he found a transistor radio that he rarely used during working hours, but tonight it would provide a vital distraction from the eerie presence of death.

Twisting the radio dial, the deputy tuned past the fading signals of the Birmingham stations. Operating at reduced power after dark, Birmingham radio could hardly be heard outside the metropolitan area. As usual, he opted for WGN from Chicago whose signal was always loud and clear. "She's About a Mover," a favorite from a few months earlier, was blasting away, followed by The Byrds' "Turn, Turn, Turn." Thank God for music, he thought, but it also reminded him of the local skating rink, one of his favorite stops on Saturday nights — it was an ideal spot to watch the area's full-breasted teenagers.

Settling by the fire, Granger gazed at the millions of stars overhead and watched his own frozen breath dissolve into the darkness. Twenty-four hours ago those Georgia folks were just beginning their journey, he thought.

The sounds of night creatures clashed with the music.

It would likely be a long night.

Channel 13's evening newscast featured film clips of local traffic ensnarled by the preceding night's freak ice storm. And complementing the story of the unusual freeze was the weather-related accident in Shelby County.

ANCHORMAN: A young Georgia couple lost their lives in a tragic automobile accident near the Shelby County community of Selton late last night. Randy Kanes has this report.

Film clips showing the retrieval of the sunken vehicle now flashed onto the screen.

KANES: To local residents, the new bridge over Kelley Creek is a welcomed improvement. But to Charles and Nancy Barnett of Columbus, Georgia, this Shelby County highway construction project meant sudden death. Hindered by last night's foul weather and a lack of sufficient warning, their car plunged into the swift waters of Kelley Creek. According to Shelby County Sheriff Chester Arnold, the re-routed section of old County Road 19 was inadequately barricaded — only a simple sawhorse barrier served to detour traffic from the previously closed and dismantled bridge.

SHERIFF ARNOLD: This appears to be a case of gross negligence on the part of the contractor, complicated in all probability by a related act of vandalism.

KANES: Representatives of Arbor Construction Company have refused to comment.

The body of 27-year-old Charles Barnett was recovered from the sunken vehicle earlier today. Dragging operations continue around the clock for Nancy Barnett, presumed dead.

Local residents turned out in force to assist in the search for the deceased woman. After lending assistance himself, Roger Albritton, Mayor of Selton, had this to say:

ALBRITTON: On behalf of the people of Shelby County and the State of Alabama, I would like to express my deepest sympathy to the family of Charles and Nancy Barnett. This apparent oversight of safety regulations on Alabama highways is deplorable, and I pledge my support to Shelby County District Attorney Albert Reynolds in his investigation and prosecution of the responsible parties.

KANES: Governor George Wallace announced late this afternoon that representatives of the Department of Public Safety will personally inspect other construction sites across the state for assurance that proper safety precautions are being observed.

This is Randy Kanes, WAPI News.

Nancy was devastated by the news.

She sat upright on the sofa in a near daze, her leg resting on a chair before her. Wayne watched the evening newscast from the floor. As a sportscaster hawked the Crimson Tide's gridiron conquest of South Carolina and the upcoming Orange Bowl, Wayne stood and clicked off the set. His face was flushed. They had reached a standstill, with Nancy stubbornly refusing to listen to him. He knew that this latest bad news would only worsen matters.

"I'm sorry about your husband," he said in a soft, consoling tone.

"Don't talk to me!" Nancy screeched, her head shaking with rage. Her tears again flowed freely, this time not only renewed from fear but for the loss of her husband. Charlie was dead. In her disoriented condition, it was something she hadn't even considered. Charlie was so big and husky . . . At any moment she expected to hear his gruff voice outside, his fists pounding on the door as he came to her rescue. Not now. Not ever. He was gone.

Though their marriage had been a failure, with tender moments few and far between, she had once loved him dearly. And despite his many faults, Charlie had been an excellent provider. Perhaps, following a divorce, they might have worked out their differences and remained friends.

Nancy's eyes were red and swollen with grief and exhaustion, her aching joints also contributing to her misery. And seated on the floor before her was the mysterious young man who had brought her to his home. Undressed her. Taken photographs of her nude body. Forcibly restrained her. Would it not also be possible that he had murdered her husband? Had he cunningly staged the deaths of the Barnetts as a cover-up? Was he sitting there silently gloating over his sinister success?

Night had fallen again. Her abductor appeared nervous and frightened, it was true. But what did he have in mind for her? Perhaps screaming this last time had been a mistake. It had accomplished nothing, instead eliciting a temporary rage from her captor. He had all but withdrawn from her, fidgeting around the small mobile home in a vain attempt to avoid the mounting problem. True, he had found his keys hanging from the aluminum window crank on the wall. He claimed they must have been knocked from the TV set and lodged there during their last scuffle. But even if she hadn't screamed, even if he had taken her away in his car, what would have kept him from driving deep into the countryside, down a long-neglected logging road, where her screams would go unnoticed? Buried within an abandoned mine shaft, her corpse might never be found.

Waves of nausea swept over Nancy. She wished she were dead. With Charlie.

And oddly enough, she was *already* dead, at least to the rest of the world. No one could possibly suspect that she was anywhere other than the bottom of Kelley Creek. No one would come looking for her. Now a widow, she felt alone and defenseless, barely managing to hang on to the last threads of sanity.

Wayne's thoughts were equally disturbing. There now appeared no way for him to avoid trouble with the law. And he had to admit that perhaps it was justified. Looking back, he couldn't believe his own stupidity. If only this morning he had rushed her to the hospital, the outcome would have been vastly different. But he had been scared. Never having been in trouble before, he had found the prospect too threatening. His own fear and respect of the law had pushed him into this. And Nancy. She had pushed him, too. He had held her too long against her will, and his guilt was now apparent. He was facing a kidnapping charge and whether he detained her a matter of minutes, hours or days, the law was the same. He and Nancy had reached a stalemate. Who could outlast the other? It seemed cruel to keep an injured woman from the funeral of her husband. Yet a lifetime prison term for himself seemed equally unfair. As long as the slightest chance remained that she would reverse her stand, he would keep her here.

As for medical attention, he needed it as much as she did, he thought, tenderly fingering the bulging knot on his forehead.

He glanced at his beautiful adversary on the sofa. She was staring ahead unblinking, as if in a trance, her passive femininity in marked contrast to the violence she had shown earlier. But who could blame her? How ironic that two innocent, well-meaning individuals who had met through a sheer twist of fate could ruin each other's lives, Wayne reflected. Who would ever have believed such a thing could happen?

Now he was forced into the role dictated by this woman. She was not to be trusted, and would have to be physically restrained. The burden would shift to her to prove her belief in him, to demonstrate beyond a doubt that she was worthy of release. Till then, she would remain under his control.

Tonight he would sleep.

Tomorrow their lives would begin anew.

8

Sunday
Day Three

When he first heard the news, Sheriff Arnold was dumbfounded. The telephone receiver clanged loudly as he dropped it to its cradle; then he shook his head in disbelief and returned to his seat at the kitchen table. Sarah, the sheriff's wife of 26 years, stuck her face in the doorway, her hair a mass of curlers and bobby pins. Having finished breakfast only minutes before, Sarah stared at her husband with impatience.

"Well — was that Thelma, Chester?"

"No, darlin'. I'm afraid not," he answered.

Dressing for church, Sarah was awaiting a call from Thelma Ritter with whom she alternated driving to the Sunday service.

"So, who was it then?" she asked.

"Business," he drawled.

Sarah stormed away to comb out her hair. She had given up years ago on squeezing police information out of Chester. The man just couldn't be broken.

Sheriff Arnold raised a cup of steaming coffee to his lips and considered what he had just learned. The purse had been found lying open about a mile or so downstream from the accident site, void of any cash and, according to Deputy Hart, hidden behind a brush thicket. Everything in it was still damp. Had the purse floated from the wreckage to be found along the shore? Or could it have been taken before the accident, and discarded prior to Friday night's heavy rain?

It could have been found by a volunteer searching for the woman's body. But women didn't carry much money — usually not more than ten dollars or so. And the volunteers were, for the most part, conscientious. For them, the prestige of having found the purse would far outweigh the value of a few lousy bucks. It seemed unlikely that any of them would sacrifice fame and self-satisfaction over such a meager amount of cash. But to be safe, he would find out how much cash she was likely carrying. She could have had a shitload of money on her. Someone could have known about it. Admittedly, the idea was far-fetched, but at this point nothing could be discounted.

Again he wondered if the purse could have been taken before the accident. If so, it suggested foul play. Hmmm. But it seemed too neat, too tidy. Still — could a clue have been missed at the accident site, something so obvious that it had been carelessly overlooked? No, he didn't think so. But there was that damned flashlight the Gibbs kid found beside the Barnett woman's shoe. The metal switch on the flashlight's plastic base showed no indication of rust, so the flashlight had been dropped recently. He had believed the two objects were unrelated. Until now. Yes, when he thought about it, foul play simply could not be eliminated. The Barnetts could have picked up a hitchhiker, someone who knew the area well and who had conceived an ingenious plot to cover up the crime: Rob them. Knock the victims unconscious. Drive them into the creek, hoping their missing valuables would go undetected.

But wait. Charles Barnett's wallet was found intact. What thief would overlook sixty-seven dollars? The man's wallet would have been the primary target. Robbery couldn't have been the motive, despite the fact that the woman's money was missing — if, indeed, she had been carrying any at all.

The flashlight and shoe had been found together. Suppose for a moment that a crime had been committed, and that the flashlight was somehow connected. Why would it have been left behind in the dark? It must have been lost . . . unless someone's hands had been needed to restrain a resisting woman. If the light had been pocketed, it could easily have fallen out.

A sex crime? It seemed preposterous, yet all the pieces fit. The man's body had been recovered, but the woman was missing. But such a scheme would require planning, and by someone familiar with the area. That would mean a local was likely involved. And Sheriff Arnold knew most of the folks in the surrounding communities on a first-name basis. No sex fiends or perverts around there, at least, not to his knowledge. But then, what about the construction crew? Whoever was responsible for leaving the old bridge unbarricaded could very well have plotted the whole thing.

With a start, Sheriff Arnold stared at the telephone, its harsh ring blaring in his ear from the nearby kitchen counter. There were just too many possibilities.

"I'll get it!" Sarah called as she hurried into the room. "It must be Thelma."

The sheriff reached for his hat and tuned in to the conversation. As soon as he discerned that the call was not for him, he walked briskly out the back door and settled behind the wheel of his patrol car.

Neither likelihood of foul play could be ignored. First, he would examine the purse and the area where it was found. Then he'd make a few inquiries as to how much cash Mrs. Barnett had been carrying. He would also review the personnel records of Arbor Construction Company.

At long last! thought the sheriff with a smile at the rear view mirror. This could turn out to be a humdinger of a case — a chance to do some real police work for a change.

A thin ray of sunshine broke through the otherwise darkened room and sent a streak of bleached light across Wayne Crocker's bed. Lazily, he opened his eyes and focused on the particles of lint that drifted through the sunbeam above his head. Inhaling deeply, he blew out a burst of air and watched the microscopic filaments scatter. It was morning now, a night of broken restlessness having finally passed.

After a quiet yawn, he grew instantly aware of the nervous tingle that burned under his skin. He told himself to calm down, that all was not yet lost. But on the opposite end of the trailer, sprawled across the sofa, lay a bound and gagged young woman who represented a major threat to his future.

Pushing away the covers, Wayne stumbled to the bathroom, relieving himself and brushing his teeth, before he stepped through to the tiny living room. She was awake, and from the appearance of dark circles around her eyes, had slept little, if at all. Her hair was matted and oily, her face reflecting both fear and grief.

Turning away without speaking, Wayne opened the refrigerator and retrieved a package of sausage and canned biscuits. He then proceeded with breakfast, humming a Beatles tune and ignoring her presence. Sausage patties sizzled in a cast-iron skillet, a splattering of grease popping out occasionally to sting his bare wrists.

"I could have watched you die," he finally said, just loud enough for her to hear. His eyes stared coldly ahead at a row of green canisters on a shelf above the stove. He couldn't bring himself to look at her. "I could've watched that car sink. I could have minded my own damn business instead of ruining the rest of my life."

Nancy watched through tormented eyes. The gag around her mouth and chin was uncomfortable, but she had no desire to speak. Her muscles ached, her stomach was tied in knots, and she was so exhausted, the words of her captor hardly registered in her mind.

Wayne flipped the sausage patties and checked

the biscuits in the oven. A tear dropped from his cheek and hissed on the hot oven door. "I saved your life and you screwed up mine forever," he said, his voice breaking.

With a warm pot holder, he pulled the hot biscuits from the oven and slammed the door hard, his frustration with her growing.

"I don't know what the hell I'm gonna do," he sobbed quietly. "God, I wish there was a way out of this."

Wiping tears from his eyes, Wayne scraped two sausage patties and two biscuits onto each of two plates, then turned to face her. She stared blankly past him, and Wayne felt a sinking hollow sensation as his eyes met hers. It was a moment of lonely desperation that he knew she was feeling, too, but for vastly different reasons.

Stepping to her side, he offered her a plate.

"Sorry I don't have any eggs," he said, forgetting that her hands were tied and she couldn't take the food. "Excuse me," he apologized, and carefully loosened the strips of fabric that bound her arms and legs. Then he removed the nylon gag and raised her to a sitting position, again placing her injured leg to rest in the chair in front of her. Nancy sniffled, but otherwise sat in silence.

"You wouldn't know what it's like to be unwanted," he said. "You're attractive, you've always had guys chasin' you. But I'm nothing but 'Mr. Average', and on top of that, I'm not very outgoing. I never know the right things to say."

She ate slowly, but appeared to be listening as Wayne reflected on his social problems.

"It really hurts to want something so bad, and have it waved in your face and then pulled away," he continued. "I've had dates, but never a steady girlfriend. I guess I want one so bad, it shows too much."

He stopped to swallow some sausage, and then gulped a drink of orange juice. Her eyes met his accidentally and quickly turned away.

"Nancy, I'm a decent person and I've never done anything wrong in my whole life. I want to settle down and raise a family, but I can't seem to find . . . to find . . ." His voice broke as he choked on the words.

"You've had love and affection," he tried again. "You know how important it is. But just imagine how awful it would be if you were my age and you'd never had it."

He took a last bite of sausage and watched her chew a biscuit. Was he getting through to her?

"I was wrong, Nancy, to look at you and take those pictures. I admit it, and God, how I regret it. But, please, put yourself in my place and try to understand the temptation. I would never have hurt you. I only wanted to satisfy my curiosity, and I thought you'd never know the difference. It was stupid, a big, big mistake. But what can I do? My future is up to you."

The next minutes passed quietly. Each continued to eat while avoiding the other's eyes as the gentle drone of an airplane hummed far overhead. Finally Wayne spoke again.

"I had no idea it would lead to this when I pulled you from that creek. I only wanted to . . . help," his voice trailed off.

Nancy stared blankly ahead. Physically and mentally anguished, she found it all but impossible to comprehend the meaning of his words. Now was not the time, and she sat as peacefully as if she were the room's sole occupant. Wayne suddenly looked up and met her stare. Their eyes locked.

"You won't even speak to me!" he growled. "I saved your goddamn life and you won't even talk to me!" He wrung his hands in exasperation, her expressionless face only irritating him further.

"All right, if that's the way you want it," he snapped, fighting an urge to reach out and shake her back to her senses. "But you're stuck with me, whether you like it or not. And you'll stay here with me until you can show a little compassion."

Fidgeting in his chair, he jumped to his feet and paced between the kitchen and living room. "And it won't be easy," he continued the tirade. "I don't trust you, either, and I don't intend to leave you free for one minute while I'm away. So you'd better get used to being tied up."

She sat without emotion. No tears. No response.

Wayne pivoted and slammed the panelled wall hard with his fist. "God help me," he moaned. "*Please* . . ."

Again he told himself to calm down, that it really wasn't her fault, only a cruel twist of fate. Slowly he regained his composure and faced her again. He had tried to reason with her, and had failed. Exhaling a pent-up breath, he managed to force a smile.

"You look awful," he said. "You need to get cleaned up."

Nancy winced at his approach, her hands clenching the blanket that lay across her lap. He stood directly before her and wrenched the protective covering away.

"Your clothes are a mess," he muttered. "I'll find something for you to wear. But first you need a bath."

She sat spellbound. Wayne stared back impatiently.

"You'll feel better when you're clean," he explained.

No response.

Wayne threw up his arms in disgust. Hell, what did he have to lose? He had disrobed her once already for safety reasons, but it looked as if she'd hold that against him forever. Whether she realized it or not, she needed a bath. Stinking, disease-ridden creek water had dried all over her body and in her hair.

What have I got to lose? he considered again. It was a hopeless case. He would give her a hot bath, then maybe she would feel like talking.

Silently he led her to the bathroom.

Sunlight sparkled across the water as Liz Farrell circled a small pond on her father's pastureland. Just ahead a flurry of wings startled her as a covey of quail fled from nearby brush. Across the pond the bare drooping limbs of a weeping willow tree swayed in the wind. On countless occasions she and Nancy had climbed that very tree, their pigtails dangling to the ground as they hung suspended from their knees around a low limb. Life was so simple back then, Liz mused, carefully skirting the edge of the pond toward the tree, and remembering the many times she and her cousin squealed at the sight of a snake in midsummer. Beneath the tree she reached up to touch the thick limb she had played on most often — it seemed like it was only yesterday . . .

Her childhood had been firmly rooted in the fifties, a decade that passed with little notice. Who could have known the turmoil and horror that lay ahead? A President lost to an assassin's bullet, young men sent to fight a war that few believed in or understood. Riots breaking out all over the country. Every day the news had been more depressing — it seemed as if people had forgotten how to *live*. And for Liz, of course, her personal life had paralleled the national disasters. First she lost her good looks. Then a lover. And now a loved one. Normally, in times of grief, a person could depend on a lover or a friend for moral support. Liz Farrell suddenly had neither, and she found herself alone in a vacuum that her parents could hardly understand.

A brisk breeze whipped the tawny branches into her face, interrupting a fresh flow of tears. Guilt gnawed at her for the self pity she was experiencing was almost as strong as her grief and she found herself torn apart by these uncontrollable emotions.

How will I feel when I cross the new bridge and see the place where Nancy died? she wondered. *When will the memories die?*

Hearing movement, Liz raised her head and saw a brown rabbit scurry along a path and into the brush, followed close behind by two tiny bunnies. Liz smiled, remembering her love of animals and the comfort they had always brought her. She thought about her cat, Sparky, and how her pet depended on her.

Maybe I'll quit my job and go away to school. Start all over again. Make new friends to replace the ones I've lost.

Drying her eyes on the sleeves of her blouse, Liz brushed off the dead weeds clinging to her skirt, and began the short walk back to the house, her spirits much improved.

With a gloved hand Sheriff Arnold dropped the waterlogged purse and its contents into a wrinkled A & P grocery bag. The surrounding area along the creek lay covered with dry leaves so whoever had rummaged the purse had left no footprints. There was, however, a curious design etched in the nearby mud, which might or might not have some bearing on the case.

"Ol' Jesse will be sorely pissed when he finds out he missed all the excitement," exclaimed Deputy Hart from the rear of the sheriff. "I bet it wasn't fifteen minutes after I relieved Jesse's guard duty that the Bates kid came runnin' up, hollerin' about a purse he'd found."

Sheriff Arnold rose from a crouched position and stretched. The new deputy had been on the force less than six months and the sheriff already knew that hiring Hart had been a mistake. Their opinions clashed more often than not.

"Why the hell was that kid out here so early?" asked the sheriff. "It must've been barely daylight."

"That's right," Hart answered, and spat on the ground. "Hell, these kids are all thrill seekers. Ain't nothin' this exciting ever happened around here."

The sheriff rubbed his stubbled cheek in deep concentration. Something didn't seem right.

"There's a house right past that cluster of pines over yonder," Hart said, pointing east. "Or a shack is more like it. Anyway, I watched the place while I waited for you, and you might have known who lives there — *niggers*."

His tone implied an automatic connection with the purse and the Barnett woman. Sheriff Arnold glanced in the indicated direction, then slowly shook his head. "So?" he responded, his blood suddenly boiling. "You've got a lot to learn, rookie-boy. Why don't you just tell me how that proves anything?"

The deputy shifted uncomfortably and lowered his blushing face. "Well, sir, you see . . . I . . . uh . . ." he stammered and looked past the sheriff. "All I meant was, we ought to question them."

"You're damn right; we'll interrogate them, and anybody else around here," Sheriff Arnold exploded. "But we don't have one ounce of evidence that could implicate anybody. Hell, we don't even know if there's been a crime! Use your head, goddamn it!"

Hart backed off as the sheriff continued to unload on him. "Besides, I know who lives there," the sheriff roared. "I've known Preacher Mason most of my life. When I was a kid my daddy hired him to help in the fields. Preacher and I picked cotton side by side for weeks. And I'll tell you one damn thing. There ain't no finer man around, colored or white."

Deputy Hart was aghast. Was his boss actually a nigger lover? It hardly seemed possible!

"I'll talk to Preacher," the sheriff said as he pivoted in the direction of the house. "You get back to your post."

Hart was fuming as he paced upstream. The sheriff had no right to talk to him that way. Shit! How humiliating — to be reamed out over a damn nigger. Nothing worse was hardly imaginable. Quickening his pace, Hart kicked at an outcropping of driftwood. *Stupid sonofabitch sheriff,* he thought. *You ain't fit to be a proper lawman, just like I've known all along. But you'll be sorry. I'll get even with you and your nigger friend.*

Swirls of pubic hair danced in the warm bathwater between Nancy's legs. She sat motionless in the bathtub, staring into space, and undaunted by the presence of her captor who had carefully eased her into position. Her injured limbs had stiffened further and grown almost numb and she hardly knew who or where she was.

Wayne glanced at the mounds of suds beneath the flowing faucet, then traced her figure with his eyes. It was flawless. She had yet to speak this morning and he wondered if she was possibly suffering from shock or some type of withdrawal. Later today, he promised himself, he would visit the local library to learn how she should be treated.

After considerable thought, he had decided again not to release her just yet. There was still a faint chance he could make her understand, and he had nothing left to lose. One more day of captivity wouldn't make him look any worse a kidnapper than he already did.

Wringing out a terry-cloth wash rag, he leaned over the tub and began to remove a hardened film of mud from her legs. "You'll feel much better once you're clean," he spoke soothingly as he scrubbed her. She winced occasionally at pressure around particularly sensitive areas, but otherwise gave no response. Slowly the bathwater turned a dingy shade of brown and her skin regained its natural glow. Noticing the scratches and minor cuts that scarred the flesh of her swollen limbs, Wayne realized the wash cloth might be abrasive to her raw flesh, and decided to use only his hands.

His fingers glided over her soft silky skin and promptly found her breasts. The feeling was divine — how soft and supple they were. And to his surprise he noted how the nipples grew erect at his touch.

Intensely aroused, Wayne wanted desperately to explore the secrets of her inner thighs, but resolved to control his feelings and wash only above her waist with his bare hand. A residue of guilt still remained along with a touch of embarrassment, about his voyeuristic treatment of her earlier. And besides, he thought, there'll be plenty of time.

His arousal partially subsiding, Wayne activated the shower head and aimed a steady spray at the top of her head. Then he slowly kneaded her hair, building a thick lather from Prell Concentrate shampoo. Her long tangled locks were matted with bits of leaves and sand that fell into the brown bathwater. Realizing that her hair would require at least two washings, he rinsed off the soap and began applying a second coat of shampoo. He enjoyed caring for her as if she were a child.

Hesitating briefly, Wayne stopped to watch her eyes. Throughout the bath she had stared ahead, fixing her attention on the shiny pink tile around the tub. Now he noticed she was slowly surveying the room. For a moment their eyes met, and he marveled at their clear liquid sparkle. He also thought he detected a slight twist of her lips. Had it been a semblance of a smile? Despite the pain throbbing in his own injured forehead, a feeling of warmth rose inside his body, a contentment that was heretofore alien to him, but a state of mind he longed to hold forever. It was a feeling of admiration. Of caring. Of *concern*.

Tentatively, he returned the smile.

"Nice doggie . . ." Sheriff Arnold said nervously. "Good boy."

Crouched on all fours, the fur about its neck standing on end, and snarling between bared teeth, the dog was guarding its territory. When the snarl changed to a deep growl, the sheriff slowly backed away, avoiding any sudden movement. Although a small dog, its teeth looked sharp and menacing, and only a fool would venture within its prescribed boundaries. Behind the dog stood the old Mason homestead, looking exactly as it always had for the past twenty years. The exterior hadn't seen a fresh coat of paint in as long as the sheriff could remember. On the front porch sat a worn wooden rocker, an old washing machine, and a stack of firewood. A missing pane in the window behind the rocker had been replaced by a thin sheet of cardboard. Poor Preacher, thought the sheriff, he does the best he can.

"*Hey, Preacher!*" Sheriff Arnold yelled. "*You at home?*"

The dog answered with a vicious bark and inched closer to the sheriff.

"Easy boy," the sheriff said softly. "Calm down, sport."

There was no visible movement within the house, and the disturbance outside would have been investigated long before now, if anyone had been at home, the sheriff realized. He checked the time — 10:15 A.M. Of course, he thought. Preacher would be in church with his family, leading Sunday School classes. Now would be a perfect opportunity to snoop around without interference — if it weren't for the damn dog.

The house sat two or three feet above the ground, supported by six pillars of brick. Underneath were piles of junk, including a chrome bumper from an Edsel, complete with a "Jesus Saves" bumper sticker.

Damn this dog! thought the sheriff. Now I'll have to come back later. But, then again, perhaps it was all just as well. Neither the Preacher nor his family were likely to have seen or heard anything from this distance.

As he pivoted and walked away, the sheriff flashed a wide grin at the dog. "Get lost, mutt," he chuckled. "Go lick yourself."

Almost a mile upstream, Deputy Hart was combing the shoreline in search of evidence. Though he knew the area had been scoured several times already, he hoped his trained eye might spot something overlooked by the others. The scene with the sheriff played over and over in his mind, feeding his anger and thirst for revenge. Another clue would turn up — it had to. All he needed was a piece of physical evidence from the sunken car, or even better, a piece of clothing or other such personal item from the woman herself. He'd find a way to link it to the nigger, even if he had to plant the damning proof himself.

With a touch of envy, he recalled the woman's shoe found by the Gibbs kid. If only he had found it first. The shoe would have been perfect. But, still, there had to be other scattered articles hidden within these muddy waters. And whatever was there, he would find it. Then he would expose Sheriff Arnold as a nigger lover, send his spade friend off to prison, and claim all the glory himself. In the next election, Hart would run for sheriff.

Everything was falling neatly into place. Deputy Hart smiled and stared ahead, past the massive new bridge to the barely visible, dismantled bridge in the distance. Charles Barnett, you stupid asshole, he thought. Thanks for takin' a dive.

James Crocker awoke near mid-morning with a ball-breaker of a hangover. From his perspective sprawled across the stinking mattress, the room was spinning end over end, the flowered print of the bedroom wallpaper merging into a single swimming pattern.

"James, you've got to stop this," a voice nagged in his ear. His wife Edith was standing nearby, calm and collected. Her figure wavered before his eyes.

"Do you even know what day it is?" she asked.

Day? he thought. Why, of course, its Fri — Saturday? He couldn't be sure. But did it really matter?

"I missed church because of you. Because I was worried about leaving you alone."

Church? It couldn't be Sunday already! The last thing he remembered clearly was leaving work Friday afternoon in a deep funk. Sylvester Granger had gotten a big raise, and it was James who had taught that asshole everything he knew, yet his own last raise had been pitiful.

"James, can you hear me? Answer me! Do you realize how *serious* this is?"

"Yeah . . . yeah . . ." he mumbled, blinking tightly to clear his vision. Now he could feel the bed sinking, as if the mattress were about to engulf and suffocate him. "*Eedie!*" he moaned, extending a shaky arm to her. "Help me, Eedie. Help . . . me."

Edith took her husband's hand. "I've helped you since the day we met," she said. "It's time for you to straighten up for a change." Fighting back tears, Edith continued, "You worry me to death, Jim. I never know when the police might come and tell me you're dead. And, God, it's been hard on poor Wayne, too. He's a good kid, James. He's always stood by me. You should be proud of that boy."

James' temper momentarily flared. "But . . . that boy . . . left me in . . . jail," he mumbled.

"And that's where you belonged," Edith interrupted. "Don't you realize you could kill yourself, and somebody else, too, when you're drunk? James, you hardly know what you're doing when you're . . . that way."

He knew that what she said was true. Every word of it. But how could he control these intense cravings? Avoid the need to escape reality? If life had provided more rewards, perhaps the bottle wouldn't seem so . . . inviting.

"If you don't promise me," she sobbed. "If you don't swear to me that you'll stop drinking, I'll leave you, James. I will. I'm not too old to change my life, and I'm not afraid to go."

He stared at her in silence. She had to be pulling his leg. After twenty-four years of marriage, only a few months shy of their silver anniversary, she would just up and leave? No way.

"I'll do it, if you force me to," she sobbed. Tears dampened her cheeks. "I'll move in with Wayne until I find a job."

Damn! Maybe she really meant it this time. But so what? It would be good for her to get out on her own awhile. After she stayed with Wayne a few days, she'd come whinin' back. Wayne . . . What was it about Wayne that kept gnawing at the back of his mind?

9

He dressed her in a pair of flannel pajamas and carefully brushed the tangles from her wet hair. Concentrating on the gentle tug against her scalp, she sat contentedly on the edge of the bed. The bath had been refreshing, the flannel, soft against her skin, relaxing. Sleepy, she tried to lie back across the bed, but the pain in her leg and shoulder prevented her.

". . . Help . . . me . . .?" she asked softly.

Wayne stopped in mid-stroke. She had finally spoken. Was she coming out of her strange withdrawal? Quickly he stood and raised her injured leg, taking care not to bend it at the knee, and swung it up and over to rest on the bed. Then he placed a pillow beneath her head. He could see the exhaustion weighing heavily in her eyes.

"Would you like to take a nap?" he asked.

She nodded and closed her eyes.

God, she was beautiful. Like a sleeping angel. Her skin was so smooth, her body perfect in every way — like a goddess.

Quietly he rose from the bed and left the room. Could this be another of her tricks? Probably not. Her fatigue was all too obvious. She would rest well.

Wayne sat on the floor of the next room and flipped through his record collection. Finally selecting *Beatles '65*, he pulled the record from its sleeve and placed it on the turntable. A ballad, "No Reply", spilled into the room. Stretching across the floor, Wayne relaxed. Much of his own fear had passed, now that he regarded himself as her defender, her guardian. He dreaded being forced to restrain her again, but it was too soon to leave her to her own defenses. The library would open within an hour or so, and he would be waiting at the door, hoping to gain some insight on her condition and how she might best be treated. She seemed to be improving, gaining awareness. That was great. Right now, she was all that mattered. He would keep her safe.

And secure.

As Nancy drifted into a deeper sleep in the next room, she heard music. It was the Beatles, her favorites, and the sound floated lazily into her subconscious, bringing with it a mellow feeling of peacefulness and euphoria. Often she had escaped her troubles through music. Silently her lips mimed the words of "I'll Be Back" as the song played far away in another world.

In the black void of sleep, she was home again. Charlie was at her side on the sofa. Rusty, her cat, was purring quietly in her lap. All was well.

Seated alone at a corner table of the library, Wayne frantically scribbled notes from an encyclopedia, growing increasingly frustrated at the lack of information available. An exhaustive search of the card file had produced nothing. Under the heading "Shock", there had been only one thin book, the primary topic of which had been electrical shock. Likewise, "Medical — Diagnosis" yielded nothing of any value. Quickly he had turned to the encyclopedia, which dealt with more symptoms as opposed to treatment. For a moment, he rested, his thoughts reverting to the mysterious woman who now dominated his life.

Nancy. What a pretty name. A delicate name that fit her well. Remembering the confusion in her eyes when he had tied her up again before leaving, he winced. Soon she could be freed, he had assured her, but for the present he had no other alternative, he'd explained.

The scene in the bathroom repeated itself in Wayne's mind. He'd pulled her gently from the tub, steadied her against a wall, and toweled her dry. Beads of water clung to her skin and rolled down her breasts, only to disappear into the terrycloth. On her hip he noticed a small birthmark, and as he crouched to dry her legs, she placed a hand lightly on his shoulder. Had it been merely to support herself? Or was it perhaps a subtle invitation? God, how he hoped her hardened attitude had changed.

But now, this very minute, she lay in discomfort inside the trailer. What little faith she had gained might already be lost. It was unfair, he knew. She was like a caged bird, and her involuntary detention could not be continued. Even at the risk of his own future, he would release her soon. Her life seemed suddenly more important than his own.

Not since Friday night had his eyes gleamed with such pride. No matter what she or anyone else thought, regardless of the consequences, he alone had rescued this beautiful woman from certain death. And her life was worth any sacrifice, because she was unlike any woman he had ever known.

I'd love to have her with me. Always. To care for her, to comfort her. To see that all her needs are met. Nothing could give greater meaning to my life.

But tomorrow, Monday, was a workday. The realization struck Wayne hard. What could be done with her while he was away for as many as nine hours? She couldn't be bound and gagged daily. The thought was cruel, depressing. It could never come to that. There had to be another way to guarantee her silence while still maintaining her safety —

Safety! *First aid . . .*

Within minutes of searching the card catalog for a second time, he found the ideal book — a first aid manual. A wealth of information was contained inside, including diagnosis and emergency treatment of shock, exposure, and bone injuries. Quickly he checked out the book, forced a smile toward the prim librarian, and burst through the door on his way home.

As he drove, he reflected on himself and his rapidly changing moods. One minute he felt a frustration and fear of her; the next, a deepening love. Her docile behavior had elicited the latter, he knew, and he hoped she would remain so.

Their present course was smooth, he thought.

And promising.

In Columbus, Georgia, a funeral was about to begin. At the prompting of close friends and relatives, the next-of-kin of Charles Barnett had prepared to bury him quickly, in order to put the ritual behind and adjust to his loss on their own terms. Whisperings around the congregation centred on the absence of Nancy's immediate family. Gossip abounded as to the unhappiness of the young couple, but most understood that her closest survivors were with relatives in Alabama, awaiting the recovery of Nancy's body.

The church was packed with friends and family. Flower arrangements of all colors and sizes crowded the pulpit as the haunting melody of the organ faded. Reverend Foster rose and stepped forward, still uncertain of the eulogy he was going to deliver. The deceased had seldom been to church, and Reverend Foster barely knew him. Nancy, however, had attended occasionally, and had recently come to him for marital counseling. The words of the Lord had comforted her with assurance that in faith would be her deliverance.

Still hesitating and finding it difficult to begin, Reverend Foster met the tear-stained eyes across the crowd. The solution to Nancy's problem in the eyes of the Lord had been death, and this weighed heavily on the reverend's mind. Now the struggle for faith had been passed to her loved ones.

In the cruelest of ways, her prayer had been answered.

The Sunday edition of *The Birmingham News* lay scattered across the living-room floor, surrounding the sofa where James Crocker lay. Occasionally Edith glanced at him through the doorway from the kitchen. Clad only in a T-shirt and dirty work pants, an offensive odor wafting from his unclean body, he was repulsive. Silently she shook her head, her face showing the strain of internal turmoil.

James scratched his head in wonderment at the front-page report of the continued search for a woman's body in Kelley Creek. Till now he had been unaware of the accident — yet he had dreamed of a peculiarly similar accident. The dream involved Wayne, and had nagged at his subconscious, until jogged by the newspaper story when it had all come back quite clearly.

In the dream, he had stumbled in the dark along the shore of Kelley Creek, on the opposite shore from his usual spot. A storm was building, and forced him to stay close to his pickup truck for shelter from the rain. Under his right arm was a fresh six-pack of Schlitz, and on the floor of the truck lay another, now empty. Suddenly the wind strengthened, rocking him on his unsteady feet. Dead leaves and dust whipped through the air and stung his cheeks. Then came the rain, a cold drenching downpour that sent him to shelter beside a massive boulder. Streaks of lightning continuously interrupted the thick darkness of night. The noise itself was overpowering, an explosion of wind, rain, thunder and rushing water.

James stared in bewilderment as suddenly an automobile appeared in the river, slowly sinking at midstream. He staggered in disbelief from behind the boulder, rain lashing against his face, and fell to his knees. Downstream on the opposite shore, Wayne appeared, waving his arms and shouting at the vehicle. James yelled to his son, but his voice was muted by the raging elements. Wayne obviously hadn't seen or heard him, instead concentrating on the automobile and someone who had escaped and was fighting the current for survival.

In the dream, the scene was obscure, visible only through intermittent flashes of lightning. James couldn't tell if the accident victim had been a man or woman, but regardless, Wayne pulled the survivor to safety. James had never felt such intense excitement. But then a bitter cold settled in, and he felt the brittle crackle of his own frozen sleeves as he bent his arms. His teeth chattered, his feet ached from the cold. The rescue scene had been quickly forgotten as James ran on wobbly legs to the warm, dry cab of the pickup truck.

Ain't that a bitch! thought James. It was almost like ESP or something, crazier than any dream he'd ever had. But why had Wayne held the leading role? James usually cast himself as the hero of his dreams. Shit, it didn't make good sense. But there had to be an explanation. Since the real accident occurred near his favorite haunt, his subconscious must have taken note of a radio report while he was drunk. Yeah, that must have been it.

Liquor could really fuck you up sometimes.

The shed was shaped like a crude quonset hut with two large front doors that opened outwardly to allow for the movement of bulky objects inside. Parked adjacent to the unsightly garage was a run-down wrecker, and the smell of gasoline and motor oil floated through the air. Zeke Allen keyed the padlock and snapped it open, then pulled the wobbling, rattling doors out and to the side.

"She's right here where we left her," Zeke drawled through a wad of tobacco. "Sheriff said to keep her under lock and key, and that's exactly what I done."

Deputy Donald Hart peered into the murky darkness inside. A musty odor hung in the air and particles of dust floated through sunbeams that seeped through cracks in the side walls. An assortment of automobile parts lay scattered along the edge of the earthen floor, but more importantly, at the center of the room rested the battered remains of the Barnetts' '63 Ford Falcon.

"Sorry to mess up your Sunday afternoon like this, Zeke," Hart apologized. "But the sheriff thought I should go over this thing one more time to be sure we didn't miss anything."

"Aw, that's all right, Don," Zeke said. "You and me go 'way back — you know I'll do anything to help."

Hart paced around the car, rubbing his chin in thought. "Nobody's touched it?" he asked.

"Hell, no — I got strict orders from the sheriff about that. But lots of folks come around to take a look. I let some of 'em peep in through the window.

Was that okay, Don? Didn't see no harm in it at the time."

The deputy grinned, knowing Zeke all too well. The old fart probably charged fifty cents per peek. "Nothing wrong with that," Hart answered. "Nothin' at all." Zeke had yet to leave his side.

Hart cleared his throat and faced Zeke. "Now, what we got here," he began, "is a confidential police investigation. Has to be done in complete privacy. Understand?"

"Sure, I get the message," Zeke said as he backed away. "Guess I'll just get on back to the house. Watch the ball game. You'll lock up for me, won't you, Don?"

"Sure, sure," Hart said, escorting Zeke outside. "Thanks again for the use of your garage. And I appreciate you comin' down here with me this evening."

As soon as Zeke was out of sight, Hart returned to the car. To hell with tromping down that muddy creek to find real evidence. Probably nothin' there anyway. But right here, in this shed, was a veritable gold mine of hard proof. All he had to do was find something the sheriff had missed on his visual inspection. Thank goodness, the vehicle hadn't been stripped and inventoried yet.

Both doors of the Falcon stood slightly ajar, having been warped and rendered virtually inoperable by the accident. Hart pulled the passenger door open and leaned inside to rummage through the glove compartment. The smell was awful, but the contents were the same as before — tire pressure gauge, soggy road maps, unused straws from McDonald's. It was all there, but nothing that could be specifically linked to the car or, better yet, the girl. And, besides, the nigger-lovin' sheriff had seen all this stuff, and might remember if a particular item turned up missing.

A dried layer of mud blanketed the interior. Bending to inspect the area beneath the front seat, Hart could tell that any loose contents had likely been swept away by the swift current. Abruptly the unbalanced passenger door swung shut, startling Hart and depositing a sprinkle of powered mud on his trousers.

"Shit!" he cursed, and took a deep breath to calm his nerves. The car stank and seemed to taunt him, almost as if it was saying, "You won't find anything here, Mr. Unscrupulous Lawman. My secrets are safe".

Got to hurry up, before the sheriff stops by.

Backing away from the vehicle, Hart stretched and regarded the wreckage again from afar. There had to be something he could use within this piece of junk. There just had to be.

Should I try the trunk? he wondered. Hell, it might not even open, and he couldn't afford to break into it. Curiously, he peeked inside the steering column. A key chain still dangled from the ignition. What the hell — I'll give it a try, he thought. I'll just have to be careful not to force it.

Hart pulled the passenger door open and again leaned inside, supporting himself as he leaned across with his left hand anchored in the crack-ridden mud of the front seat. As he reached for the keys, several loose strands of pine straw tumbled into the small opening where the lower seat adjoined the upper half. He pressed harder on the seat and peered into the opening at its back. Soggy chewing gum wrappers appeared. A wicked smile crept across Hart's face. If anything had fallen from the woman's purse or the man's pocket, it could still be hidden in this back section of the seat. Using both hands for more pressure, he pushed the cushioned upholstery harder and found a comb, two quarters and a penny. Interesting. Carefully, he worked both hands further along the seat until his heart almost sank at the sight of a small object. Jewelry. A gold-plated band of some kind. With his right hand he twisted the metal strip free and backed away toward the garage door for better light.

Oh, this is perfect, he thought. Absolutely *perfect*! He rolled the tiny bracelet in his palm, noting the corrosion that marred the band in several places. Wetting his thumb with saliva, he wiped away a film of mud and grime from a front flat section and held his breath. An engraved heart appeared, and inside its borders were the initials "N.S.B." — *N*ancy *S*ue *B*arnett.

"Whooo-eeee!" he whooped. Nothing he found could have been better than this! Pacing about with nervous excitement, he pocketed the bracelet and closed and locked the garage doors. Now to clean this little jewel, he thought, and get it inside the nigger's house. Hot *damn*!

Sheriff Arnold smiled through the screened order window of the local Burger Shake restaurant. Inside young Trudy Kates was busily preparing his usual hamburger, French fries and chocolate shake.

Trudy's long auburn hair hung loosely over a white smock that disguised her shapely figure.

"I swear, Miss Trudy," the sheriff drawled. "You look prettier every time I see you. When are you gonna get yourself a husband?"

Trudy blushed and flashed her long eyelashes nervously. She knew it was true — she was more attractive now than when she was named Senior Beauty three years earlier. Still she remained outwardly modest.

"Oh, sheriff, that's sweet of you," she said as she pushed the lawman's lunch through the sliding door of the countertop. "Maybe someday I'll surprise you."

"The only thing that surprises me is that some fellow hasn't snagged you already," the sheriff chuckled.

"Have a nice day, sheriff," Trudy called as he carried his meal to a shaded redwood picnic table.

The town appeared peaceful today, as were most Sundays. Harry Wilson, son of the local dentist, circled the Burger Shake parking lot in his metallic blue GTO, its chrome wheels glistening in the sun. Two weeks earlier the sheriff had been lenient with the boy, ticketing him only for speeding, when an arrest for reckless driving had probably been more appropriate. Maybe it had done the boy some good. Embarrassedly, Harry spotted the sheriff, dropped his speed considerably and waved, his face visibly red even from the sheriff's vantage point.

Oh, hell, thought the sheriff, returning to his meal. Life goes on.

As he'd been tied up with Jeb Stevens, President of Arbor Construction Company, the sheriff was famished and his late lunch was revitalizing. Munching on French fries, he maintained a steady vigil of the passing traffic, nodding hello to one and all, as almost every car was familiar to him.

Stevens had been evasive about his company's safety precautions at the construction site. The accident had struck a public nerve, and a criminal negligence suit appeared likely. Under the advice of an attorney, he refused to discuss the tragedy and informed the sheriff that, not until a court order was received, would his company's personnel records be available for inspection. The sheriff tried in every way to "smooth-talk" the nervous executive, but to no avail. Even now, though, the lawman knew his efforts with Stevens had been only half-hearted. The "foul play" aspect of the Kelley Creek accident was a long shot, lacking in substance.

Returning to his meal, the sheriff finished off the burger and fries, slurped the milkshake dry, then tossed the paper refuse into a nearby garbage bin. He stood, took a deep breath, and stretched. Possibly he could catch Preacher Mason at home about now. Preacher might still shed some light on the subject. But as he slid behind the wheel of his car, a confusing thought occurred to him: The woman's shoe and the flashlight had been found on the *opposite* shore from the purse. The car had plunged into the creek from the east, and the purse had also been found on the eastern side. But the shoe, which matched another found inside the car, was discovered on the *western* shore. Would an alleged abductor have forced her to remove her shoes and leave them inside the car? No, she must have been inside the car when it entered the water. Assuming that to be the case, a sex crime should logically be ruled out. The purse and shoe could have been swept from the vehicle and drifted to opposite shores. That was possible. A closed patent leather purse with air trapped inside could float indefinitely. More and more this explanation seemed to fit. Someone had merely found the purse and ransacked it. But the shoe, on the other hand, could hardly have floated. True, the current was strong enough to deposit the shoe practically anywhere. But logically — would such an object lacking in buoyancy likely to have been found in such close proximity to the accident site? It seemed more probable that the shoe would be carried further downstream, if indeed, it ever surfaced at all. It just didn't make much sense. But then again, what if the woman had escaped the car and made it to the shore while still wearing one shoe? The passenger window had definitely been rolled down, and the woman was missing. But that was silly — of course she hadn't made it to shore — she would've turned up by now.

Sheriff Arnold shrugged. If there had been foul play, it had taken place against all probabilities. He felt annoyed at himself for having pursued it seriously in the first place. But law enforcement had to work that way. Every theory must be investigated and put to the test. And a case could unwind through several blind alleys before the truth was finally known.

Twisting the key in the ignition, the sheriff raced the engine and watched a cloud of exhaust smoke rise through the rear view mirror. Trudy waved goodbye from behind the plate-glass window and Sheriff Arnold grinned. Chester, you dirty ol' man, he thought. You shouldn't be thinkin' such things about Miss Trudy.

Assembling a splint around Nancy's injured leg had been easier than he'd expected. With the help of the first-aid book, Wayne's childhood Boy Scout training had come back to him quickly.

He relaxed a moment to examine his work. Fabric strips held the thin wooden slat firmly against her leg — tight, but not excessively so. Next he would assemble a sling for her shoulder.

"Does that feel all right?" he asked.

She nodded, her eyes unblinking and finally empty of tears. Upon his return from the library, she hadn't appeared as upset as he might have expected. She seemed to be accepting the situation more. Or had she simply given up?

Wayne breathed a sigh of relief. The book described in detail the symptoms and proper treatment of shock. At first he was frightened, reading that during the late stages of shock, a victim would appear apathetic, unresponsive, vacant — just as she had been this very morning. But somehow, perhaps by the grace of God, she had come out of it. Unknowingly, he had treated her condition properly. It was with satisfaction, he read that the prescribed treatment for exposure was the removal of wet clothing. Likewise, the removal of restrictive undergarments improved blood circulation, a necessary procedure for shock victims. He had kept her warm, given her orange juice and plenty of rest — all of which had brought her through. But he had been lucky, so very, very lucky. Had her condition worsened only slightly, she might not have lived through the first night. Shock, he'd read, can be fatal when left untreated.

She smiled again as he gently placed a blanket over her lower body. He massaged her temples lightly and stroked her silky hair. She's beginning to trust me, he thought. She's an angel.

And she's mine.

10

A line of rowboats parted the calm waters of Kelley Creek as dragging operations continued. Hurriedly, Deputy Hart paced along the path to the water's edge, hoping his absence had gone·unnoticed. As he had been placed in charge of the search efforts, Hart had been nervous about leaving long enough to rummage through the mangled car. But now, he could relax. Reflecting on the discovery of the bracelet, Hart smiled and waved at Ned Peters who was reeling in a grappling hook at midstream. Everything was falling into place.

"Any luck, Ned?" Hart yelled.

"Hell, no," answered Peters with a tone of disgust. "Pulled in a couple of dead dogs — that's about it."

Hart stepped between two boulders at the shoreline for a better view. "Got any ideas?" he yelled.

"Sure, I got ideas," Peters growled. "Ain't gonna find nothin' here. Ought to be further downstream."

Hart nodded in silent agreement. If the body had been in this general vicinity, it should have been found by now. "Stay with it awhile longer," he yelled. "Youngblood has a team a mile or so downstream."

"Youngblood?" laughed Peters. "That bastard needs a map to find his own asshole!"

The scattered laughter of nearby rescue workers carried faintly across the stream, for Ned's good-natured humor was a welcomed relief.

"Get out of here!" Hart gibed, with an obscene gesture to his buddy. It was time to hike downstream and check on Youngblood, and as Hart turned away, Ned's voice trailing behind him, "Hey, fellas — ol' Deputy Don is sure enough worried now. He's headed for the bushes to find his own asshole!" An accompanying roar of laughter slowly faded.

Ned Peters is a real character, thought Hart. Cheerful son-of-a-bitch, that's for sure.

Just ahead lay the favorite swimming hole of the local boys. A long section of steel cable hung from an overhanging oak tree and gently swayed with the breeze. In the summer this place would be packed with screaming teenagers, drinking and carrying on. Wouldn't it be funny, Hart thought, if the woman's body were never found, and one hot summer's day some smart-ass kid dropped from that steel cable right on top of her rotted corpse? Hell, that would be one hell of a sight to—

From a short distance downstream came a frantic yell. Shielding the sun from his eyes, Hart gazed

ahead — young Reggie Martin was racing breathlessly toward him.

"Deputy!" the boy yelled again.

"Right here, son," Hart answered.

The boy bounded forward, picking up speed as he
huffed for air, his face red with exhaustion, his feet
slapping rapidly against the packed soil of the
shoreline. Finally Reggie reached Hart and collapsed against a nearby tree to catch his breath.

"What's goin' on?" Hart asked. "Did Youngblood
send you?"

"Yessir," panted the boy. "Mr. Youngblood said
for me to find you quick." Reggie hesitated for a
deep breath, then continued. "They found her,
Deputy. They found the dead lady."

Nancy lay awake in the bedroom, listening to the
dull clatter of pots and pans from the kitchen where
Wayne was doing the dishes. The surges of pain had
finally faded, only to be replaced by an irritating
soreness and she now felt as if her normal thought
processes were returning. But there were so many
details. And it was difficult to discern recent
memories from what might have been only vivid
hallucinations.

Nancy closed her eyes, breathed steadily, and
tried to concentrate on one fact at a time. First, her
current physical condition. Without question, she
had been injured. But what had been the source of
her injury? Was it the result of a beating from
Wayne? Or had she actually been an accident victim? While Wayne had roughed her up in their
earlier altercations, she could not recall him inflict-

ing brutality on her in any form or fashion. On the other hand, sketchy images of an automobile accident flirted with her consciousness. Obviously, there had been a mishap — that realization had occurred to her earlier, she suddenly remembered. But she had never come to a firm conclusion as to whether or not Wayne had orchestrated the whole thing.

The news report on television had omitted any hint or suspicion of foul play. But, of course, if the whole thing had been carefully planned and executed, the authorities could have been easily fooled.

Or had the TV news been part of an elaborate dream? God, it was so confusing! Tears trickled from Nancy's closed eyes. She wished she could open them and find everything back to normal. Even the problems with Charlie had been easier to deal with than this unending frustration of not knowing what had happened in her life over a period of . . . *days*? She had lost all concept of time.

Wayne was humming as he worked in the kitchen. He seemed such a kind and gentle man, and yet, his behavior was unpredictable. Where and how he had entered her life remained a mystery. And even though he had bound and gagged her . . . once? Twice? It was difficult to imagine Wayne doing harm to her. But there were the unexplained photographs — or had they also been unreal?

Nancy raised her right hand to her forehead, the soreness of her arm irritated by the movement, and slowly massaged her temples — this intense concentration was giving her a headache and she had irritated her sore arm by moving it. Perhaps she should try to go to sleep.

But, no. All these things must be sorted out in her mind. It was vital that she understand her situation, so she would know how to react to Wayne.

Was Charlie really dead? It seemed more and more likely. But she couldn't worry about that right now. Her own safety was at stake and she decided not to dwell on any thoughts that might distract her from her current situation. It was sad to think that Charlie might have been killed — but, no, she wouldn't entertain those thoughts at all. And any consideration that Wayne could have murdered Charlie, well, that was preposterous. Despite what little she knew of her captor, she felt confident he wasn't capable of murder.

But maybe that was assuming too much. Wayne could possibly be a psychotic, a split personality. In a blood-freezing instant, Nancy couldn't help but remember mild-mannered Norman Bates in that terrifying movie "Psycho" she and Charlie had seen a few years earlier.

Suddenly Nancy became aware of the tension that had stiffened her sore body as she had been trying to gather her thoughts. This mental agony was accomplishing nothing, she thought, as a familiar heaviness slowly settled over her eyelids, sleep gradually returning. But as she wavered along the boundaries of consciousness, she knew one thing for certain: Although her life might still be in danger, she felt the threat was not quite as immediate as before.

Sheriff Arnold gazed thoughtfully at the trail of dust kicked up from behind the departing ambulance.

Inside the emergency vehicle was a female corpse, nude with multiple stab wounds. A group of rescue workers loitered along the creek, their numbers increasing as news of the shocking discovery spread.

"What do you make of it, Sheriff?" asked Luke Fletcher between chews on a plug of tobacco.

Sheriff Arnold turned to the crowd, which immediately quieted for his response. "Now, listen, all of you," he said in a loud, stern voice. "I don't have much to say about this. All I know is that this body belonged to a young colored girl, obviously murdered and possibly raped — we'll have to wait for the coroner's report. This new investigation will keep me busy awhile, so I'd suggest that you folks get back to searchin' for the Barnett woman while I look into the other girl's death."

The group noisily dispersed, their various grumblings and complaints drifting back to the sheriff's ears. "It's only a nigger," he heard someone say. Another wondered aloud, "What the hell has happened to our community?"

That same question dominated the sheriff's thoughts. This was the first non-domestic murder to occur in Shelby County in over a decade. And complicating the issue further was the wide-spread racial unrest in Birmingham that was beginning to spill over into Pell City and surrounding areas. The Klan had been relatively inactive in Shelby County, or so the sheriff thought. Regardless, just a few short days ago he had hoped for a new challenge. Now he had almost more than he could handle.

A few feet away Deputy Hart mumbled softly to a small group of passers-by. The sheriff couldn't catch the gist of the conversation, but discerned that every other word was "nigger." With rising impatience, he considered how to deal with the prejudiced deputy. He felt like reprimanding the young lawman on the spot. But public sympathy toward negroes could be dangerous. Unfortunately, most local residents were as biased as the deputy. No, he'd have to contend with Hart later, in privacy. Give himself time to calm down and approach the situation logically.

"Hart!" he yelled and motioned for the deputy to break away from his audience. Realizing from the tone of the sheriff's voice that he was in trouble, Hart sheepishly trudged to his boss's side.

"Yessir?" Hart answered.

"Hart," the sheriff began, staring coldly at his subordinate, "I want you to get back to the courthouse and file a report on this. Check any missing persons bulletins to identify the victim."

Hart nodded, avoiding the sheriff's eyes.

"I'm gonna try to catch Preacher Mason at home again," the sheriff continued. "And I'll see you later this afternoon. But in the meantime," the sheriff leaned closer and lowered his voice, "*try to keep your damn mouth shut*."

Verbally beaten, Hart ambled slowly to his squad car. His heart raced as he slid behind the steering wheel. The sheriff was definitely on his case. He'd have to be extra careful.

Sheriff Arnold pivoted and faced the creek. That bastard has got to go, he thought. Ahead the curiosity seekers were breaking up, some walking back to their cars parked aside the narrow dirt road, others resuming their search along the creek for the

Barnett woman's body. Sheriff Arnold gazed downstream. Couldn't be more than a half mile to Preacher's house, he thought. Might as well walk.

Along the way a number of volunteers, recognizing the sheriff was in deep thought, gave him a wide berth. For a moment the lawman considered turning back when he was faced with the first of the many detours caused by the numerous downed trees littering the shores, but he forged ahead.

Integration would be spreading soon to Shelby County. It was inevitable. Already several Birmingham schools had been desegregated amid protests and violence. Why do people have to be so damn cruel and inconsiderate? the sheriff wondered. There was no common courtesy and respect offered anymore. Racial prejudice had been passed from generation to generation in the South. It wouldn't go away overnight. But was there really any need to assign blame? Bigotry was wrong, as anyone who took the time to understand the other side would plainly see. But life in the Deep South had always centered strongly around the family unit. Kids believed, without question, what they were told by their parents. And, unfortunately, most parents had taught their children wrong.

Sheriff Arnold recalled the distress he himself had experienced when at age twelve he had asked his Dad, "Pop, why are niggers bad?" His Pop had had no answer, instead offering the vague excuse of "Says so in the Bible." But young Chester had known that wasn't true. His parents had led him to dislike and distrust colored people for no good reason. But Chester's bitterness toward his parents had faded when he finally understood. Decent,

God-fearing people, who would do no harm to anyone, they were only passing on to him what their folks had taught *them* decades ago. His parents were too old and set in their ways to change, he had decided. But he could alter his own views. And, he had determined, no longer would he automatically accept anyone else's philosophies without question.

Sheriff Arnold stared ahead and waved at Ned Peters who was now paddling alone in a canoe. People were the cruelest of all living creatures, he thought as he trudged along. Young Chester had learned early not to speak out in defense of the coloreds. The resulting white backlash could be deadly. For years, he had kept his views to himself, feeling strongly that one person alone could do little to change a whole region. Even now his sympathies remained secret for he knew when he first took office that more could be accomplished this way. Were he to verbalize his true feelings, he would merely be defeated in the next election. But as long as he held office while keeping his views to himself, he could at least assure equal justice to the colored folks of Shelby County. On that issue, he would never budge.

Just ahead a young colored boy was tossing rocks into the creek at passing driftwood. Probably one of Preacher's boys, he thought.

"Howdy, pardner," the sheriff greeted the young boy. "Are you one of Preacher Mason's boys?"

The young lad jerked at the sight of the lawman. Awed by the husky figure of authority, he nervously answered, "Yessir."

Sheriff Arnold squatted beside the boy. "Is your Daddy home?"

"Yessir."

"Well," said the sheriff, "I'd like for you to do me a favor. I need to talk to your Daddy a few minutes, and I want you to keep that dog of yours from chewin' on my leg. Think you could do that for me?"

"Yes-*sir*!" the boy grinned, standing now proud and erect. Sheriff Arnold followed as the boy began to jabber. "He ain't no bad dog. Ain't never bit anybody. 'Ceptin' me."

"What's your name, son?" the sheriff interrupted, keeping a watchful eye out for the dog.

"Nathaniel," answered the boy. "I want to be a fireman when I get big."

Ahead the dog bounded from the house to greet his master, then quickly crouched, growling on sight of the sheriff.

"It's all right, Skipper," Nat said, reaching down to stroke the animal's back. "The sheriff here is our friend."

Grudgingly the dog allowed the two to pass. Around a bend in the trail, the house came into view. Seated on the front steps was Preacher Mason, dressed in a white shirt and faded blue slacks, knife in hand, whittling on a small block of wood.

"Got company, Pa," Nat proudly announced.

Preacher looked up with a start and dropped the knife. Then, regaining his composure, he stood and offered a firm handshake.

"Good to see you, Mr. Sheriff," he said. "How have you been?"

Sheriff Arnold smiled. "No complaints. How about yourself?"

"Aw, the Lord's been mighty good to me,"

Preacher answered. "Been real good to me. What brings you out this way?"

Leaning informally against the top step, Sheriff Arnold watched as Nat raced away, chasing Skipper who had playfully run off with the boy's catcher's mitt.

"Been some strange things goin' on around here," the sheriff began. "Guess you heard about the accident."

"That was a real shame, Mr. Sheriff," Preacher answered. "But those two Georgia folks is knockin' on the doors of Heaven right now."

The sheriff hesitated, then continued. "The woman's body hasn't been recovered yet, but her purse was found not far from your house, over by the creek. Somebody took what money was inside."

Preacher raised his head, a look of surprise on his face. "Yes?"

"Have you seen or heard anything unusual around here in the past few days?"

Preacher searched his thoughts, then nervously answered, "No sir, can't say that I have."

Sheriff Arnold gazed through the open front door and windows of the house. There seemed to be no movement inside. "Where's the rest of the family?" he asked.

"Well, the missus is over at Uncle Walt's. He ain't been feelin' too good, and she's helpin' Aunt Maggie take care of him. Lurlene, she's my oldest, she done up and got married last year. Livin' over in Bessemer now."

"Don't you have an older boy, too?"

"Demetrius? He ain't here."

"When will he be back?"

"Don't rightly know. That boy is in and out all the time."

Straightening up, the sheriff took a deep breath. "Preacher, about a half mile upstream, we found a teenage colored girl's body."

Stunned, Preacher stood silently, his mouth hanging open. "Colored girl, huh?" he finally muttered.

"Murdered. Stabbed. From the looks of her body, she ain't been dead more than two or three days at the most. Do you know of anybody around these parts that might be capable of such a thing?"

Preacher shook his head slowly. "Not right off, no sir," he said, his lips quivering. "But that scares me, sheriff. That scares me real bad. I hear talk about the Klan."

"We'll find who did it," the sheriff reassured him. "I'd like for you to ask the missus and your older son if they've seen or heard anything unusual. I'll stop by again tomorrow and have a chat with them."

"Yes sir, Mr. Sheriff," Preacher answered. "I sure hope you find him quick."

The sheriff turned and headed for the creek. "You take care now, you hear?" he said.

Preacher reached a shaky hand to retrieve his pocket knife from the ground. "You, too, Mr. Sheriff. You, too."

Efforts to withhold from the press the discovery of Mrs. Barnett's purse had proved unsuccessful. Sheriff Arnold attributed this to the fact that the situation had gotten out of control, thanks primarily to Deputy Donald Hart. By late afternoon, the sheriff was besieged by reporters from as far away as Huntsville and Columbus, Georgia. "No comment" was his response, recognizing with a degree of reluctance the danger of allowing journalists to speculate. But what else could he do?

The body of the young colored girl had been identified as seventeen-year-old Bertha Mae Sampson of Leeds, Alabama, reported missing since Thursday night. Miss Sampson's murder, impacting on top of the Barnett investigation, had brought confusion to the minds of all concerned, including Sheriff Arnold. Could the two events be connected? The answer would have to come later, the sheriff thought with exasperation, knowing he would be hounded by the media for an answer today.

As twilight settled over the area, Sheriff Arnold parked his patrol car beside Highway 231 for a brief rest. For the first time in years, anxiety was coursing through his body. Having sent an enraged WBRC-TV news team back to Birmingham minutes before, the sheriff's pulse had yet to slow. Taking a deep breath, he glared at the oncoming traffic. A few automobiles had begun to switch on their headlights. Tomorrow, this entire operation must be reorganized, he thought. The day's developments had caught him off-balance. The sting of embarrassment still burned when he considered the inept picture he had presented to the public.

Tonight he'd do some serious planning.

"Don't you worry about Uncle Walt," Maybelle Mason said, noting her husband's grave expression as she slid into the front seat of the car. "He's gonna be just fine."

Preacher steered the old '53 Chevy down Uncle Walt's driveway back to Selton Road. He had stopped to pick up his wife on the way to church in nearby Pineville. After his usual complaint about having to wear a bow tie, young Nat had fallen asleep in the back seat.

"It ain't Uncle Walt what's worryin' me," Preacher said as he switched on the headlights. "It's Demetrius."

"Oh, he'll come home. You know he will," Maybelle said. "The boy just needs attention. That's why he invents those crazy stories."

Preacher stared at his wife, his lips trembling, his eyes filling with tears. "Sheriff Arnold come by this evenin'," he said. "I'm afraid we got real trouble this time."

Maybelle shifted uncomfortably. She had feared this day would come. Every night she'd pray for the Lord to give guidance to young Demetrius, to lead him away from the troublemakers he palled around with and ease the boy's rebellious spirit. "What do you mean?" she asked.

Preacher wiped tears from his cheeks. "Bertha Mae's dead."

"Oh, Lord, no—" his wife moaned.

"And that ain't all," he continued. "The sheriff says they found a purse not far from our house. It belonged to that white woman that was in the accident the other night. But I don't believe the sheriff thinks it was no accident. Not by the way he was talkin', anyways."

"Oh, God, no," Maybelle moaned. "Oh, Lord, please don't let Demetrius be mixed up in this!"

Preacher guided the car to a stop along the road. "Hush now," he said. "You'll wake the boy."

Maybelle glanced over the seat at Nat, asleep in the back. He was such a precious boy. Surely the Lord would protect him from evil. Grasping for support, she slid closer to her husband and held tightly to his arm. "But we don't know for sure that Demetrius was involved," she whispered. "He was talkin' out of his head when he ran off."

"Woman, he *had* to be involved — you know what the boy *said*!" Preacher snapped. "Now, get a-hold of yourself. We got to go on to church, just like nothin' happened. And then we got to find him."

"But what will you do with him?"

"I'll do what the Lord tells me," Preacher said, then took a deep breath. "If Demetrius broke the law, he'll have to be punished. It's out of our hands."

Slowly he steered the car back onto the pavement, wondering what effect his emotional turmoil might have on tonight's sermon. No one must know of his family problems.

Nothing could interfere with the Lord's work.

Wayne quietly approached the darkened bedroom and took two cautious but determined steps inside.

"Are you awake?" he whispered.

Amid the rustle of bedsheets he heard Nancy's response. "Yes."

Slowly he stepped to the foot of the bed and settled into a comfortable seated position. Outside a myriad of crickets sang as Wayne's vision adjusted to the dark of night. A glimmer of wandering moonlight was reflected from her staring eyes.

"I think we should talk," he said.

Nancy gazed wonderingly at his obscure form. "Okay . . . if you want," she answered.

Wayne breathed a sigh of relief, then glanced at the nearby light switch. "Would you like the light on?" he asked.

"No —" she answered sharply, then explained, "I like the dark . . . and the moonlight."

Wayne fumbled nervously with the loose fringe of the bedspread. "Nancy, you know I really—" but then he stopped. She looked so soft, so feminine in the moonlight. Momentarily breathless, he finally continued, "I want you to try to understand. Please?"

Her eyelids lowered. "Understand what?" she asked.

Now Wayne looked away, staring out the window. A glowing cloud passed before the moon, and the wind swept gently through the trees. How could he make her understand?

"It's all true, what I told you before," he said. "I saved you from drowning and brought you here for shelter. You saw the report of the ice storm on the news. There was really nothing else I could do."

Her face remained expressionless.

What was she thinking? Wayne wondered. Was she once again blocking out everything he said, refusing to believe him?

"I'm sorry about what I did, Nancy. But I never had any bad intentions. I know the way everything happened, I must seem awfully guilty. But won't you please try to understand?"

Nancy refused to speak, and Wayne noticed her lower lip quiver nervously for a moment.

"Listen to me — please!" he implored. "I've taken

care of you. Do you honestly think I would hurt you?"

Finally she looked up at him and their eyes locked for one burning moment. Then clearing her throat, she slowly forced out, "Why . . . are you keeping me here?"

Turning from her sight, Wayne said, "I want you . . . to believe that I've . . . meant you no harm. I want you . . . to *like* me."

"*Like* you?" she screeched, her sudden outburst startling him. "*Like you?* I *despise* you! I don't know what's happening to me anymore. All I know is, I want to go home and *you won't let me!*"

"I'm sorry . . ." he mumbled, trying to disguise his disappointment, "I'm so sorry."

"Don't be," she blurted, turning her head quickly away. "You'll get what you deserve."

Her vicious tone made Wayne feel tense, once again. How could she speak to him in such a way? Had he completely misjudged the subtle changes in her attitude he thought he had perceived?

Closing her eyes and massaging her temples, Nancy then took a deep breath, and apologized. "I'm sorry," she said. "I didn't mean to be so blunt. But if you want me to understand you — why not put yourself in *my* position for awhile? I've been hurt, I've lost my husband, and I'm a prisoner. Can you even begin to imagine how I feel?"

"You don't deserve this, I know," he said soothingly. "And I promise I'll take you home soon."

For the first time she perceived his insecurity and lack of confidence, and again, she could have sworn he was being sincere.

"I'd give anything to change those few moments

before you woke up and first saw me. That was the biggest mistake of my life," he said. The darkness hid his blushing cheeks. "I know it must have been awful for you, but I really didn't do anything — honest."

"It's all right," she interrupted. "As crazy as this all seems, at times I feel half-way convinced that you're telling the truth."

Wayne's face brightened. "Please try — to understand, I mean. It's important that you know what I'm like. Not only to keep me out of trouble, but because I care about you. I've enjoyed having you here."

Noticing the glitter in her eyes, he felt uneasy. Was she lying to him again? There was too much at stake to trust her just yet.

"They said on TV you were from Georgia. Were you just passing through?" he asked.

Relaxing, Nancy settled her head into the pillow. "I was coming to visit my cousin Liz—"

"Lizzie Farrell?" Wayne interrupted. "God, I've known her for years!"

"Really?"

"Sure! I even dated her once, a couple of years ago. She's nice."

Nancy turned to face him again. "Wayne?" she asked.

"Yes?"

"Are you going . . . to tie me up . . . tonight?"

Wayne frowned and hung his head. "I really wish I didn't have to," he said. "But I think it would be best if I did. Besides, you're not able to walk, and if you tried to get up, you could hurt yourself."

Nancy huffed in exasperation. "But it's so uncomfortable," she said. "I promise I won't leave the bed."

For a moment he seriously considered her request. But then a vision came to mind, of a police car sliding to a stop in front of the trailer.

"No!" he said sternly. "Don't ask. I'll leave off the gag, if you promise not to scream. But, for now, you'll have to be tied, for both our sakes."

As Nancy sulked, Wayne silently admired her. He wondered if perhaps she liked it when he exerted his control, and thought it was masculine. Finally he reached for the nylon strips on the nearby dresser. "I know it's early," he said, "but you need all the rest you can get."

Nancy shrugged. "All right, I won't complain," she said. "But would you help me to the bathroom first?"

"Sure," he said. He leaned forward to brush aside a lock of hair that had fallen into her eyes.

"And Wayne —?"

"Yes?"

"Would you play that Beatles record again while I fall asleep?"

Stars littered the heavens in such numbers that the sky looked like a fake backdrop for a cheap motion picture. From nearby Kelley Creek, croaking frogs joined in an off-beat chorus with crickets by the thousands. Dark and forbidding, the Mason house stood amidst these cheerful night sounds, eerily silent except for the snarling growl of an unseen dog.

Parked in front of the house, in his squad car Deputy Hart sat fumbling nervously with a flashlight. He swallowed hard, pausing to listen. As he'd expected, no lights were on inside, because the family was away at evening church services. But the dog was an unforeseen complication.

As the steady tick of the cooling engine died, Hart pulled the door handle with just enough force to disengage the latch. The slight click of the handle brought with it a vicious increase in pitch from the dog. Where is the hairy bastard? Hart wondered. His eyes were only now adjusting to the darkness. Finally the moon wandered from behind a cloud and spread a dim but even glow over the landscape.

Hart rolled down the window. As far as he could determine, the growl seemed to originate from the front porch. He snapped on the flashlight and aimed its beam — the dog lay crouched at the top step, its white teeth glistening in the light. "Shit!" Hart cursed, feeling for the bracelet in his shirt pocket. He needed to get inside the house, to put the jewelry in a place that would be easily seen when he came back the next day.

Carefully, he eased from the car, hoping the dog would back down. But as he approached the house, the animal seemed all the more determined to attack. I could kill the fucker, he considered, and slowly reached for his holster. His hand dropped to the butt of his revolver, but rested there. The bullet could be traced to his weapon — that would be too risky. Quickly he scanned the area for a board or a club. Nothing was within easy reach. "Shit!" he cursed again. The dog responded by inching forward, with a show of teeth even more threatening than ever.

Pulling the bracelet from his pocket, Hart held it tightly in his right hand, as if to give himself motivation, for he knew another opportunity to find the Mason home empty might come too late. Cautiously he eased forward, slowly closing in on the dog. I'll kick his balls if he attacks, he thought, keeping a wary eye glued to the animal at all times.

"Nice doggie," he crooned, but to no avail — the growling intensified.

Shifting the bracelet to his left hand, Hart drew his service revolver with his right. A hard rap with the gun barrel would convince the dog to keep his distance, Hart decided, taking a deep breath and quickening his pace.

Suddenly the dog sprang from the porch, sailing through the air and colliding with the surprised deputy. Hart sprawled to the ground, screaming and kicking in self-defense as he tried to avoid the animal's fangs. Somehow he managed to grab the loose skin on the dog's back and succeeded in keeping its gaping jaws from his face. But, wrenching its head around, the dog sank its teeth twice into Hart's arm. Despite the pain shooting through his damaged arm the lawman managed to aim a glancing blow of the gun at the animal's skull, stunning him long enough so he could escape.

Abandoning his mission, Hart jumped to his feet and raced for the car, barely making it inside before the dog attacked once more. Safe at last, wheezing to catch his breath, Hart holstered his weapon. Then he remembered — *the bracelet!* He aimed the flashlight, its beam reflecting from the shiny metal chain near the base of the front steps. The glimmer of jewelry promptly caught the dog's attention. Diverted, the animal padded forward, tongue lapping, and grasped the bracelet in its mouth, then scampered back to the front porch.

"Well, I'll just be goddamned," Hart muttered, wincing at the pain in his arm. The wound would need treatment against rabies, he realized, angrily twisting the ignition key and throwing the transmission into reverse. First, he'd go home and change his clothes. Then he'd drive his own car to an out-of-town hospital for emergency treatment. The bracelet was in place on the premises, and that's all that mattered. Tomorrow he'd return in an official capacity and find the damn thing.

Lying awake on the sofa, Wayne watched the trees swaying in the moonlight. Nancy had behaved herself in the bathroom and hadn't complained when he tied her to the mattress. Now, hours later, Wayne was still unable to sleep. He'd made up his mind — he wouldn't report to work tomorrow. He'd call in sick until this situation was resolved. Perhaps he could still find a respectable way out.

Wayne yawned. Although his eyes were heavy, his mind was so alive with thoughts and visions that sleep evaded him. Nancy's so pretty, he thought. Now that much of his fear of her had finally disappeared, he enjoyed having her around, and he knew she'd realize soon that he hadn't made any real moves on her. Then they could go their separate ways.

A cold wind slammed against the trailer while Nancy slept soundly in the bedroom. And as morning approached, over a hundred miles away in Columbus, Georgia, a crisp, white frost blanketed the fresh gravesite of Charles Barnett.

11

Monday
Day Four

Awakening at sunrise to the crow of a rooster, Preacher Mason readied himself for a busy day. Seated at the breakfast table, he sipped cautiously at a steaming cup of coffee, as Maybelle, leaning against the kitchen sink, stared at her husband through bloodshot eyes.

"You ought to get out there and find him, or we'll never get no sleep," she scolded her husband through a stifled yawn.

Preacher hung his head, repeating for the third time, "I've got to work today. I'll look for him after I get off."

Although Preacher had been the janitor of Selton High School for almost fifteen years, he still earned only slightly above the minimum wage. But for an uneducated Negro in the rural South, he felt it was the best he could do. Besides, it provided a steady income that he couldn't afford to jeopardize.

"Those boys in Leeds — they're bound to know where Demetrius is—" Maybelle began.

"Those boys in Leeds probably *ain't in Leeds* no more," Preacher interrupted. "They're hidin' out, just like he is."

"But we don't even know for sure what they did."

"No, we don't," Preacher mumbled. "We don't know nothin'. But I'm not about to lose my job over it. The rest of us has got to eat. And if the boy is guilty, he's got to pay the price. It ain't for us to judge — that's the Lord's job."

Unable to withstand the anguish, Maybelle flung herself around her husband, holding him tightly as a reservoir of tears unleashed. Lovingly, he patted his wife on the back.

"He'll come home on his own," he soothed her. "And that'll be best for all of us."

But at the back of his mind, guilt nagged at his conscience. *The proper thing for you to do under the eyes of the Lord, Preacher, is to tell Sheriff Arnold what you suspect.*

Already Sheriff Arnold felt relieved. At the meeting in his office that had broken up only minutes before, Deputy Granger, as he'd expected, had quickly grasped the urgency of the two investigations. Hart, however, had sat, sullen and unresponsive, and after the sheriff had dismissed Granger, he'd taken the young lawman aside, and had given him notice that his job was on the line. The sheriff sat, savouring the return of his control. He knew Granger would be busy talking to Nancy Barnett's parents who were still staying with the Farrells in Selton. He was hopeful that they'd be able to tell Granger how much money Mrs. Barnett had been carrying, and whether or not her husband was inclined to pick up hitchhikers. Hart, on the other hand, would be at the accident site, directing the search efforts further downstream. And while all this was taking place, the sheriff planned a short drive to Leeds, in Jefferson County, to talk with Bertha Mae Sampson's parents. It would be a busy day, but at least the wheels of justice were turning again.

Hart's attitude seemed to be worsening. This morning the deputy had complained of a bruised arm and requested time off until the swelling went down. Sheriff Arnold had merely laughed at the notion, attacking his subordinate for his lack of dedication to his job. It seemed that Donald Hart had not yet learned that there were few people who could put things over on Sheriff Chester Arnold.

Taking a ruled pad from the center drawer of his desk, the sheriff carefully noted Hart's recent acts of carelessness. When the facts were substantial enough to document Hart's dereliction of duty, he intended to take it to the county personnel board.

The sheriff grinned as he put the notes away. Soon, Hart's tour of duty would be re-routed — from Kelley Creek, without a paddle, to Shit Creek, without a boat.

After sleeping almost twelve hours, Nancy awoke calm and refreshed. She lay in silence, her mind blank. Not once did memories of her deceased husband enter her thoughts. Nor did she recall the accident or her first frightening encounter with Wayne.

Instead she felt as if she were living in a dream world and had been reborn as a completely new being. Realizing with pleasant surprise that Wayne had already untied her, she concentrated her energy into her right leg. Moving the leg from side to side, she was encouraged when she managed to raise it slightly before surrendering to the pain. Next she tested her shoulder, but found it too sore and swollen to work with. Instead, she ran her fingertips across the bump on her forehead and discovered that it, too, had diminished.

As the aroma of breakfast drifted from the kitchen, Nancy took a fresh look at her situation. Her injuries were not as serious as she had once feared, but the resulting soreness still impaired her movement. Instinctively, though, she knew that she could walk, or at least stagger, if she had to. And that fact must be kept secret from Wayne. If there was to be another chance to escape, she'd have to catch him off guard, and that would be easier to do if he perceived her as bedridden.

More and more Nancy wanted to believe that Wayne was harmless, although chances were good that he was suffering from some type of mental disorder. For now, she would simply play him along, gain his confidence, then escape at the first opportunity. And if a relatively risk-free chance didn't materialize soon, she supposed she would have to force one.

Vaguely, she remembered earlier attempts to disable her captor. She had struck him in the head once, and later, tried to cut him with a razor. But she had been weak then. Now her strength was slowly returning, and along with the element of surprise, she should be able to escape when the next occasion arose.

Nancy leaned over the side of the bed and craned her neck to see down the hallway.

"Wayne?" she called, then heard the metal clatter of a spatula dropped into the sink, followed by quick footsteps to her door.

"Yes?" he answered with a look of concern.

"Would you help me to the bathroom, please?"

Wayne smiled and jumped to her assistance. "Certainly. Do you feel like lying on the sofa while I finish breakfast?"

Nancy returned his smile. "That might be nice."

Yielding to her desire for privacy in the bathroom, Wayne returned to the stove to check the scrambled eggs. The brightness of his face revealed all — she had smiled, with no sign of fear!

"I'm finished," she yelled and he bounded to her side. Even though her hair was tangled and her breath was foul — she was still dazzling to him. Today there was a previously unseen sparkle in her big brown eyes. Seated on the toilet, but still clothed in the flannel pajamas, she looked up to him again.

"Wayne . . ." she began, obviously reluctant and embarrassed, "I need some . . . personal things . . . from a drug store."

"Yes?"

She looked away. "Nothing much. Just a toothbrush and some makeup . . . and . . . and . . . sanitary napkins."

"Sanitary napkins?" he questioned.

"You know," she hesitated, and then, after a hard swallow, whispered, "*Kotex!*"

Wayne's face flushed. He wiped his forehead,

then stuttered, "Uh . . . y-y-yes. I'll go into town l-l-later this morning."

Nancy was blushing, too. She avoided his eyes and muttered, "I really would . . . appreciate it."

Still hot around the collar, Wayne took a deep breath. Jesus! Buying Kotex would be absolutely mortifying. But somehow he would manage.

Regaining her composure, Nancy looked up at Wayne. "Smells like the eggs are burning," she grinned.

"Oh, no!" Wayne raced back to the kitchen to find a crusty mass of lumpy black eggs in the skillet. Turning off the burner, he opened a nearby window to ventilate the smoke, while from the bathroom, Nancy laughed, soon to be joined by Wayne as he marveled at the marked change in her attitude.

When the smoke cleared, he hurried back to her side. She smiled and Wayne could feel his eyes filling.

But this time they were tears of joy.

Willpower, Liz Farrell reminded herself as she scanned the kitchen table which was spread from end to end with food offerings from sympathetic neighbors. Deliciously fragrant cakes and pies of all varieties also lined the adjacent countertop. Nancy's parents, Ralph and Helen Anderson, were staying with the Farrells, and many of the local residents fondly remembered the Georgia couple from when they had lived in the area years before. But what a painful homecoming the two had faced, Liz thought, watching them through the doorway as they sat on the living room sofa. Martha Farrell sat at Helen's side, trying to comfort her sister for the loss of her only child. Resisting temptation, Liz turned away from the table, and whispering "Mom?" motioned for her mother to come to the kitchen.

Martha looked up, and concerned by her daughter's harried look, excused herself and came into the kitchen. Sympathetic about the many misfortunes her daughter had suffered through in recent weeks, she extended a loving hand to Liz.

"Mom, something has got to happen soon," Liz said, taking the proffered hand. "None of us can stand this kind of tension much longer."

"I know," Martha answered. "I wish Tom hadn't gone to work today. I told him we needed him at home, but you know how he is about—"

"Mom," Liz interrupted. "I just called the Robbins Mortuary in Columbiana." She wiped away a tear, and then continued. "I asked what kind of funeral arrangements are usually made when a body is missing. And they said *none!* I can't believe it, Mother. That means this agony goes on and on until they find Nancy. *If* they find her. Does Aunt Helen know that?"

"No, honey, I'm sure she doesn't," said Martha, tenderly squeezing her daughter's palm. "I didn't know it myself."

"We need to talk to her then."

Martha looked up sharply. "No! We can't do that! She's not ready for that kind of talk!"

"Will she ever be?" Liz asked. "Mother, no one loved Nancy more than me. But we're in our third day of mourning already, and we've got to get on with our lives. I stayed off work today myself — I could use a whole month off — 'cause all this is driving me crazy—"

"I know what you mean," Martha sobbed, embracing her daughter. "We've got to put this tragedy behind us. But let's give Helen a little longer, at least until this afternoon, all right? Then we'll talk to her. Maybe we can ask Brother Martin to stop by."

Liz nodded, but the thought of Brother Martin leading the family in prayer was less than appealing.

At the moment, Liz was quite angry at God.

Declining an invitation to eat with the usual gang, James Crocker ate his brown bag lunch alone. Chewing on a ham and cheese sandwich beneath a pine tree on the company grounds, he contemplated his life. Work was a pain in the ass. Day after day, same old shit, and no opportunity for advancement. Lazily, he poured more coffee from a red thermos. Edith had been bluffing again. Hell, he knew she'd never leave. And besides, what was wrong with him taking an occasional drink? He worked hard for a living! No one understood — especially Wayne. Vaguely remembering his scuffle with the boy over the weekend, he recalled his son's aggressiveness. It had been totally out of character for someone who had never before displayed anything other than docile behavior. And that crazy dream kept creeping back. Something about that vision just wouldn't go away.

James poured out the remainder of his coffee and recapped the thermos. Hell, maybe he'd been too rough on Wayne. There was no need to hold a grudge, and besides, soon he might really need the boy's help. So this afternoon he would stop by his son's trailer. If Wayne was receptive, James might consider an apology. Hell, he and Wayne were a team. They'd never stayed mad at each other very long.

James stood and stretched, then eyed his friends trudging back to their respective work stations as the end-of-lunch whistle blew. God, I'd love to shove that whistle up the foreman's ass, he thought.

A gang of older Negro boys, loitering at their lockers, leered at Sheriff Arnold as he paced the halls of Moton High School in Leeds. Still too hysterical to gather their thoughts, Bertha Mae's parents had provided little information. He had learned only that Bertha Mae hadn't come home from school Thursday, which hadn't alarmed them much at first. In recent weeks, she had entered a defiant, rebellious teenage stage and had acted against their wishes on several occasions. But her parents also suspected she might be involved with a bad crowd. Her sudden withdrawal from her parents was unusual for her. And just as Jerry and Amanda Sampson had begun to realize the severity of the problem, it had been too late. So now Sheriff Arnold was seeking out the girl's classmates in order to determine who might have seen her last. He doubted she had left school alone.

The sheriff stared through the dirty glass door of Room 101. The teacher, a tall, white-haired and feeble colored woman named Mrs. Beekins, was slashing at the blackboard with a piece of chalk, trying to simplify a mathematical equation for a largely uninterested class. Just as he was about to interrupt, a man's voice boomed from down the hall.

"Sheriff?"

He turned to face a slight, middle-aged colored man wearing black horn-rimmed glasses and a friendly smile. "I'm Lester Banks," the man said. "The principal. Sorry I missed you back at the office."

"That's quite all right," Sheriff Arnold smiled. The two shook hands and the sheriff noted the strong, firm grip for a man so small. "Mr. Banks, I'm Chester Arnold, Shelby County Sheriff. I guess you know why I'm here."

The little man hung his head. "A terrible shame," he said. "In her first two years, Bertha was a model student. But I noticed a change in her when school started up this past September. Her teachers noticed it, too, and brought it to my attention. I was planning to call a conference with her parents when . . . this happened."

"Don't blame yourself, Mr. Banks. Teenagers can be awfully difficult to handle. I'm sure that if Bertha were still alive, you'd do everything in your power to help her."

"Thank you, Sheriff."

"But right now I've got to find out who killed her. And I believe some of her classmates could point me in the right direction."

"We'll be happy to cooperate," the principal said.

Sheriff Arnold stood, deep in thought for a moment, and then faced the small colored man again. "Mr. Banks," he began, "if you don't mind, I'd like for you to sit in on the questioning of a few students. I believe they'll disregard the racial barrier and feel more comfortable if you're present."

"I'd be happy to," Lester Banks agreed as he pulled open the classroom door.

Inside the students were snickering at Mrs. Beekins, whose backside sported a circular patch of chalk dust.

With her arms around a basket of wet laundry, Maybelle Mason kicked open the front screen door and trudged outside to hang the clothes to dry. As the door arced to its limit, its rusty spring screeching from the strain, Skipper bounced to his feet and pranced indoors, wagging his tail and carrying a saliva-coated bracelet in his mouth. The dog padded across the hardwood floor, leaving a fresh trail of muddy paw prints, and sprang to the worn velour sofa in the living room, where he rolled on his back, spreading a mess of dirt and grime across the fuzzy nap. Abruptly, the dog's ears raised pointedly. The woman was coming back, her footsteps drawing nearer.

Setting the empty laundry basket on the front porch, Maybelle wiped her forehead, and then stood for a moment surveying the line of clothing fluttering in the wind. Then she pulled the door ajar, the scratchy door spring grating on her nerves.

Curious, Skipper tilted his head and the bracelet slipped from his teeth, dropping into the crack between the two large sofa cushions. Fire leaped from Maybelle's eyes as she took in the messy scene.

"You mangy animal!" she screeched. "Get out of my house *right now*!"

Cowed, the dog jumped from the sofa, his ears drooping. The woman barred his way, but suddenly she side-stepped, and kicked the animal's rib cage.

With a frightened yelp, Skipper darted outside to safety.

"Git out!" she screamed again, then stomped to the kitchen for a mop. Returning, she ranted and raved at the sight of the soiled sofa — it would take her all afternoon to remove the grime.

Skipper, the incident quickly forgotten, padded to his water dish near the edge of the porch and calmly lapped a drink.

In the privacy of the tiny bathroom, Nancy Barnett relaxed in warm, sudsy bathwater, revelling in the slippery feel of soap against her skin.

In the next room, Wayne was thumbing through his record collection. "Nancy? How about the Beach Boys?" he asked in a loud voice.

"Which album do you have?" she answered.

"All Summer Long".

"I like that one," she said.

Wayne placed the record on the turntable and eased the tone arm down to the first cut. "I Get Around" reverberated through the trailer. Wayne reached for his guitar and attempted to strum along, but the beat was too much for him. Shaking his head in pleasant surrender, he laid the instrument aside and drummed his fingers on the tile floor.

The bathroom door teased at the corner of his vision. Behind it was the most attractive, appealing woman he'd ever met. And now that he'd grown acquainted with her, he'd begun to feel the same nervous sensation he always had when the opposite sex was near.

"Nancy?" he called with an unsteady voice.

"Yes?"

Wayne cleared his throat. "Is there any way you can get by without the . . . uh . . . *you know*."

"Kotex?"

"Yeah . . ."

"Well, I suppose I could. But I'd rather not," she said. "I haven't actually started yet, but I'm due any day."

"Whew!" Wayne exclaimed. "I'll pick up the other stuff this afternoon, but I'll wait for that until you really need it. All right?"

"Sure," she chirped. Running her right hand down the length of her soapy legs, Nancy thought about Wayne's timidity. She slid further into the water, the suds rising to meet her chin. Could he have planned this whole thing? It seemed unlikely. Obviously the situation would have to be resolved soon. She wondered how he might react if she casually asked to leave. It seemed they understood each other now, and if she tactfully phrased the request, he might go along. If he refused, she'd simply wait for the right opportunity to surprise him with her concealed strength.

Nancy shrugged and eased her fingertips between her legs. For now, there was no reason to hurry. The right moment would come soon. Then she could face the other mounting problems in her life.

She knew the time was near.

Maybelle glanced at the kitchen clock, her face lined with worry as the familiar sound of the family car whined to a stop outside. 2:30 P.M. — Preacher was home early. Curious, she stepped through the living room and met him at the door.

"Why are you —?" she began, then stopped. The answer was written in anguish across his forehead. Preacher was a man of principle, of high moral and religious virtue. And not even his love for a troubled son could lure him from the path of righteousness.

"I left a message for the sheriff to stop by and talk to us this evenin'," he said. "We got to tell him, May. We just got to."

Though she knew it was hopeless, Maybelle tried to change his mind. "Why?" she questioned. "Can't you even try to find the boy first? And talk to him yourself?"

"What for?" he snapped. "What am I supposed to do when I find him?" Preacher slouched into a ladderback chair and stared into space. "I been thinkin' about Bertha Mae's mamma and daddy," he said. "They lost their young 'un. And even though it was the Lord's will, can you imagine how they feel right now?"

Maybelle stood silently by.

"I lived by the teachin's of the Good Book all my life," he continued. "And I ain't about to stop now."

"But he's your son!" Maybelle pleaded.

"Makes no never mind," Preacher shrugged. "Besides, I tried to find the boy. When he didn't come home Friday, I went out looking for him — you know that. Got caught in that awful weather and almost froze to death. I've done about all I can do."

Wiping her eyes with a dirty dish towel, Maybelle turned and looked out the kitchen window. Outside young Nat was playfully chasing his dog. Maybelle glanced back at her husband, then quickly turned away from him. Preacher's faith had seldom been a problem between them, but now it was almost unbearable. The man just didn't know where to draw the line between church and family. And when it came to religion, there was no changing his mind. He would send his own mother to the devil if he felt it was in the best interest of the Lord.

"So, you're gonna turn Demetrius in, are you?" she snapped.

"No!" he answered angrily. "Try to *understand*, woman. I ain't turnin' nobody in — I'm just gonna tell the sheriff what I know, that's all."

"Same difference," she mumbled beneath her breath.

Preacher stood, reaching high atop a kitchen cabinet for his favorite carving knife. "Ain't no use to talk about it no more," he said.

And Maybelle knew he was right.

12

Though the squad car's emergency light and siren were off, the speedometer needle drifted between seventy-five and eighty miles per hour. Behind the steering wheel sat Deputy Hart, gloating at his strange twist of luck. After being relieved of duty at the accident site, he had returned to the courthouse and happened to see a note on Sheriff Arnold's desk. It was a message from the nigger, asking the sheriff to stop by his house. Anxiously Hart seized the small slip of paper and decided to make the call in the sheriff's absence. And what could be wrong with that? The sheriff was away investigating the latest murder and could be detained for hours. For all practical purposes, the deputy was only filling in, as he should. He would be firm, but polite, all the while keeping a keen eye out for the bracelet. More than likely, the engraved jewelry was still on the front porch in the dog's bed. When he first arrived, Hart would visually survey the porch before knocking. If he caught sight of the bracelet, he would wait to "discover" it upon leaving. If he failed to see the bracelet, he would make an excuse to sit on the porch so he could casually survey the area as he talked. If the bracelet was anywhere in view, he would spot it and confront the nigger on the spot.

Hart grinned and barked a sinister laugh. Hell, this was working better than he'd planned!

Braking the car, he turned onto the narrow dirt road that led to the old shack. The automobile bottomed out, swaying along the deep ruts of the unmaintained road bed, until the house came into view, nestled among a thicket of pines. Hart brought the car to a stop, its wheels sliding a foot or so in the dirt yard. Stay calm, Hart told himself. Don't do anything to make the sheriff mad.

Just as Hart exited the car and slammed its door shut, the dog bounded from an unseen hiding place and raced directly toward the lawman, snarling between gritted teeth. Caught by surprise, Hart reached for his weapon and wielding its heavy butt, grazed the animal again on the skull.

"Somebody put this damn dog on a leash!" Hart yelled, as Preacher hurried outside to investigate the commotion. The lawman's heart was bumping hard against the badge on his chest.

"Skipper — You leave the man alone!" Preacher scolded the dog and wrestled him to the ground. "Nat!" he yelled. "Come and put this dog in the shed!"

Nat appeared from nowhere and grasped the animal's collar, but Skipper dug his heels into the dirt with a firm determination to stand his ground. Finally, Nat dragged the dog to the shed, Skipper's paws etching a trail of claw marks behind.

"Sorry 'bout that," Preacher apologized, extending a hand of friendship to the deputy. Hart dusted his clothing with both palms, then reluctantly took the proffered hand.

"I'm Deputy Hart," he said coldly.

"Glad to meet you, Deputy," Preacher smiled. "I'm Horace Mason, but most folks just call me Preacher." The colored man hesitated, then drawled, "I was expectin' Sheriff Arnold."

Hart stared the man down. "Sheriff's busy," he snapped. "Now, just what is it you needed to see him about?"

Preacher swallowed hard. This man wasn't like Sheriff Arnold, he sensed. Not at all like the sheriff.

"Well . . . I . . ." Preacher stuttered. "You see, the sheriff was out here t'other day and we was talkin' about something, you see, and I just remembered something else and—"

Hart pulled a small notebook from a shirt pocket and said, "Okay, let's have it."

"Well, sir, I'd kind of like to talk to the sheriff if you don't mind," Preacher stalled. "You see, me and the sheriff go way back, and it's kind of personal, you see."

Hart looked the colored man sternly in the eyes. "Mister, you're wasting my time," he growled. "Now, I suggest we sit down and get on with this. I ain't got all day."

The heavy soles of Hart's shoes clomped hard against the wooden steps of the porch, as the colored man followed reluctantly behind. Hart scanned the entire length of the deck and saw no trace of the bracelet. Choosing a flimsy rocking chair beside a hair-ridden blanket where the dog obviously slept, Hart sat down, still holding the eyes of the colored man with his stare.

"Now let's get one thing straight," Hart said. "I don't put up with no horse shit. Now, what've you got to say?"

Preacher hesitated. Demetrius might well have done wrong, it was true. But this Deputy Hart was an outright, hard-nosed bigot who plainly enforced the law by his own standards. Under no circumstances would Preacher subject his son to such abusive treatment. Preacher summoned courage from the Lord and matched the deputy's stare. "I done told you once," he said. "I asked for Sheriff Arnold and I ain't talkin' to *nobody* else."

Taken aback by the colored man's show of assertion, Hart stood, and kicked at the dog's hairy blanket. It partially unrolled to the right, but there was no bracelet to be seen. Shit! he cursed to himself. No telling where the dog might have dropped the damned thing.

Spitting over the side of the porch, Hart stared at the colored man's rickety chicken coop across the way. "You know," he growled. "You ain't exactly cooperatin' with the law."

Preacher took one step forward. "Now, I done told you, Mister Deputy. I ain't got nothin' much to say anyhow, but what I do got to say, I'm gonna say to the sheriff. I ain't got nothin' against you, but I've known that man since he was just a boy and I want to talk to him."

Hart turned and briskly descended the steps. "You've wasted enough of my time," he complained, then halted as his feet touched the barren soil. "But I'm gonna look around this place before I leave. And I'll tell you somethin' else," he added with a pause for effect, "you ain't seen the last of me."

"Go right ahead. Help yourself," Preacher said as he pulled open the front door. "I ain't got nothin' to hide."

Deputy Granger sat in the living room of the Farrell home, fumbling nervously with his broad-brimmed hat. It was the first time Sheriff Arnold had entrusted him with duties involving close emotional contact with the public, and even though the situation was difficult, Granger wanted to earn the sheriff's respect. Seated beside him on the sofa were Ralph and Helen Anderson, Nancy's parents, clinging to each other in awkward desperation. Across the room sat Martha and Liz Farrell.

Granger considered what he'd learned — virtually nothing, which also happened to be approximately how much cash Nancy was believed to have been carrying. And Charles, it seemed, had an aversion to hitchhikers, labeling them all as "lazy, good-for-nothin' hippies."

Now came the difficult part of the conversation. Granger felt his chest tighten as he pondered the sheriff's message and how it might best be delivered. Leaning closer to the distraught couple, he spoke softly to them as Liz and Martha looked on sympathetically.

"There's something you both need to understand. In water-related accidents, the . . . missing persons . . . are usually recovered rather quickly." He paused to clear his throat, then continued. "We've searched around the clock since the accident and haven't found Mrs. Barnett yet. To me, that means it could take a whole lot longer. Or possibly . . . never."

The Andersons' sobs grew louder, their embrace tighter.

"What I'm trying to say," Granger added, "is that it doesn't do any good for the two of you to sit around and wait. You're only torturing yourselves, and you'd both feel a lot better if you got back into your normal routine. You owe it to yourselves and your families."

Across the room Liz nodded in agreement.

"But we can't just—" Helen began to blurt but Granger interrupted her. "I know the thought is unpleasant. And all I'm suggesting is that you think about it, all right? Your daughter wouldn't want you to suffer like this. She'd want you to go home and get on with your lives."

Having noticed Liz's open concurrence, he looked to her for support. "Wouldn't you agree, Miss Farrell?"

"Yes, I would," she said without hesitation. "I know Nancy would want it that way."

Granger slowly rose to his feet, pleased with his performance. "If there's anything I can do, please call me," he said.

At the sound of the couples' mumbled thanks, he turned for the door. Liz followed him outside.

"I appreciate what you did in there," she said with a smile. "I've been thinking exactly the same thing myself."

Granger regarded the young woman with admiration. Though her eyes were red and swollen and her hair was a mess, she held a certain unique appeal. His friends often laughed at his attraction to heavy-set women. But here was one he'd like to know better.

"Miss Farrell," he said. "Is it all right if I call you Liz?"

"Certainly."

"I—" he began, then paused. He wanted to ask her if he could see her socially, but realized the timing was wrong. Perhaps later another opportunity would arise. "I'm glad we met," he said instead.

Liz smiled. "So am I," she said.

The afternoon had passed uneventfully, the trip to Vincent for Nancy's personal supplies having posed no problem. Wayne picked up a few extra items, including a hair brush, a package of bobby pins (though he didn't actually know if she used them) and a box of chocolate-covered cherries. He had apologized profusely for tying her up again prior to leaving, assuring her that it would be the last time. Nancy had not uttered any complaint and upon his return, smiled innocently as he loosened the nylon strips. She seemed pleased with the gifts — especially the candy — and expressed her appreciation warmly. Wayne then massaged her neck and shoulders, assuring her that her comfort was important to him.

Now she lay sleeping in the bedroom, her steady breathing barely audible above the hum of the refrigerator. Wayne reached for a sweater from a corner coat rack in the living room and quietly stepped outside. The air was brisk and refreshing, and he inhaled deeply, absorbing the sounds that surrounded him — a crow cawing as it soared high above, the bark of a distant dog — and the whine of an approaching automobile.

Suddenly his Dad's pickup rolled into view, bouncing slowly along the narrow roadway toward the trailer. Wayne's heart froze. What could he do? If another altercation should awaken Nancy, she was unbound and free to call attention to herself. And there was no time to dash inside and secure her. Would she do such a thing?

Wayne swallowed hard as the truck rolled to a stop. He'd have to remain calm and be careful. Stay in control of the situation. Avoid any disagreement, talk quietly, and keep his father outside.

James Crocker exited the truck and slammed its door. "Hello, son," he said, his face red with embarrassment. James sauntered toward the boy, both hands in his pockets, his head hung low. "I'm real sorry about last week," he said, his voice soft and cottony. "Guess I got juiced to the gills again."

Wayne met him twenty feet or so from the trailer's door.

"No harm done," Wayne said, forcing himself to give a friendly nudge to his Dad's ribs. Placing his left arm around his father's shoulder, Wayne steered him from the trailer.

"I know I make it awfully hard on you and your mother," James continued. "But I ain't got many other faults."

Wayne laughed. "Yeah, but your drinking alone is bad enough," he said. Wayne led his Dad around the far end of the trailer, to a small butane tank at the tongue of the trailer hitch. Knowing their voices shouldn't carry as far as the bedroom, Wayne rested his right foot on the protruding metal lip.

"I'm not as bad as you think," James said defensively.

Their eyes met briefly, then James looked away. "Let's not talk about that," he said. "Let's go inside and watch TV."

"No!" Wayne blurted quickly. "I . . . uh . . . I've been workin' inside. Just waxed the floor." Swallowing hard, Wayne pocketed both hands, jingling his car keys.

Although James thought the boy seemed awfully nervous, he decided to let it pass. "All right," he said instead. "Why don't you come to the house for supper? Your mother ain't seen you in days."

Wayne shuffled his feet in the loose soil. "I've got a lot to do around here. The place is a mess."

James looked up sharply. "What's so goddamn important about this fuckin' place? Nobody sees you anymore!"

"I just want to take care of my investment, that's all."

"Hell, you weren't that concerned when you lived at home!" James huffed, then pivoted quickly toward the front of the trailer. "I want to see what's so damn important."

Panicking, Wayne wedged himself between his father and the door. "N-N-Now Dad, let's n-n-not get into another fight. Why don't you just go home and we'll try this again later, okay?"

"The hell I will," boasted James as he reached for the door.

Wayne slapped his father's hand away from the doorknob.

"You little shit!" James growled, reflexively drawing back a fist to deliver a punch. Wayne dodged the errant blow and tackled his father low, sending them both sprawling to the ground. Then, his pulse pounding, his adrenalin at its peak, he scrambled over his father and pinned the older man's flailing arms to the ground.

"Listen to me!" he said between gritted teeth. "You get outta here and *leave me alone!*"

James eyed his son in shocked dismay. Was the boy insane? In silence, the two remained motionless. Finally James closed his eyes and shook his head. "I don't know you anymore," he mumbled. "You're not my son — I ain't never *seen* you before!"

Loosening his grip, Wayne removed his weight from his father's stomach. "Please go," he sobbed.

James staggered to his feet and dusted dirt from his clothing. Then without a word he returned to his truck, shaking his head as he drove away.

Wayne sat in the dusty soil, his hands shaking as they reached to dry his eyes. Then came the click of the doorknob. The door opened slightly, and Wayne turned to see Nancy's face peering outside.

For hours he wondered what might have happened if her timing had been a few minutes earlier.

It was late afternoon when Sheriff Arnold arrived at the Mason home, tired and dismayed by the testimony that had led him there. At least two of Bertha Mae Sampson's high school friends had mentioned the name of Demetrius Mason, with whom she had been seen recently on numerous occasions. The most disturbing revelation came from Ellie Parks, who reported that Bertha Mae had planned to see Demetrius the evening she disappeared.

The drive from Leeds to Selton had been difficult for the sheriff. He considered Preacher Mason far too decent a man to be faced with such a family crisis. But he knew Demetrius Mason wasn't the first son of a holy man to rebel against a strict religious upbringing. And now that Demetrius appeared to be linked to the final hours of the Sampson girl, the sheriff couldn't help but wonder if the boy were involved in the Barnett accident. After all, the purse had been discovered near the boy's home, its contents ransacked.

When the sheriff brought the car to a stop outside the run-down home, young Nat bounded around the corner of the house and raced up the porch steps to announce his arrival. Almost immediately, the boy's father appeared at the door, his face haggard with worry.

Sheriff Arnold regarded the man with deep concern — he looked as if he'd aged twenty years overnight. Not knowing how to begin, the sheriff waited for the colored man to speak first. The two hesitated, in silence, then finally Sheriff Arnold slammed the car door and cleared his throat. Preacher stepped across the porch, wiping his brow.

"Hope I didn't make that deputy of yours mad," he mumbled.

"How's that?" Sheriff Arnold asked.

"Your deputy. I hope I didn't make him mad when I wouldn't talk to him this evening."

"I don't understand." The sheriff stood perplexed. Which deputy? And for what reason had a deputy come to the Mason home? Sounded like something Hart would do.

Preacher motioned the sheriff up the front steps. "Didn't you get my message?" he asked.

"I've been out all day."

"Oh," Preacher responded. "Well, you see, I called around lunchtime and left word for you to stop by. Then this Deputy . . . Hart is it? . . . came by instead and he got kind of huffy when I told him I'd only talk to you."

Sheriff Arnold scratched his stubbled cheeks. So Preacher did have more to say. That explained his uncharacteristic nervousness last Sunday.

"I didn't get any message," the sheriff said, "but I do know that your son appears to be connected with the Sampson girl."

Preacher swallowed hard.

A gust of wind twisted through a nearby stand of pines and brought with it the first splattering raindrops of an evening shower. A rumble of thunder shook the front windows of the house.

"Better get inside afore we get soaked," Preacher offered as he pulled the front door open. Maybelle entered the living room from the kitchen as the two stepped inside. She appeared sullen and unfriendly, hardly nodding at the sheriff as she reached for a string hanging from an overhead bulb to switch on the light. Briefly the sheriff remembered his own childhood home where there were no wall switches, his reminiscence cut short by a sudden flow of tears from Preacher's wife. The sheriff settled into a straightback chair, facing the two on the sofa.

"I know this must be difficult for you," he began, watching Preacher try in vain to comfort his wife. "But it'll be best for everybody if you'll just tell me what you know."

Preacher patted his wife affectionately. "The man's right," he told her. "You know we got to do this." She made no response. Staring past the sheriff at a portrait of Jesus on the wall, Preacher began, "When I got home from work last Thursday—"

"No!" Maybelle screamed. "You ain't tellin'! I won't *let* you!" Her arms struck out weakly at her husband to no effect. Then she stood abruptly and left the room. As she rose from the sofa, a small bracelet fell from beneath the cushion to the floor. Preacher scooped up the chain and tossed the jewelry to the coffee table. Sheriff Arnold casually noted an engraved heart. Then he looked back to Preacher.

"Will she be all right?" he asked.

Preacher shook his head. "I don't rightly know. I ain't never seen her so tore up afore." Preacher breathed deeply. "Mind if I calm her down?" he asked.

"Go right ahead," the sheriff answered.

The poor man's world was falling out from under him, the sheriff knew. Preacher, who had always been a strong family man, was now pitted against both a son and a troubled wife. From the bedroom came the sound of muffled voices, increasing in volume and tempo. Sheriff Arnold glanced back at the engraved heart. N.S.B. The initials didn't fit anyone in Preacher's family. N.S.B. . . . N.S.B.—

A loud crash came from the bedroom — then the sound of tumbling furniture, the breaking of glass.

Startled, Sheriff Arnold jumped to his feet, then froze. Aimed directly at him were the double barrels of a shotgun, with the quivering finger of a nervous woman dangerously near its trigger. Behind her, in the bedroom, Preacher struggled to his feet. "Lord, *no!*" he moaned. "Maybelle, honey — you don't know what you're doing!"

Maybelle peered down the double barrels wavering in her grasp. "Nobody's gonna do nothin' to my boy," she said. "*Nobody.*"

From the cover of nearby shrubbery, Deputy Donald Hart watched the Mason home with curious fascination. Hiking along Kelley Creek to avoid being seen, he'd been drenched by a sudden downpour. He shivered in the chilly evening air, his teeth almost at the chattering point, as he peered ahead. The kid he'd seen earlier was playing in the front yard beside an abandoned Ford mounted atop four concrete blocks. Hart smiled at the sight of the dog, still caged in the shed away from the house. But the animal sensed his presence, and was now thrashing wildly inside the shed.

Hart turned his attention back to the house. He was fortunate to have gotten so close. In fact, were it not for the noisy dog, he could probably hear the conversation inside. But the dog growled relentlessly. Hart cursed the animal again and again. His plans were falling apart. He'd intended to eavesdrop, hoping to learn what the old nigger knew and turn it to his own advantage. But Hart hadn't planned on running into the sheriff. It was just too risky to get any closer with his boss inside. If he were caught, there'd be some tall explaining to do.

The sun was falling slowly in the horizon, the temperature dropping fast. Hart shivered in his wet uniform. He couldn't stand the exposure much longer, even though he was intrigued by the sound of a scuffle inside the house. The old nigger and his wife were arguing, he could tell.

Reluctantly, Hart turned and ran toward the creek, fleeing toward the warmth of his car. Fate had delivered another nasty blow, for he had fled just before the action began inside the Mason home.

Nat Mason hurried inside to investigate the commotion. With all the energy of youth, he bounded up the front steps, sailed across the porch and yanked the door open wide. His eyes met his mother's — she was holding Pa's shotgun, aimed straight at the sheriff! As her attention was diverted by her son, Preacher caught her from behind and snatched the gun away. Young Nat broke into tears, and Sheriff Arnold quickly swept him out of the room.

"Son," the sheriff said. "I want you to play outside awhile."

"But my Mama—"

"Your Mama's fine," the sheriff said. "We'll take care of her."

Sheriff Arnold ushered the boy to the door and gently pushed him outside, then closed and latched the door.

"Whew!" exclaimed the sheriff, glancing back at Preacher. "Ain't nothin' more dangerous than a hysterical woman."

"Mister Sheriff, I'm awful sorry," Preacher began. He stopped and scanned the lawman's face. It looked hard as stone.

"This is a serious offense. You understand that, don't you?" the sheriff said.

Preacher nodded. Maybelle stood motionless, still restricted by her husband's grasp.

Sheriff Arnold returned to his chair. "I'll tell you what," he said as he sat down. "We'll forget this little incident ever happened if you folks will cooperate."

Preacher shook his wife until, with obvious resignation, she finally nodded. Then he looked over to the sheriff. "I intended to do that all along."

"I know you did," the sheriff said calmly. "Now, why don't you just tell me the whole thing from the beginning."

Preacher ushered Maybelle to the sofa where she reclined, sobbing quietly.

"Demetrius started takin' up with bad company a few months ago," the colored man began. "Particularly with some hooligans from Leeds. I talked to the boy over and over, but it didn't do no good. He just wouldn't listen. You know how boys can be, Mister Sheriff," he said, pausing.

Sheriff Arnold nodded, and Preacher then continued.

"About two weeks ago when them Leeds boys come by for Demetrius in that ol' pickup truck of theirs, I heard 'em laughin' and talkin' outside. They was sayin' as how Bertha Mae Sampson was willin' to do nasty things with them — you know?"

The sheriff nodded again.

"I stepped out on the porch to give them boys a good sermon and they just ran off laughin'. Demetrius was right in the thick of it, too. And that hurt me, Mister Sheriff. That hurt me real bad."

As Preacher broke off to step into the kitchen for a wet wash rag to wipe his wife's face, Sheriff Arnold's attention strayed to the bracelet lying on the coffee table.

"I gave him a good talkin' to after that," Preacher said, resuming his story after he had attended to his wife. "But the boy was disrespectful and laughed in my face. And besides, he said Bertha Mae was all talk and wouldn't do nothin' with them after all."

Preacher paused to allow the sheriff to catch up with the notes he was frantically scribbling in a small spiral notebook.

"Last Thursday when I came home from work, Demetrius was edgy. He flitted all around this place like he was hopped-up on somethin'. I never knowed the boy to be interested in drugs, Mister Sheriff. But nothin' surprises me no more. Them Leeds boys was capable of anything and they could easily drag poor Demetrius into something, too. The boy just didn't have no mind of his own. Anyway, them hooligans drove up again and I told Demetrius not to leave this house. But he mocked me and said Bertha Mae was just a tease, but that they was gonna make her regret it real soon. And that boy had a wicked look in his eye, Mr. Sheriff. It scairt me pretty bad."

The colored man sighed and squeezed his wife's hand.

"I figured he was just mouthin' off," he went on. "But when he didn't come home that night, me and the missus got worried. Next night when there was still no word from him, I went out lookin' for him. Got caught up in that ice storm, an' almost got kilt myself. But I never did see no trace of him."

Looking the tortured man in the eyes, Sheriff

Arnold knew he was speaking the truth. Preacher shook his head, then added, "He didn't kill that girl, Mister Sheriff. He might've done some bad things, but he couldn't kill nobody."

"I hope you're right," the sheriff answered, then flipped the notebook back to his earlier notes on the Barnett accident. "When I talked to you Sunday," he continued, "you said you didn't know anything about the Barnett accident. That still correct?"

"Oh, yessir."

"Even though Nancy Barnett's purse was found not a hundred yards from your house?"

"That's right, Mister Sheriff. None of us heard nothin'—"

Preacher broke off as the sheriff suddenly leaned forward to grab the bracelet from the coffee table. He turned the engraved heart over between his fingers, then looked sternly at the colored man. "Who does this belong to?" he asked.

Preacher eyed the trinket. "I ain't never seen it afore," he mumbled.

"And you?" the sheriff interjected as he held the jewelry toward Maybelle.

"Me neither," she answered coldly.

Preacher glanced at the lawman in wonder. "Why do you ask?" he questioned.

Sheriff Arnold turned the engraved heart toward the colored man and pointed to the etched letters. "N.S.B." he said. "*Nancy Sue Barnett.*"

Preacher slumped against the back of the sofa, as Maybelle turned enquiringly to each man, still uncertain as to what was happening. Finally, Preacher leaned forward. "But that don't make sense, Mister Sheriff. Demetrius ain't been here since Thursday. And that accident happened Friday—"

"I'm not accusing anybody of anything," the sheriff interrupted. "For all I know, this could belong to someone else. Just a coincidence that the initials match. Stranger things have happened."

Preacher breathed a sigh of relief.

"But as for Demetrius being away," the sheriff went on, "nobody was at your house Sunday morning. I know, because I stopped by. Demetrius knew you'd all be at church, too. He could easily have come inside to gather some of his things."

The sheriff rose to his feet and eased toward the door. "I'll need to take this with me," he said, referring to the bracelet. Preacher nodded his approval. "And I want you and your wife to check very carefully to see if any of Demetrius' things are missing."

Preacher nodded again, but Maybelle, still reclining on the sofa, shook her head violently from side to side. Sheriff Arnold noted her objection. "Ma'am," he said to her. "It's important that we find Demetrius. Now, I doubt that your son's a killer. But those friends of his most likely are. And they just might decide they'd be better off if your son wasn't around any longer. Understand?"

Mrs. Mason stared blankly ahead, but the sheriff knew his message had been received and understood. "I'm real sorry about this," he said. "You folks are fine people."

Stepping outside to the porch, Sheriff Arnold heard the vicious growl of the dog from a nearby shed. He turned to Preacher and asked, "Do you have any idea where Demetrius might be?"

"No, Mister Sheriff," Preacher answered. "I done looked everywhere myself."

Sheriff Arnold flipped his notebook open again to a clean page. "You'd better tell me the boy's known hangouts anyway," he said.

13

As darkness settled over the trailer, Wayne hurriedly washed the dinner dishes. Nancy sat upright on the small sofa. The television was on, but at low volume, and Nancy wasn't watching it. Instead, she was observing Wayne with admiration. He seemed so natural in the kitchen, and he was an excellent cook. He was also mannerly. Intelligent. In a strange way, she felt relieved that it had been him who had rescued her from the river. He'd taken good care of her. And her ordeal had certainly lessened the impact of her own injuries and the loss of her husband. But what exactly did Wayne have in mind for her? He still hadn't leveled with her. And now that her strength was returning, she felt restless.

Wayne dropped a wet dish towel neatly over a rack beneath the kitchen cabinets and breathed a sigh of relief. "Glad that's done," he said with a smile.

"Wayne, we need to talk," Nancy said.

"All talk and no action?" he answered jokingly. This afternoon she'd noticed an increasing relaxation in Wayne's manner. He was obviously feeling more at ease with her and had begun to tease her with good-natured sexual innuendos.

"I'm serious," she said. "Let's talk."

Wayne sat on the sofa beside her.

"You know this has got to end," she said.

Wayne frowned and avoided her eyes. "I suppose so," he mumbled.

Nancy reached out and touched his cheek. "I appreciate what you've done for me," she said. "Aside from our first night, you've been a perfect gentleman, except for—"

Wayne turned to hide the tears in his eyes.

"Don't feel sorry for yourself—"

"But you don't understand," he interrupted. "I'm a grown man, and this is the closest I've ever been to a woman."

"That's difficult to believe," she said with a touch of sincerity. "You're a good catch. You've got many good qualities. I would think you'd have lots of girlfriends."

"Don't try to con me," he snapped.

"I'm only being honest," she countered.

Wayne wiped his eyes and admired her pretty face. "You're special, Nancy. I feel so good with you. I've never felt this way before."

Nancy blushed and averted his attention.

"I mean it," he went on. "I'm a different person when I'm with you." He chuckled to himself and sighed. "All those times I was rejected by the snobby girls at Butler's Lake would be worthwhile if I could have someone like you."

Nancy perked up at the last comment. "I used to go to Butler's Lake when I visited Liz in the summer."

"No kidding!"

"Sure!" she laughed, her face suddenly red with embarrassment. "Once I went down the slide into the water and my *top came off*! It was just *awful*!"

Wayne laughed, then added, "That's funny! You know, I remember hearing the guys at school talking about a girl's top coming off at Butler's Lake during the summer. I must have been thirteen or fourteen years old. I always seemed to miss out on things like that."

Nancy blushed and turned away from him.

Wayne hung his head. "That's the story of my life," he said.

Suddenly Nancy found herself stirred by compassion. Wayne was a kind, gentle man, a truly decent human being.

"I believe in you," she said softly, reaching over and squeezing his hand. "Let's end this now, and put our lives back together."

To cap off an especially good day, Donald Hart shed his uniform and drove to Terrie's Lounge for a beer. It was one of his favorite off-duty haunts. Even the smoky, stagnant air over the bar failed to bother him as he reflected on the most recent developments.

It seemed that the ever-bumbling Sheriff Arnold had somehow found the missing bracelet inside the nigger's house. How it got there, Hart had no idea. Nor did it matter that the nigger preacher himself was not the suspect, but instead, the nigger's son.

What was important was that his original hunch had
paid off. He'd known all along that those niggers
were involved in a crime of some kind. Though a
warrant had yet to be issued, the boy was wanted in
connection with the Sampson murder, and for questioning in the Barnett case. Even before Sheriff
Arnold had taken the bracelet to the Farrell home
for identification by the Barnett woman's parents,
Hart had leaked the news anonymously to the press.
Before the dust settled on both cases, he would surface as the true force behind their solutions. In the
meantime, he'd do his damnedest to find that
Mason boy and whip his ass before dragging him to
jail.

Funny, Hart thought. This afternoon everything
had been a disaster. But somehow the pieces had all
fallen into place.

Hart burped and, sliding off the bar stool, flipped
a dime to the countertop for a tip. Tonight's late
newscast would be starting soon, and he wouldn't
miss it for the world.

Nancy could feel herself panicking. She was lying in
bed beneath the covers, clad in the same flannel pajamas, and Wayne was bashfully undressing. Moon-
beams danced through the darkness across the
wrinkled bedsheet as Nancy frantically considered
what to do.

"Wayne, please," she whispered. "I'm afraid
you've misunderstood — I never meant for this—"

After convincing her of his innocence, Wayne had
then misinterpreted her sympathy toward him. It's
no wonder he has problems with women, Nancy

realized — he doesn't know how to read a woman's signals! Quietly he slipped beneath the blanket beside her.

"Please, Wayne, don't spoil it now," she pleaded. "Don't do something you'll regret."

Wayne pulled the blanket below her waist. "I just want to be close to you," he whispered.

He put his arm around her and hugged her body close. Feeling the change in his body caused by his physical excitement, she tactfully pushed him away.

"Wayne!" she scolded him. "If you don't leave me alone, you'll blow everything!"

He stopped and Nancy could see the hurt-puppy look in his eyes. And although she couldn't understand why, a rush of compassion washed over her. Tears streamed from her eyes; her body trembled. She knew she was strong enough now to jam her knee between his legs and run. But in a mysterious, and unexplainable way, she wanted him. She wanted to feel his arms around her, to bask in the warmth of human concern and affection, but she wouldn't allow herself to give in.

Wayne leaned over to kiss her, but she forced him away again. He swallowed hard, and then stroked her hair. "It's all right," he said.

"No," she moaned. "I'm not — I shouldn't—"

"Yes," he urged her on. "We depend on each other. And you know how I feel about you."

Silently, Nancy turned away. Wayne reached around her shoulder and began to unbutton her flannel top. She lifted her hand to stop him, resting her palm over his fingers but finally allowed him to continue. His hand reached inside to squeeze her left breast, its nipple pointed and erect. Both reveled in the pleasure of his touch, and Nancy's head began to roll softly from side to side against her pillow as Wayne licked and caressed her nipples.

Her body tingling with excitement, Nancy began to gasp for air, relaxing her weight against the mattress, then tensing again as his hand slid beneath the elastic band of her pajama bottom.

She looked into his eyes, barely visible in the darkened room. "I want to," she panted, "but I *can't*."

His fingers traced circles through her pubic hair, moving further down to the moistness of her vaginal lips. As he touched her ever so tenderly, her body trembled with intense arousal. She recalled the discomfort of Charlie's crude initial touch. He had forced his hand inside her pants and groped for self-pleasure, with no regard to her feelings. But here was a sensitive man of little experience whose every movement elicited waves of sexual pleasure. And she suddenly realized it was because Wayne honestly cared for her, no matter what her feelings were toward him. His fingers were not merely exploring — they were making love.

Wayne pushed the pajama bottom past her hips and over her knees. Filled with confused emotions, Nancy squirmed. She was hot and wet and no longer able to control herself.

Wayne, however, was beyond the point of no return. Slowly he mounted her and directed his penis between her legs, the tickle of pubic hair wildly exciting against his rigid shaft.

"Wayne," she moaned. "Can't we wait?"

The sticky warmth of her vaginal lips teased his erection. Awkwardly he tried to enter her, but found himself tensing with sexual release. His back arched, and his legs stiffened, as semen poured across her stomach. He gasped and collapsed on top of her. "I'm sorry," he panted, suddenly ashamed. "Please forgive me."

Nancy sniffled in the dark, her body limp and un-fulfilled, but thankful that by the grace of God, the act had not been consummated. Wayne stumbled to the bathroom for toilet tissue to clean up the mess, and when he returned, she was crying softly. Wiping her dry, he begged for forgiveness. "Please don't think badly of me," he pleaded.

She rolled away, still crying softly into her pillow.

Carefully, he spread a blanket and quilt over her heaving form. "Nancy," he whispered softly. "I . . . love . . . you."

Scooping up his clothes from the floor, he left the room and closed the door. After he had washed in the bathroom, Wayne dressed and then stepped into the living room. The television was playing at low volume, and as he reached to turn off the set, a news anchorman's words caught his attention: "Steve Willard has more about that dramatic break-through in the investigations of three Shelby County deaths."

His eyes glued to the dim screen, Wayne leaned closer to the set and turned up the volume.

WILLARD: Although the Shelby County Sheriff's Office refuses to comment, an uniden-tified source told WBRC News late tonight that at least four suspects are wanted in connection with the death of young Bertha Mae Sampson, a Negro teenager whose body was discovered during the recent search for Nancy Sue Barnett, the victim of last Friday night's freak automobile accident. But now the question arises, was it, indeed, an accident? Our source assures us that one of the suspects is also wanted for questioning in regard to the Barnett accident. Evidence has supposedly been uncovered that, at least circumstantially, links the suspect to the accident victim. Again, the Sheriff's Office refuses to either confirm or deny these allegations. Regardless, this latest development has no bearing on the district attorney's pending negligence charge against Arbor Construction Company.

Wayne snapped off the set when the newscaster shifted to another story, then extinguished the light and reclined on the sofa in deep thought, his hands behind his head. Their informant was obviously wrong, he knew.

Carefully he got up and tip-toed down the hall to peek into the bedroom. She appeared to be asleep. Groping his way back to the sofa, he relaxed again. Although Nancy had been upset by his lack of control, he knew she'd get over it, just as she had before. At first it hadn't seemed possible that she would ever express any feelings for him. But she hadn't resisted. And never had he been more surprised and pleased.

As he reviewed their physical interlude, Wayne's penis grew erect again. Nancy was everything to him. And in time she would feel the same. But that would be difficult. Sooner or later she'd be discovered. A trailer was no place to hold someone captive.

Of course, they could run away . . . The more he thought about it, the more appealing it seemed. He could withdraw what little money was left in his bank account and simply vanish. He'd always wanted to see the Smoky Mountains. They could live deep in the backcountry until Nancy was ready to accept him as her husband. And considering her improved state of mind, it shouldn't take long.

The thought of having her forever brightened Wayne's thoughts. He tried to sleep, but found himself wide awake with excitement.

Not far away, huddling alone in thick, inky darkness, Demetrius Mason also tried to sleep—anything to keep his mind from his own misery. He could hear an occasional bat flutter by, but in the total absence of light inside the cave, he could see nothing. The steady drip of water was maddening, but at least the temperature remained constant, protecting him from the winter outside. Wounded and starving, he waited, his energy ebbing fast. He had yelled for help until his voice had grown hoarse, and had finally given up. His stomach ached with waves of pain, and countless times he licked seeping water from cracks in the rock walls around him. The blood that flowed from his side had long since dried to a crusty paste.

They had left him for dead, he knew. And although he had lived longer already than they had expected, he realized he was quickly running out of time.

14

Tuesday
Day Five

By early morning an APB had been issued across the state of Alabama for the following persons:

Terrell "Jason" Thomas — Negro male, age 19, 6'2", 190 lbs., prior arrests including assault and battery, and breaking and entering

Henry Lee Carny — Negro male, age 18, 5'10", 175 lbs., only prior charge being child molestation which was subsequently withdrawn for reasons unknown

Demetrius Louis Mason — Negro male, age 19, 5'11", 160 lbs., no prior record

Rufus Rayburn — Negro male, origin and prior record, if any, unknown

All units were alerted for a faded red 1957 Chevy pickup, license 1A-22601, one headlight and front grill smashed, and a missing tailgate. Law enforcement officials in both Jefferson and Shelby Counties expressed confidence that, as the fugitives were rank amateurs, they would be apprehended soon.

A red-eyed Sheriff Arnold reported to work at sunrise following only three hours of sleep. Two journalists were waiting outside the courthouse, only to be rudely pushed aside by the angry lawman as he stormed inside. Feeling reasonably certain that the leak to the press had originated from Hart, he snatched the private notebook from his desk and poised himself to write. Unfortunately, the script flowed slowly, as there was little in the way of concrete testimony to record. The sheriff slammed the desktop in disgust, sending a corner metal ashtray clanging to the floor. Wearily, he ran a nervous hand across his receding hairline.

Hart was getting to him, there was no doubt. In an effort to calm himself, he relaxed his weight against the back of his chair. Was he being entirely objective about Hart? The sheriff felt a growing dislike for the man and feared he might have let his personal feelings influence his professional judgment. But he knew Hart was not to be trusted, and vowed, once again, to rid the county of Hart's inept service. He would have to be patient, until the facts were substantial enough to speak for themselves. Then he would ask the personnel board for Hart's removal. Until then, he would assign Hart only routine drudgery so that the bored deputy would decide to leave voluntarily.

The sheriff reached for a bottle of aspirin in a bottom desk drawer and trudged to the nearby water cooler. Perhaps it was time for him to retire.

"We're leaving," Wayne announced as he packed clothing and other personal items into grocery bags. Nancy looked on in bewilderment, trying desperately to understand.

"What . . . do you . . . mean?" she muttered.

"I mean we're leaving," he answered, a blank expression in his eyes. "We're heading for North Carolina, into the mountains where no one will find us. Where we can live normal lives again."

"But Wayne—"

He wasn't listening. The cool morning chill rolled inside the open door as he exited to load the automobile. Nancy peeked outside — the trunk was almost full. Clouds of frozen vapor floated from Wayne's mouth and nose as he stepped quickly through the frigid air between the trailer and the car.

"But Wayne," she cried. "I don't want to go! You can't do this!"

He stopped and gazed at her wildly. "Why not?" he said. "It's the only way, as far as I can see."

Nancy grabbed his arm as he reached for another sack of clothing. "Wayne," she pleaded. "You misunderstood last night. I've been under a lot of pressure and—"

"So have I," he interrupted. "And we both need a rest." Carelessly, he jerked away and carried the sack and his guitar outside. He forced the sack into the trunk and slammed its lid shut. Then he placed the guitar in the back seat among books, records, shoes and other assorted paraphernalia. Next he opened the hood and checked the oil.

Nancy's mind was racing with panic. What could she do to change his mind?

Wayne slammed the hood and came back inside. Nancy was huddled in a corner of the bedroom.

"Wayne?" she sobbed. "This is *kidnapping*!"

He stopped beside the bed and regarded her briefly, then sat. "According to you, it's that already."

"But, Wayne, I trust you now — or at least I did."

He reached for her, but she wrenched away.

"It's all right," he said calmly. "You don't have to go. If you really hate the idea, I'll let you out somewhere along the way."

Nancy eyed him with a fixed stare. What had happened to him during such a short span of time?

"I'll be away awhile," he continued. "To the bank, and then to pick up a few supplies. Then we'll be on our way."

"Wayne—" she pleaded.

"And that reminds me," he added. "I'll get the . . . the . . . Kotex . . . for you when we stop in another town along the way."

Collapsing onto the cold tile floor, Nancy realized she had forgotten about her impending period. Either she was pregnant or the stress of recent events had caused a shift in her menstrual cycle. She suspected the latter, since she and Charlie had shared a dismal sex life of late. Desperately, she turned her attention to the task at hand. What would be her best course of action? To attempt another escape, or try to reason with Wayne again?

He reached for her and helped her to her feet. "I want you to rest while I finish packing," he said. "We'll have a long ride ahead of us."

Nancy trembled at his touch, but meekly obeyed.

After suffering through an unusually restless night, James Crocker awakened at sunrise and quietly slipped from the bed without disturbing Edith. He'd tried unsuccessfully during the periods of sleeplessness to discount a growing suspicion that haunted his mind. Still confused, he had decided to investigate. Now he found himself trudging on foot, the frosted grass crunching beneath his shoes as he hiked across the pasture, over the hill to Wayne's trailer.

The more he'd thought about it, the more convinced he'd become that the vision of Wayne's rescue efforts seemed too real to have been only a dream. And since Friday, Wayne had acted strangely. Normally the boy was proud to receive visitors into his home, to show off his handiwork. But on James' last two visits, his son had aggressively kept him at bay. Never had James seen such forcefulness from the boy. And it had been impossible to reach Wayne by telephone — he'd claimed his line hadn't been repaired since the ice storm, yet James knew that was a lie — all the neighbors' service had already been restored.

James' growing concern had finally gelled the night before, when a news report suggested that there might have been more to the Barnett deaths

than a mere accident. The idea was outlandish, to
say the least — but could Wayne be holding the
Barnett woman inside his trailer? Noting the increasing numbness in his feet from the frigid earth,
James shuddered at the thought. Sure, the prospect
was outrageous. But since he'd sobered up and picked his own memory, James would swear on a stack of
Bibles that he'd seen Wayne pull that woman out of
Kelley Creek. Of that, he was quite certain. But
what could Wayne have done with her? And why
would he hold her against her will?

With a growing need for answers, James topped
the hill behind Wayne's trailer. Only the backside of
the small mobile home came into view, that and
Wayne's car, parked in its usual spot, but with the
trunk suspiciously open. James hid behind a massive
oak and watched his son carry personal items from
the trailer and load them into the car. Was the boy
going somewhere?

A sickening feeling wrenched James' guts. God in
heaven — why would the boy have reason to flee?

Easing himself down, James sat on the cold
ground at the base of the tree. There was too much
to comprehend. He needed a drink in the worst way.
But it was liquor that had created the distance between himself and his son before. Perhaps if he
hadn't drank so frequently, he would have been a
better father. The very thought of what Wayne
might be involved in was alarming. But Wayne was
his own flesh and blood. He'd stand by his son to the
very end, if need be.

Feeling his lips quiver, James rubbed his hands
together briskly and watched the trailer. The lights
were on inside, as the morning sun was still dim.

And as Wayne raised the hood of his car to check the engine, James' heart leaped — a shadow crossed the curtain inside the trailer. Someone was in Wayne's living room, possibly the Barnett woman. Something strange was definitely going on down there.

His suspicions all but confirmed, James began the cold journey back to his own home. He'd wanted to ease closer to the trailer, to learn more, but found the frigid morning air too threatening. Instead, he would go back to the house for warmer clothes and return later in his truck. Perhaps he could stop Wayne before he got into deeper trouble.

But at first sight of smoke rising from the chimney of his house, James stopped, paralyzed by a horrible thought.

Perhaps the shadow in Wayne's trailer belonged to the missing colored boy. And maybe Wayne was in cahoots with the nigger, and had engineered the whole thing.

Relieved to have escaped Sheriff Arnold's icy stare, Deputy Donald Hart solemnly steered his squad car through the narrow empty streets of Columbiana en route to Selton. During the morning's meeting there had been an unmistakable tone of both caution and dislike in the sheriff's voice, whenever he'd addressed him. The asshole's trying to get rid of me, Hart realized as he gripped the steering wheel tighter. This case has got to blow first, he thought, before the son-of-a-bitch gets a chance to dump me.

This morning it had been obvious that the sheriff favored Granger and had shifted many of the latter's menial duties over to him. Granger was an okay guy, rather drab but generally likable. But Hart knew Granger couldn't match his own ability. Granger was too soft — that was his peer's major weakness.

Turning onto Highway 25, the police vehicle headed in a northeasterly direction. Hart's mind continued to wander as he proceeded to his first call of the day, a nuisance assignment the sheriff had given out of pure spite. Jeb Cramer had complained for days that he wanted to file an official complaint against kids trespassing on his property. The irate farmer had phoned the sheriff's office three times during the past week. Sheriff Arnold had intended to speak to Cramer personally since the two had been acquainted for years, but the sheriff had been sidetracked by the Barnett and Sampson investigations. Hart had met Cramer once before and recognized the man as a loud-mouthed smart aleck. Sheriff Arnold had likely gloated over the opportunity to pit Hart against Cramer.

Hart grimaced as the highway unrolled before him. Reviewing the list of routine calls the sheriff had given him, he knew there'd be little time for tracking down the fugitives. But then, he'd also realized that the suspects had likely fled the state already. He shrugged and tapped the steering wheel lightly. How could he manage to take credit for these cases? Nothing fresh came to mind, but he knew a solution would come soon. In recent days his run of luck had been unusually smooth. There was no reason for the streak to end now.

Multi-colored plastic pennants fluttered in the early morning breeze around the Pell City Raceway ser-

235

vice station as Wayne guided his Chevy across the air hose that rang a loud bell inside the small office. Jumping out of the car, Wayne reached for the "regular" gas pump, glancing up at the rack of glasses and dishes that had been re-stocked for premium giveaways. Leonard Stokes, Wayne's boss, stepped quickly from inside the office. He was a tall, skinny man, long-faced and wearing his usual grease-stained baseball cap with the bill turned up.

"Hold on, hot shot," Stokes warned Wayne. "You ain't workin' here no more. You're a paying customer now, just like everybody else."

Wayne silently relinquished the gas nozzle, then stared at a stack of oil cans as he listened to the rhythmic smack of chewing gum in Stokes' mouth. Gasoline fumes permeated the air — it was a smell Wayne had gladly forgotten these past few days.

"Ain't got no use for undependable boys," Stokes continued. "Your ass is fired."

Wayne grinned at the thin man. "I'm cryin' my heart out," he said.

Stokes glanced through the back window of the Chevy at the pile of personal belongings stacked in the rear seat. "You goin' somewhere?" he asked.

"Yeah," Wayne answered glumly. "I'm movin', and I want my paycheck."

Stokes topped off the tank and returned the nozzle to its receptacle on the gas pump. "Can't help you there," he said. "Have to mail it to you later."

"Mail it?" Wayne growled, his temper flaring. "I'm leaving town and I need that money now!"

Stokes glanced at the gas pump. "Sorry," he drawled. "That'll be $4.60."

"Listen, I'm serious," Wayne pleaded. "I need the money now."

Stokes turned away. "No can do," he mumbled. "You know my bookkeeper has to draw all my checks. Take out taxes and shit. You know that."

Wayne swallowed hard, his patience wearing thin. "Clean the damn windshield," he ordered the man.

Stokes ignored the command and studied his former employee. The boy had always seemed meek and timid, never this demanding. "I'll make a deal with you," Stokes said. "We'll settle in cash. But for half of what I owe you."

"Fuck that!" Wayne snarled.

"It's that or nothin'," Stokes beamed. "I'll throw in $4.60 for the gas you just bought."

Wayne shook his head in disgust. The crook had him over a barrel. "All right, all right," he gave in. "I'll settle for half a week's pay in cash."

Stokes pulled a roll of bills from his pocket and counted out a twenty, and five one-dollar bills. Wayne took the money and tucked it into his wallet.

"Where you headed?" Stokes asked.

Wayne scowled at the man and flipped him an upturned middle finger as he slid behind the steering wheel. After a quick stop at the bank, he'd pick up Nancy and they'd be on their way.

After secretly calling his employer and asking for a day of vacation, James Crocker grabbed his lunch pail from a kitchen counter and kissed Edith goodbye. For all she knew, James was going to work as usual. But her husband had a secret mission — to save his son from a confrontation with the law. Running would accomplish nothing. Somehow, he would convince Wayne to face up to his responsibilities, admit his error and make amends in whatever way possible. Wayne was an intelligent, reasonable young man who would surely listen to reason.

James opened the door of his truck and waved to Edith who stood smiling on the front porch, unaware of her husband's suspicions. Today was her turn for volunteer work at a local nursing home, and she'd be gone until late afternoon. He would protect her from the truth as long as was practical, James decided, turning the ignition switch. The engine sputtered, then roared to life at fast idle, its manual choke pulled out to the maximum. Driving along, James mulled over the feeling of fatherly responsibility that had settled over him. He knew he'd disregarded the well-being of his family for too long, and perhaps now he could rightfully resume his role as Wayne's guardian.

For a moment, he remembered the fishing excursions with an adolescent Wayne. The hunting trips. Christmas. The boy's graduation. Where had the years gone? James shrugged, knowing the answer all too well. An era of his own life had been bottled and sealed in a Tennessee distillery. But such shameful thoughts were no strangers to James Crocker, who, despite his feelings of guilt, had always found himself back on the bottle again.

Perhaps this time would be different. Hell, recently he'd kept away from the hard liquor and stayed primarily with beer. That was at least *some* improvement. He laughed to himself as the truck rattled down the bumpy dirt road toward Wayne's trailer. Shit — he needed a drink already.

Nat Mason sat at his desk absorbed in deep thought, oblivious to Mrs. Rankin's boring geography lecture about the climate of eastern Europe. The boy chewed nervously at his fingernails, scribbling occasionally on a ruled pad as if taking notes, while his teacher's monotonous voice droned on.

Demetrius was in trouble. Nat didn't know exactly what his brother had done, but he knew it was serious. Ma and Pa had stayed in their bedroom since last night's visit from the sheriff, and all he'd been able to hear was bits and pieces. Ma wasn't feeling well either. She wasn't herself. The image of her holding a gun on the sheriff still burned in the young boy's mind.

But what troubled him most was the purse. He heard the sheriff mention that the purse was found close to the house. Did they think Demetrius stole it? If that was his brother's crime, Nat could clear the air by confessing that he'd found the purse floating in the creek, and took the money himself. Losers weepers, finders keepers. But would the sheriff then not think that he, Nat, had stolen the purse? Nat shivered at the thought. The idea of going to jail himself was terrifying.

Nat sank lower into his desk, seeking solace from a Fantastic Four comic book hidden in the back of his loose leaf binder. He would do some serious thinking before he admitted his own involvement. No telling what Pa would do if—

"Would you like to share with the class, Nathan?" Mrs. Rankin's voice screeched into his ear. She was standing beside him, staring down at the comic book.

Nat cringed and slowly closed the notebook, rolling his eyes from side to side.

"Nathan — answer me!" she snapped.

"N-N-N-No, Ma'am," he drawled sheepishly.

"Well, I think you should," she said in a cold, stern voice. "Take your funny book to the front of the class and read to us."

Nat stared at her in disbelief.

"Go on," she nagged.

Reluctantly Nat dragged himself to his feet and trudged down the aisle amid the scattered snickers of his classmates.

Demetrius was suddenly the farthest thing from his mind.

At the sight of the squad car pulling to a stop in front of the house, Jeb Cramer turned from his partially dismantled tractor inside the barn, dropped a wrench onto the hay-strewn earthen floor and wiped grease from his hands onto a soiled rag. Angrily, he marched from the barn and yelled, "Well, it's about goddamn time!"

Hart diverted his attention from the neat white house bordered by neatly trimmed shrubbery and glanced in the direction of Cramer's voice. A barbed wire fence surrounded the barn and stretched over the distance, enclosing a herd of cattle. Piles of cow manure dotted the terrain, its odor permeating the air.

Cramer owned one of the larger spreads in the Selton area, including one landmark in particular that lured youngsters like a magnet. In the side of a rocky wooded hill was a cave, with interconnecting tunnels and home to thousands of bats. Cramer had warned the kids repeatedly to stay away, fearing for their safety and his own liability. Twice he had attempted to block the cave entrance, but both times the pesky kids managed to slip through anyway. Now Cramer was ready to do legal battle if necessary to keep the juveniles off his property.

"I hear you're havin' trouble with cave explorers again," Hart answered with forced politeness.

Cramer strolled forward and spat on the ground. "Where's that good-for-nothin' sheriff?" he asked in a jesting tone.

Hart stepped forward and the two shook hands vigorously as Hart introduced himself. "I'm Deputy Don Hart," he said. "I believe we met a couple of years ago, but you may not remember —"

"Hell, I never forget a face," Cramer said tamely. "I appreciate you comin' all the way out here."

Hart smiled. Cramer was warming up to him. This assignment might not be such a pain in the ass after all. He turned his head 180 degrees and admired the countryside. "Nice spread you've got here," he said with a nod. "Where's the cave?"

Cramer motioned for the deputy to follow him across the front lawn. From this new vantage point Hart noticed the land dipped for a hundred yards or so away from the house, then rose steadily farther away.

"You see that hill there?" Cramer asked, pointing in the distance.

Hart nodded.

"Cave's on the other side. Runs underground

all the way below my house and farther. I want those kids out of the damn thing. They might get hurt, and I sure as hell don't want to get sued."

Hart nodded again. "Ever think about blocking the entrance again?"

"Shit, yeah!" the man said. "But nothin' short of cavin' the damn thing in will keep 'em out."

"So, what about cavin' it in?"

Cramer eyed the deputy with impatience. "Hell, I don't want to do that," he said. "Might need it for a fallout shelter some day."

Hart shrugged and pulled a small notebook from his shirt pocket. "Do you have signs posted? Have you verbally warned these kids?"

"Yes, yes, yes."

"Can you give me any of their names?"

Cramer stroked his chin, trying to recall which kids frequented the cave most. "Let's see now — only one I know for sure is Tommy Martin. And I've seen that damn Gibbs boy down there a couple of times. Hell, I don't know!"

Hart pocketed the notebook. "I can talk to their parents, if you like."

"Please do," blurted Cramer, adding, "And I wish you folks would patrol this area more often. Then you might happen to catch them damn kids sneakin' around. Hell, just look for their bicycles on the side of the road."

"We'll do our best," Hart mollified the man as he returned to his car. Hart opened the door as Cramer spoke up again.

"Oh, yeah," he said. "Lately there's been a bunch of niggers goin' in there. Big, mean-lookin' guys, you know? Don't know if they're playin' hookey from school or not, but I don't like 'em hangin' around here. Makes the wife nervous."

Hart's attention quickened at the last remark. "Just when did you last see these niggers?" he asked.

"Oh, must have been Friday or Saturday. Can't remember which. Saw three or four of 'em headed for the cave through the woods. I was gonna run 'em off, but, hell, there was four of them and one of me. And one of 'em looked meaner than hell."

"Did you happen to see when they came out?"

"Hell, no! I got better things to do. Didn't stand around waitin' for 'em, if that's what you mean."

Hart eased into the driver's seat and closed the door, then remembered another important question. He rolled down the window and yelled to Cramer, who was sullenly walking away.

"One more thing," Hart yelled. "Was there a car parked along the road that day?"

Cramer stopped to think. "Don't rightly remember," he said. "Might've been an ol' pickup truck. But I could be wrong."

"Remember what color?"

"Shit!" Cramer roared. "I don't even remember for sure if there *was* a damn truck. How the hell could I know what color, for God's sake?"

Hart shrugged off the man's insolence. "I'll check it out," he said as he twisted the ignition. He backed the car onto the main road and stopped, then took a flashlight from the glove compartment and checked its batteries. They were excellent. Then he laid his service revolver aside the flashlight on the passenger seat and pressed the accelerator.

The squad car rounded the curve, then came to a stop at the side of the road. To the right Hart saw a narrow trail twisting through the heavily wooded hillside toward an outcropping of rocks. Silently he exited the car, flashlight and revolver in hand. Feeling certain the trespassers had long since departed, he hoped valuable evidence might be found. Enough to put him in good graces with the press anyway.

The gentle sound of cattle echoed over the hilltop, as Hart took a deep breath and entered the path.

15

James Crocker's heart sank as he steered the pickup truck into his son's driveway. Wayne's car was gone. He was too late.

Cursing at himself for taking so long to get away from Edith, James stopped the truck and quickly got out. As the cooling engine ticked behind him, he carefully regarded the boy's trailer. Suppose I should look around, he thought. Couldn't hurt.

Stomping to the front door, James twisted the knob. It was locked, just as he'd expected. He tugged the door harder, hoping to jar it open, but it wouldn't budge.

Next he tried the back door, with the same result. James spat on the ground and trudged over to the bed of his truck. Hell, he'd find a tool to pry the damn door open. As he sorted through the scattered collection of rusted tools, James noticed out the corner of an eye that the curtains in the back bedroom were pulled slightly apart.

The window was too high off the ground for him to peek through, so he surveyed the area for a suitable object to stand on. In a small clearing away from the trailer stood a fifty gallon drum in which Wayne burned his trash. James knocked the barrel over, spilling ashes and partially burned garbage over the ground. Then he rolled the container to the bedroom window, turning it bottom end up on the ground below. Next he braced himself against the trailer walls with soot-blackened hands and clumsily climbed atop.

Craning his neck, James peered inside.

Its opening approximately five feet in diameter, the mouth of the cave receded in a frozen yawn into the rocky hillside. Fallen leaves covered the entrance floor along with beer cans, ashes from long abandoned campfires and a scattering of depleted flashlight batteries. Hart stepped through the rubble into the quiet darkness, bending over for several feet until the tunnel enlarged enough to accommodate his height. Cryptic messages scarred the cavern walls from generations of visitors who had documented their presence by defacing the vulnerable stone.

Hart directed the flashlight beam up, down and around. A massive stalactite hung from the ceiling, its pointed end chipped away by souvenir seekers. Ahead, the chamber sprouted a smaller second passage which veered to the right, away from the main catacomb. The floor of the cavern grew increasingly wet.

Every few steps Hart stopped to listen, hearing nothing, save for the steady, rhythmic dripping of water. Climbing a slippery incline, the deputy braced himself against the wet walls to maintain his balance as he continued ahead.

Abruptly Hart entered an unusually large underground chamber, its ceiling thirty to forty feet above his head. The flashlight beam appeared thin and weak as it traced a maze of cracks in the cavern walls and settled on a cluster of bats, hanging upside down from the ceiling. Hart stopped and swallowed hard. Although the temperature was warmer than outside, the air was clammy and damp. He considered yelling to see if anyone happened to be inside the cave, but realized he would lose the element of surprise if by some wild chance the suspects were still there.

A pile of refuse caught his attention near the base of a large flat rock. Hart picked through the litter — wax paper wrappers from sandwiches, potato chip bags, beer cans, a Dr. Pepper bottle — nothing of any substance, though more than one person had obviously eaten here within the past few days. But, of course, that wasn't unusual — spelunkers often carried food. Hart leaned against the rock, noticing dried streaks of crimson that trailed over the edge. It looked like — *blood*. The flashlight beam followed a scarlet trail up the side of a large rounded boulder to a ledge six feet or so above the flat-topped rock. And hanging over the ledge, perfectly still, was a human arm.

Startled, Hart retreated and drew his weapon. Realizing the hand belonged to a colored man, the lawman planted both feet firmly and pulled back the hammer of his revolver. Steadying his aim with both hands, he took a deep breath.

"Freeze!" he yelled, readying himself to squeeze the trigger. The figure remained perfectly still.

"You!" he screamed again, louder this time, his voice breaking into a nervous twang and echoing in the cavern depths. "On your feet!"

Still nothing.

Cautiously he leaned his weight against the stone wall beneath the ledge, extended an arm upward, and barely reached the overhanging fingertips.

They were cold and stiff, and without a doubt, very dead.

Maybelle Mason was confined to bed, her blood pressure dangerously high. Preacher stayed home from work, attending to her needs and trying in every way to calm her nerves. Over and over she accused him of betraying their son whom she continued to maintain was innocent. Preacher patiently sat at her side, wondering why the prescribed sedative had yet to take effect.

"Now, honey, don't fret no more. Try to get some rest." Preacher gently pushed back the locks of hair from her forehead. "I believe the boy's innocent, too. And if he is, the law will protect him."

"Huh!" she huffed. "You know better than that! What with lawmen like that Deputy Hartz running around."

Noticing a slight droop in her eyelids, Preacher smiled. She was finally succumbing to sleepiness. "It's Deputy *Hart*," he corrected her. "But that don't make no difference. We got to cooperate with the law."

"No . . . I . . ." her voice drifted lazily.

"The law and the Good Book, they should work together," he reminded her.

But his last words were lost to her in sleep.

Steering the Chevy along the bumpy drive, Wayne panicked at the sight of his father's pickup truck parked outside the trailer. And there, below the bedroom window, was his Dad struggling to free himself from the trash container whose bottom had obviously collapsed from his weight. Wayne brought the Chevy to an abrupt stop and bounded forward, his heart pounding against his chest.

James Crocker's face was a mask of pain. Jagged edges of rusted metal from the barrel's bottom had ripped through his trousers and pierced both legs. Dark stains of blood soaked the torn fabric.

"Wayne!" James gasped. "Get me out of here!"

Wayne worked diligently to free his father's legs. The rusty metal was brittle and broke away when pushed down, but a few fragments remained impaled in James' thigh.

"Watch it!" James blurted at the burning pain when Wayne held his father's shoulders and helped him from the filthy container. Quickly examining the wounds, Wayne could see that they were serious and would need treatment and shots as infection from such dirty cuts was highly likely.

"What are you doing here?" Wayne demanded. "Why aren't you at work?"

Still leaning his weight against his son, James' lungs heaved as he tried to catch his breath. "You saved her, didn't you?" he said in a breathy tone. "You saved that Barnett girl."

Wayne stood paralyzed.

"I saw you," James continued with a hard swallow. "I was drunk as hell. But I was there Friday night, across the creek."

Wayne's head suddenly began to ache. He hadn't planned for this. His Dad could spoil everything. "I . . ." he began, but found himself suddenly lost for words.

"She's inside the trailer." It was more a statement than a question. "That's why you've acted so funny lately." James paused, trying to read the strange expression on his son's face. "I saw somebody's shadow in there this morning while you were outside. She's in there."

His father's hip was bleeding badly. Wayne suddenly felt sick.

"No . . . you're . . . wrong," he stammered, turning quickly away. "You've got it all wrong."

James wavered on his feet, then gasped at the sight of blood pooling at his feet. "Son, you've got to . . . *help me—*"

Wayne's skin tightened with a burning fear. What could he do now? His Dad needed help.

James sank to his knees, his complexion pale. Without hesitation, Wayne hooked his hands beneath his Dad's shoulders and dragged him to the door. With the door opened wide, he pulled James up the steps and laid him to rest on the living room floor. A smear of blood trailed behind James' left leg.

Grabbing the first-aid book he'd checked out from the library, Wayne rushed to the bathroom closet for strips of old rags to devise a tourniquet.

James' head was wobbling now, his tongue continually moistening his lips. Wayne tore his father's left trouser leg to the hip and found a large gash on the outer thigh. Blood oozed steadily from the wound, and there was barely enough space between the cut and his Dad's crotch to tie off the tourniquet and slow the circulation of blood.·

Wayne worked frantically, his hands awash with crimson, until finally the blood ran in a smaller stream. James' head was rocking from side to side, and he mumbled incoherently, "Where's . . . the girl? Where's . . .?"

Wayne froze. A cool rush of fear tingled down both arms and met at his chest. Where was she?

He leaped to his feet and ran to the bedroom.

The nylon strips lay in a loose pile on the floor.

The bed was empty.

Mrs. Hargrove, the Weems Elementary School principal, took the thermometer from young Nat's mouth and held it near a lamp for a better view. "No fever," she said, then turned to the boy. "Nathan, are you sure you're sick?"

"Yes, Ma'am," he muttered. "It's my stomach."

Mrs. Hargrove shrugged and reached for a pad and pencil on her desk. "Minute ago you complained of being hot," she said.

Nat avoided her eyes. "Yes, Ma'am. But now it's my stomach."

She scribbled a brief note on the pad, tore off the sheet and handed it to him. "Give this to your teacher and you'll be excused for the rest of the day," she said with a sigh. "I'll call your Mama," she added, reaching for the telephone.

"We ain't got no phone," Nat interjected.

The principal exhaled in exasperation. "Then how do you expect to get home?"

Nat shrugged and pocketed both hands. Mrs. Hargrove glanced at the wall clock over the door. It was almost 10:30 A.M. "Can't you wait just a little while longer?" she asked.

"Oh, no, Ma'am," he answered with an exaggerated grimace. "It's gettin' real bad now."

"All right, all right," she conceded. "I'll drive you home myself." A spark flashed in the boy's eyes. "But you'd better not be lyin' to me."

Wayne floored the accelerator en route to the nearest doctor in Vincent. Perhaps along the way he would find Nancy. But then again, she could easily have traveled in the opposite direction. And what would he do if he found her? Talk to her again, and plead with her not to report him to the police? Or force her inside the car and proceed with the original plan after dropping his Dad off for medical treatment?

The elderly Crocker was unconscious now, slumped against the front passenger seat, his blood spilling slowly to the front mat. He had lost a lot of blood, Wayne knew, but it was difficult to concentrate on his father's condition when his own future was also in jeopardy.

Wayne sped past Meyers Lake, ignoring young Tommy Martin who recognized the Chevy and waved hello from a boat a few feet offshore. Wayne wiped his brow. The movement of the automobile made his stomach pitch and roll, and the smell of blood only added to his feeling of nausea.

Finally Wayne could drive no further, and pulled off to the side of the road to vomit.

The corpse's overhanging arm was slightly misshapen from the drainage of blood to its lowest extreme. Hart braced himself against the inclining boulder beneath the ledge and carefully eased the body to the ground. Retrieving the flashlight from its resting point, he examined the remains, noting multiple stab wounds in the abdomen. A search of the deceased revealed no wallet or other documentation — the victim had apparently been robbed.

The dead Negro could not be readily identified as Demetrius Mason. Unfortunately a photograph of the suspect had somehow bypassed Hart on circulation through the courthouse. Another of the sheriff's demeaning acts, Hart suspected.

With his right foot, he rolled the body away to face the stone wall. A faint stench of death irritated Hart's nose, although decomposition had been mercifully slowed by the cool temperature of the cave. Hart smiled. Again, lady luck had shined upon him. Soon he would bathe in the glory of still another major break in this case.

Anxious to report his latest discovery, Hart turned to leave the cave and froze in his tracks. There, in a small recessed area he'd blindly passed only moments before, lay a second body.

It was almost lunchtime when Deputy Granger knocked on the door of the Farrell home. Liz had asked him to stop by and speak to Nancy's parents again. Distraught over speculation that foul play might have been involved in the disappearance of their daughter, the Andersons had since lost any emotional gain derived from Granger's earlier visit.

Liz hurried to the front door and slipped outside to speak with the deputy privately. "I'm so glad you came," she said with a smile. He grinned back at her and then timidly looked away, but quickly regained his professional composure.

"It's nice to see you again," he said. "But I really don't know what else to say to the Andersons."

Liz invited him to sit in the front porch swing. She settled beside him and set the swing in motion. "What do you think really happened?" she asked.

Silent at first, Granger finally opened up. "I really can't say," he said. "The Sampson case seems pretty airtight. But we're stumped about your cousin. It's the damnedest thing I ever heard of." He paused a moment, staring ahead in deep thought. "The Mason boy was involved in some way in the Sampson death. And then there's the bracelet that implicates him in the Barnett case. And, of course, there's the purse."

Liz looked at the deputy with increasing admiration. "But what doesn't make sense to me," she began, "is that these boys were so careless in the Sampson murder that they were immediately identified as the killers. But if Nancy's accident was only a cover up — well, the whole thing had to have been planned so precisely, it seems too advanced for amateurs. See what I mean? The two acts just don't go together."

"Exactly," Granger interjected. "It makes no

sense at all. But when the suspects are arrested and your cousin's body is found, we'll put all the pieces together."

Liz sighed and glanced at the front door.

"I agree, there's really nothing new you can tell Aunt Helen," she said with dismay. "But I can't stand this much longer. She's driving me crazy."

"Do you work?" Granger asked.

"Yes," she answered. "At Smithson's Flower Shop in Pell City. But if I stay off work much longer, I could lose my job."

"I see," he mumbled.

"I could adjust to Nancy's death better if I were working. But Mom is just not strong enough to handle Aunt Helen alone."

For a brief moment their eyes met. Both blushed, and then looking embarrassed, Liz continued. "I feel guilty for thinking this, but I still wish my aunt and uncle would go home. It only makes the whole thing worse for everybody while they're staying here."

"Well," Granger said. "I suppose we should get on with it." As the two stood and started toward the front door, Granger placed a hand on Liz's left shoulder.

She looked up at him and smiled.

Wayne squeezed the steering wheel tighter as he drove back to the trailer. He felt guilty about leaving his Dad in such a serious condition with Doc Sanders. He'd made the feeble excuse that he was driving back to pick up his Mom, and promised to be back at the doctor's office within minutes. Even as he'd spoken, Wayne had known his Mom was working in Pell City today, miles away in the opposite direction.

But he'd get back to his Dad — just as soon as he rounded up Nancy and returned her to the trailer. How long could she have been gone? How far was she physically capable of traveling without help? Wayne feared that someone had picked her up along the road. If that happened, what would she say? What in heaven's name would she tell the authorities?

Soon he sped past Meyers Lake, past his trailer, to investigate the road toward Pell City. She would be wearing his clothes — he remembered the flannel pajamas piled on the floor beside his bed and clothes hanging from the dresser drawers that had been hurriedly yanked out and left open.

The loaded Impala screamed around a curve, spraying loose gravel from the fresh pavement and shifting the contents of the back seat into a crumpled heap. Wayne righted the car's course and floored the accelerator, topping the hill at Linda Greene's house, where at a party several years ago, he had received his first kiss.

Wayne applied the brakes and skidded the car to a stop. There ahead, at the low point between this and the next hilltop, was a new Chevy II he didn't recognize, stopped at idle. And at the passenger side, climbing into the front seat, was a slender form with long hair trailing in the wind, wrapped in a plastic sheet of some kind.

It was her.

Once Nancy disappeared inside, the car pulled away.

Wayne collapsed against the seat. It was over. Tears streamed down his cheeks. But why did it have to end this way? Why hadn't he voluntarily released her? He had told Nancy if she didn't want to go all the way to North Carolina, he would let her out somewhere along the way. And he had *meant* it. Or at least he thought he had.

Slowly he turned the car around and drove aimlessly in the direction of his home. But somewhere along the way, he decided to run. It was a chickenshit thing to do, he knew, but the idea of being hauled into custody was more than he could handle.

As he drove past the narrow driveway to his trailer for the last time, pleasant memories of the improvements he'd planned played in Wayne's mind. But life in Selton was a thing of the past. Now he would take to the highways until a solution came about.

And if an answer never came, he supposed he'd just keep running.

Nat Mason threw his arms around his father's waist as the two stood on the front porch and watched Mrs. Hargrove drive away. Preacher scrubbed the boy's head with his knuckles, his usual show of affection, and said, "It ain't right to lie, son. I know you're worried about your brother and all, but—"

"I took the money," Nat blurted through a burst of tears. "I found the purse and I kept the money. Demetrius didn't do it, Pa. Honest!"

Preacher led the boy into the house. "You're not lyin' again now, are you?" he asked.

"No, Pa," the boy sobbed. "Last Saturday mornin' I found the purse floatin' in the creek." Nat pulled a wad of crumpled bills from his pocket and handed them to his father. "It's *bad* money. I don't want it no more."

Preacher took the money, tossed it to the coffee table, and scratched his head in deep thought. "Son, did you know about the bracelet?"

"What bracelet?"

"It was a heart. On a chain. Did it come from the purse? Or did you find it some —?"

"No, Pa," Nat interrupted. "I ain't seen no bracelet."

Preacher hugged the boy tightly. "I love you, son."

"Did I do wrong, Pa?" Nat asked. "Will I go to the *Booger Man*?"

"It was wrong to take the money what didn't belong to you. And it was wrong to lie to Mrs. Hargrove," Preacher answered. "But you ain't goin' to no Booger Man."

Preacher hugged the boy again, wondering where his oldest son might be.

Hart dragged the second corpse into the clearing of the dark passage and stretched it flat on its back. Similar stab wounds were present, but this was a heavy-set boy, obviously one of the three from Leeds and not the Mason kid. The smell of decomposition carried faintly through the musty air, as Hart directed the flashlight beam to the enclosed area where the body had been. There was no sign of additional evidence. He examined the hands of the second corpse and found raw, tender breaks and tears around the knuckles. Fragments of skin were embedded under the fingernails. This one had fought for his life, had probably witnessed the first stabbing and knew what was coming.

So it now appeared that two fugitives had fled together. The instigator of all the violence must have been Rufus Rayburn, the suspect about whom little was known. None of the others had a record of violence. Rayburn and his buddy had likely decided the other two were only in the way, so they'd offed their companions and ran. But as careless as they'd been so far, they'd leave a trail. They'd be caught soon.

Suddenly a noise sounded from deeper within the cave. A scuffling, sliding sound, with rocks and dirt spilling to the floor. Hart froze. Was it man or beast? He positioned the flashlight forward and held his weapon steadily in position. The revolver wavered before him, ready to spit death at any moment.

Slowly he crept toward the noise, keeping his body flat against the stone walls for protection. He entered another chamber, smaller than the first, and stopped to listen. Heavy, forced breathing sounded from nearby. He circled the room with the flashlight beam and found the frightened, dying eyes of a third Negro youth, glaring from a ledge above the cavern floor.

"Hold it, nigger," Hart growled.

The boy tried desperately to speak, but couldn't.

Hart glared into the bloodshot eyes that pleaded for help and felt a growing hatred burn inside. Slowly he stepped closer beneath the ledge, and held the revolver directly in the boy's face. He pulled back the hammer, its dull click exaggerated in the quiet catacombs.

"Time to join your buddies," he snarled.

16

The telephone clanged loudly as Sheriff Arnold dropped the receiver to its cradle. The call was from Sheriff Ames of Dale County in south Alabama. The suspects' pickup truck had been found abandoned on a country road near Ozark. Blood stains were caked across tufts of cotton from rips in the worn plastic seat cover.

Sheriff Arnold hung his head. Just as he'd feared, there had been more violence. The seating restriction of a pickup truck had forced elimination of at least one member of the runaway gang. And a young, inexperienced boy like Preacher's son had only complicated matters for the others. He had likely been the one to die.

Leaning back in his chair, the sheriff considered the few delinquents he had been involved with. How easily they were drawn into crime. But those who

262

ran from family problems usually ended up embroiled in far greater trouble.

Preacher should be told about the danger his son was in. But his wife would hardly be able to withstand such a shock. Reflecting on his years of law enforcement in Shelby County, the sheriff now appreciated their relative tameness. Now the world was changing fast, and the stress caused by a more mobile society was difficult to cope with. Fast cars, interstate highways, planes. The criminal element could strike and move so quickly that a more sophisticated approach to investigative pursuit was now required. Perhaps it's time to turn in the old badge, he thought, and take early retirement.

But he had to see this one through. And now that they knew in which direction the fugitives were headed, they'd be easier to follow. Already Sheriff Ames was checking out a reported stolen car. Ames sounded young and energetic on the telephone. Dedicated. A good man.

Sheriff Arnold stood, stretched and stepped over to the steaming coffee pot on a nearby table.

Perhaps it would soon be over.

At first, afraid that Wayne might find her along the paved road, Nancy walked along a crude trail through the woods. But finally, as exhaustion settled over her weakened limbs, she knew she would need help. Fortunately, as soon as she reached the road, this kind old man she was now sitting beside had stopped for her.

Nancy sat in silence as the terrain of her youth rolled past. She ran a trembling hand through her tangled hair, recalling how she had finally managed to escape to the safety of this elderly gentleman's care.

Following their physical interlude the night before, Nancy had been appalled when Wayne tied her again before leaving. His nerves were fraying, she could tell, and he was becoming dangerous not only to himself, but to her as well. He's doing this out of love, a twisted kind of love, she reminded herself, trying not to resent his most recent actions.

In his harried mental state, Wayne had also grown foolishly over-confident and careless. The nylon strips around her wrists had been loose, and with little effort she escaped her bonds. But dressing had been a problem. Not only were her limbs still sore, but the only clothing to be found was the sweaty outfit Wayne had worn the day before. His other clothes were already packed in the car. Nancy slipped into the soiled jeans and flannel shirt, then searched for a pair of shoes.

Wayne's closets had been thoroughly emptied. A pair of smelly socks lay curled on the bathroom floor and as she sat to put them on, Nancy decided to check under the bed. Against the far wall, matted with dust and fuzz, was a pair of ragged tennis shoes without laces. Nancy quickly brushed them off, then slipped them on and used two of the nylon strips that had previously bound her wrists to secure the shoes on her feet. They were too big, and walking in them felt awkward, but Nancy realized she had no choice.

Knowing it would be cold outside, Nancy made a quick search for a coat or jacket, but found nothing. Finally, she wrenched the shower curtain from its rod, sending plastic hooks flying through the air. Then, wrapping the plastic sheet around herself, she left her place of captivity.

Outside, she found herself in unfamiliar country-side. But as she adjusted to the sunlight and scanned the horizon she oriented herself by the sight of a long-familiar landmark — the Selton water tower, barely visible above the trees in the distance. After a moment's concentration, she had remembered the direction she should travel and painfully trudged ahead.

The driver glanced at her from the corner of his eye.

"Are you sure you're all right, young lady?" he asked.

Nancy cleared her throat and gazed out the side window at sights that vaguely registered in her memory. "I'm fine," she answered.

The man was obviously curious about her appearance, but she refused to talk. At the moment, her thoughts were centering around the comforts of a warm bath and the love of her cousin, aunt and uncle.

The Chevy II rolled to a creaking stop.

"Here's the Farrell place," the man said as he switched off the ignition. "I'll help you inside."

Nancy tugged the door handle. "No, thanks. I can manage just fine," she said. "But I really appreciate the ride."

"Well," the man said as he lit a cigarette. "Tell ol' Tom that Arny Hankins said hello."

Nancy slammed the car door and stood alone, taking in the view of the house and surrounding land that stirred a million memories. The Chevy II whined to a start and slowly pulled away.

Chickens pecked, carefree in the yard. To the far left, in the adjacent field, was the small pond and willow tree where she and Liz played when they were kids.

Nancy took a deep breath. I'm here, she thought. *I'm finally here.*

Parked in the driveway was her parents' car. Tears leaked from Nancy's eyes. All of her loved ones were here.

Except Charlie.

Demetrius inched back against the cold stone wall, and taking a deep breath, courageously stared the deputy squarely in the eye. What he saw was a look of hatred and evil that seemed to come straight from hell. The revolver wavered in his direction. The man's face, aglow from the beam of the grounded flashlight, was covered with beads of sweat and he was trembling so much that the revolver wavered in his hand.

Carefully, the frightened youth slid both feet against the hefty rock he was partially hidden behind. Then, thankful for the lawman's hesitation, he took a deep breath, and pushed with every ounce of his remaining strength.

The boulder tumbled forward over the edge, surprising the deputy who moved too slowly to escape its path. Demetrius cringed at the sound of the man's ghastly scream, and an errant gunshot that ricocheted off the stone walls.

Painfully, the boy pulled himself to the edge and peered over. The penumbra of the dislodged flashlight faintly illuminated the grisly scene. The deputy lay flat on his back, the boulder embedded in his chest, and a trickle of blood spilling from his lips.

Demetrius felt his stomach convulse, the resulting pain bringing him closer to unconsciousness. His mind spun in confusion as he relaxed his head against the cold, damp wall.

By the time the flashlight batteries finally weakened, Demetrius, too, had eternally joined his companions.

Relieved by the news that his Dad was going to be all right, Wayne hung up the phone in the telephone booth. The nurse had questioned him sternly as to why he had left in such a hurry, and why he wasn't coming back. Wayne hadn't responded, telling her, instead, to relay a message to his Mom and Dad. Tell them, he said, that I'll be going away for awhile. Tell them that soon they will know why. And tell them, above all else, that I love them, that I'll miss them, and that I'm truly sorry for what I've done, that I wish more than anything I could erase everything that has happened.

The nurse had sounded abrupt and impatient, and Wayne hoped she had gotten it all down. But somewhere down the road he would call his Mom. By then, she would have been questioned by the police and would be over the initial shock of learning that her only son had become a fugitive.

Wayne stepped from the telephone booth and returned to his car. The nervousness, the tension and fear of being caught — they were getting him down.

He swallowed hard and turned the ignition. He was never meant for this kind of life and he knew that somewhere, in some faraway town, he just might pull up to the local police station, walk inside and say, "I'm guilty. Send me home."

But for now, Wayne needed a few days to think things over. California sounded nice. He'd wanted to go there all his life, but had never had the chance. This would likely be his last opportunity.

Within hours Wayne had accumulated road maps of Alabama, Mississippi and Arkansas from service stations he'd stopped at along the way. Poised behind the steering wheel, his travels had just begun.

Nat Mason sat alone on the front porch, rocking in quiet solitude. Skipper lay sleeping at his feet. In Nat's lap was Pa's worn Bible. Carefully, he leafed through its pages, then set the book aside.

His brother was dead, he knew. Only moments ago, a sensation had overcome him, a tingling in his body, and an emptiness deep within his soul. It was as if, in his dying breath, Demetrius had reached out to his younger brother. Follow the word, a voice had said to him.

Follow the word.

Nat wandered along the creek, confused by the brief but powerful message. What could it mean? But, upon returning home, when his eyes rested on the family Bible, the meaning became all too clear. Nat felt a warmth rush over his young body, as if he were cleansed inside and out. He wondered at what age his Pa first received The Calling, and what immediate changes came over *his* life.

Slowly, Nat stood and descended the front steps, stopping on the barren soil to gaze skyward. Towering cumulus clouds drifted slowly by, aglow from the light of the hidden sun.

Demetrius was gone, he knew. But his life's mission, to touch his younger brother's heart and soul, had been accomplished.

Nat smiled at the heavens. He most definitely would follow the word.

Two hundred miles south at a Dothan service station, Rufus Rayburn stuffed ten and twenty dollar bills into his coat pockets with his left hand as he menacingly waved a knife with his right.

"Open the safe!" he growled at a frightened attendant.

"I-I-I-I don't know how," the young man pleaded.

Rayburn stepped forward and jabbed the point of the knife into the young man's stomach, passing through the victim's shirt and immediately drawing blood. The man winced at the onslaught of pain and staggered against the counter.

"Open the fuckin' safe," Rayburn repeated, "or I shove it deeper."

Clutching his stomach, the attendant watched the blood ooze over his palm and trickle to the floor. Then he glanced quickly at a .38 revolver hidden behind three cartons of cigarettes beneath the countertop. He knew his energy was fading fast.

Screeching tires sounded from outside where a car

skidded to avoid collision with an offending automobile. As Rayburn reflexively turned his head toward the noise, the attendant summoned all his remaining strength and lunged for the hidden weapon. Packages of Marlboros and Winstons scattered to the floor, and the attendant could see the shiny blade of the knife glittering in the fluorescent light, as the thief, reacting quickly, stabbed the attendant's thigh. Sprawled across the floor, the injured man brought the revolver into firing position, leveled it at his assailant's face and emptied two quick rounds that ended the wrath of Rufus Rayburn.

The letter was almost finished. Liz Farrell was writing to Jeffrey, a former pen pal from Rochester, New York with whom she'd fallen out of contact over the past couple of years. The thought had recently struck her that young Jeff might well have been drafted and if he was serving in Vietnam, might be badly in need of a friend back home. Wherever he might be, if his parents still lived at the same address, perhaps they would forward the letter to him.

Liz felt foolish at being stumped by how to sign the damn thing. "Love Ya!", which they'd both used before, seemed too juvenile at this stage of life. Finally, she settled on "Sincerely". Funny, she thought, how the simplest solutions were often the last to come to mind.

Ignoring a gentle knock at the front door, she heard her mother's footsteps tapping down the hardwood hallway to answer the door. She heard the blinds on the front door rattle open, then a brief moment of silence. Finally her mother gasped and uttered, "*Nancy!*"

So her body had been found at last, Liz thought. What a relief! But then her mother's excited voice broke into sobs — oddly enough, sobs of *happiness*. "Nancy!" she said it again. There was a commotion at the door and Liz could hear Aunt Helen burst out, "Oh my God — *she's alive!*"

Liz scrambled to the living room and couldn't believe her eyes. There Nancy stood, as alive as she'd ever been! But she was dressed very peculiarly and there was something different about her — the vibrancy she'd always been noted for was gone. But where on earth had she been?

Liz pushed past her mother, but Aunt Helen and Uncle Ralph were clinging to their daughter's side like leeches, moaning and crying uncontrollably. Finally, Nancy peered over her mother's shoulder, tears streaming from her eyes.

"Lizzie!" she sobbed. "Oh, God, it's so good to see you."

Liz forced herself between Helen and Ralph to deliver a sharp hug. Trying to push them away, Nancy said laughingly, "Hey, folks — I can't breathe!"

Ralph escorted his daughter to the sofa and for a moment silence filled the room — everyone stood spellbound. Finally Helen sniffled, wiped away her tears and asked, "Nanny, *where have you been?*"

They waited breathlessly for her response, as Nancy, taken off guard, wondered what to say. There simply hadn't been time to think about it.

"I don't know where to begin," she muttered, drying her tears. "Well, there was this accident, and . . . and . . ."

Nancy stopped in midsentence, confused by the emotion building inside her. It was an empty, lonely feeling and she suddenly found herself overcome with sadness.

"What's the matter, honey?" her father whispered, placing an arm around her shoulders, and noticing how pale and weak she looked.

In her mind Nancy saw Wayne, not as a monster or a kidnapper, but meek and timid, plain and simple *Wayne*. Where was he now?

She burst into tears, her chest heaving so hard that her relatives promptly vacated the sofa so she could lie down.

Her face etched with worry, Helen stared at Martha. "Please call a doctor," Helen said, her voice cracking from the strain.

The Mason household stood ominously still and quiet in the late afternoon as Sheriff Arnold stopped his patrol car outside. Shutting off the ignition, he sat behind the steering wheel, the tick of the cooling engine the only audible sound until, suddenly, the boy's dog rounded the corner of the house, growling. Swinging the screen door to its outermost limit, young Nat bounded from inside the house, and led the dog to its familiar shed. Skipper twisted and turned in the boy's grasp, making every effort to escape, but finally succumbed to Nat's sheer determination.

Preacher stepped from the house to the front porch wearing an uneven smile. But why? What could the man possibly have to be happy about? Sheriff Arnold watched questioningly from behind the steering wheel.

As the sheriff slowly got out of the car, Preacher descended the front steps. "Mr. Sheriff, there's somethin' you need to know about that purse," he said. "You see, my youngest boy found that purse and took the money. He told me about it just this evenin'. And Demetrius, you see, he had nothin' to do with—"

The sheriff hung his head and motioned to the front door. "Can we go inside?" he asked softly.

Observing the lawman's solemn expression, Preacher rushed up the steps and opened the door for the sheriff to pass through. Sheriff Arnold stood inside the living room and glanced through the doorway into the kitchen. "Is Maybelle able to get up?" he asked.

Preacher slowly shook his head. "She ain't been doin' too good. The doctor, he gave her some medicine to make her sleep."

"We'll let her rest, then," said the sheriff with a deep sigh.

"Did y'all find my boy?" Preacher asked. "Can I see him?"

Sheriff Arnold fumbled with his hat and avoided the colored man's eyes before finally locking stares. "Preacher, your boy died this evenin'."

A blank expression seized Preacher's face. "Dead? But how? Who —?"

"Rayburn did it. He killed his three companions, then took off on his own. He was already wanted for rape and murder in Tennessee, we learned. But he's dead now, too. Got shot during an attempted holdup down in Dothan."

A trickle of tears glided down the dark man's cheeks. "But . . . he was so . . . young and innocent."

"I know he was," the sheriff said. "Just made a mistake gettin' mixed up with the wrong crowd, that's all."

Preacher sniffled, covering his face with both hands. "It was the Lord's callin'," he sobbed. "It was time for Demetrius to go. And it's not for us to question, but to—"

Suddenly Preacher stopped and stood frozen, gazing out a nearby window. "Damn!" he suddenly cursed. "Shit!" he roared, getting down on his knees to the floor, and pounding the flimsy coffee table with his fist.

Sheriff Arnold looked on, open-mouthed and at a loss for words.

Abruptly, his chest heaving, Preacher began to wail loudly and pitifully. His eyes overflowed as he lifted his face to the ceiling. "Forgive me, Lord," he cried. "I've served you good, and I don't mean to be disrespectful. But I can't help but be angry with You, Lord. Please forgive me. I'm just a man, Lord. Just a wore-out, ol' man . . ." he cried, his voice tapering off to deep sobs.

Drying the tears from his own eyes, the sheriff then helped the bereaved father to his feet and seated him on the sofa. With a ballpoint pen he scribbled a telephone number on a scrap of paper and offered it to Preacher.

"If there's anything I can do, call me," he said.

Preacher took the paper and nodded.

"Is there somebody I can notify to come and stay with you? To comfort you and your wife?" the sheriff asked.

Preacher shook his head. "The Lord gives us all the comfort we need," he sobbed.

Sheriff Arnold stood, patted the sorrowful man on the shoulder, and stepped away, hesitating at the door. "I lost a deputy today, too," he said. "Died of a rock slide in the cave where your boy was found." The sheriff noted the pain and anguish in the bereaved father's face. "But he wasn't half the man your son was," he added.

clockface on a chest of drawers across the room. Abruptly the furnace clicked on again. She concentrated on the vibration of its metal grill in the hallway.

It seemed as if morning would never come.

Reports of the astounding appearance of Nancy Sue Barnett spread quickly across the southern region, many smaller broadcasting stations deeming the story newsworthy enough to interrupt normal programming with a special bulletin. Representative of the newscasts was the following from WBAM, Montgomery:

"As a dramatic follow up to last week's bizarre but tragic automobile accident in Shelby County, Sheriff Chester Arnold announced early this morning that Nancy Barnett, presumed dead, has been found alive and well. Searchers along Kelley Creek, where the Barnett automobile plunged over a dismantled bridge, had been baffled by unsuccessful dragging efforts. Sheriff Arnold refused to elaborate on the whereabouts of Mrs. Barnett for the past several days, but stated that the probe continues.

"Meanwhile, speculation hints of a conspiracy in the death of Charles Barnett. Sources close to the Barnetts confirmed that the young couple had been embroiled in marital problems for quite some time. Sheriff Arnold again refused to comment on this or any other aspect of the accident.

278

"In a related story, Shelby County District Attorney Albert Reynolds insists that this latest development will have no bearing on negligence charges against Arbor Construction Company. Reynolds maintains that the safety of Alabama highways remains high on his list of priorities."

As he approached Texarkana on Highway 82, Wayne envisioned a grainy photo of himself plastered across the front page of *The Birmingham News*, with a headline that read, "Kidnapper Sought in Disappearance of Accident Victim". He wondered how much of the story had been released to the public, and exactly what his parents knew. Of course, Dad had already figured it out. Was he cooperating with the police? Were detectives now swarming over his empty trailer, taking fingerprints and gathering evidence for prosecution?

It was his mother he was most worried about. He'd left her alone to deal with an unreliable husband who would become even more of a burden following his injury. For weeks, Wayne had expected his Mom to move in with him temporarily, to escape her husband's abuse. But now she was likely ashamed and embarrassed by her son's actions. And that's what hurt most. Aside from the pain and anguish he'd caused Nancy, his own mother would now suffer as well.

He had to talk to her, to try to explain.

Soon he found a convenient telephone booth and got several dollars in change from a nearby service station. With the operator on the line, Wayne deposited the appropriate coins and waited for the connection. How would he begin? What exactly would he say?

The telephone grew sweaty in his grasp. His heart pounded harder, his mouth was cottony, his lips trembling. The telephone began to ring at the other end of the line. One ring. Two. Three. And then, no longer able to take the tension building inside, he slammed the receiver to its cradle and ran to his car.

In the far off reaches of his mind, James Crocker heard the telephone ring. Its clanging sound aggravated the spinning confusion inside his head. He rolled over in bed, opened his eyes, and smelled his own vomit.

"Answer the goddamn phone!" he yelled, unaware that Edith was away at her sister's.

After three short rings, the telephone stopped and James returned to a deep, distant sleep.

Edith Crocker was overjoyed at the news of Nancy Barnett's reappearance. Edith had been acquainted with the Farrells for years and remembered a time long ago when Martha had stopped by the house for a brief social call. Accompanying her was her young daughter, Lizzie, and Nancy, her niece. The two girls were so cute, dressed in matching cowgirl outfits, pigtails dangling below their necks — Edith remembered the scene well because, at the time, she'd wanted Wayne to come out and talk to the girls. But he'd locked himself in his room, too bashful to speak, and Edith, embarrassedly, had had to apologize for him.

So now Nancy was alive, almost as if she'd return-ed from the grave. Proves you should never give up, Edith thought, as her own problems came back to mind.

There was still no answer at Wayne's trailer. Edith hung up the phone, surrendering a last hope that he might have returned home. Should she report his disappearance to the police? But, of course, Wayne couldn't get in touch with her — he had no way of knowing she was in Talladega. Perhaps she should go home and demand that James leave the house. Then Wayne would have a chance to call before she reported him missing. Annie would naturally try to talk her out of it. And if it weren't for Wayne, she wouldn't even consider going back.

But it seemed the only proper thing to do.

Though Nancy's eyelids remained heavy, she slowly forced them open. Bedside conversations seemed to come to her as if from a distance, and her head felt light and dizzy, her vision blurred.

Slowly, steadily, the images around her bed began to come into focus. A nurse was taking her blood pressure. She saw a policeman, her cousin Liz, Aunt Martha and Uncle Tom, her parents — they were all at her side, flashing broad, happy smiles. She tried to speak, but the words failed to come.

God, she thought. I feel like Dorothy in *The Wizard of Oz*. Could it all have been a dream? So much had happened . . .

"Nancy?" her mother said. "Can you hear me, honey?"

"Mom?" she whispered.

Helen Anderson leaned over to embrace her daughter as the others crowded close by.

"Excuse me," the nurse called to the group in a stern voice. "You folks'll have to spread out, so the patient can breathe."

Ralph Anderson squeezed his daughter's hand and felt teardrops tickle his chin. "Nanny, it's nice to see you smile again," he said.

Her parents huddled at her side until Deputy Granger cleared his throat, hinting for an introduction.

"Oh, I'm sorry," Ralph apologized. "Honey, this is Deputy Jesse Granger from the Shelby County Sheriff's Office."

Granger nodded. "I'm pleased to meet you, Ma'am."

Nancy glanced at the uniformed officer, then scanned the other faces in the room.

"He'd like to ask you a few questions," her father added.

The house reeked of beer and vomit when Edith arrived, and James sat on the living room sofa, his shoulders slumped, his face stubbled with two days' growth.

"Get out," she said calmly as she entered the room.

He looked up from the television with a questioning glance.

"Get out, I said," she repeated.

"Now, Edie, let's not go through this again—"

"If you're not out of this house in five minutes," she interrupted, "I'm callin' the law."

"Aw, shit — leave me alone, will you?" he drawled.

Edith went to the bedroom for a change of clothing and gagged at the smell of the puke-ridden bed. She held her breath as she gathered slacks and a blouse from a closet and quickly went into the bathroom.

James returned his attention to the television where he had just learned that the Barnett woman had mysteriously reappeared. Wayne had been involved with her disappearance, he was certain, though the trailer had been empty and the boy's name had yet to be mentioned in any newscast. Obviously the cops were keeping it quiet, for some reason. Hell, who could figure out why the law did things like that? But at least the woman was alive. And James believed that his own confrontation with Wayne might have saved her. Since the girl would tell everything, there was no need for him, James, to get involved.

Edith returned to the living room in her clean outfit, waving away the putrid fumes that violated every corner of the house. "I'm worried about Wayne," she said. "Have you heard from him?"

"He's all right," James answered.

"How do you know?" she snapped. "Have you heard from him?"

James leaned back on the sofa and snarled, "The nurse said he was goin' away for awhile. Said not to worry."

Edith stared him down. "Why didn't he tell *me*?"

"Hell, I don't know," James slurred. "Shit, give me a break."

She opened her mouth to deliver a verbal beating, then stopped short and flashed a cold stare instead.

James stalled, considering his next move. Maybe it would be best if he *did* get out of the house, give Edith a chance to cool off. By suppertime, she'd welcome him home.

"All right," he said, "I'm leavin'." He shrugged and headed for the door. "Bye, Sugar Babe." James leaned against the door and blew her a sarcastic kiss before stepping outside.

With her husband safely outside, Edith flipped through the yellow pages for a locksmith to come out and change the locks.

Midway across the plains of western Texas, Wayne cringed at the sound of a blasting siren. In the rear view mirror, at fast approach, were the flashing red strobes of a police vehicle.

Well, this is it, he thought, preparing himself for the worst. How would it feel to have a gun waved in his face, to be frisked and handcuffed like a common criminal — when he'd never been in trouble in his entire life? How would it feel to be thrown into a cold, damp cell, to be surrounded by the lowest of the criminal element? Wayne shuddered at the thought, his teeth clenching.

But in a flash the police vehicle overtook Wayne's Chevy and forged ahead into the approaching night. Wayne breathed a sigh of relief. He'd been mercifully spared.

On this second evening of his flight from home, Wayne reflected on his long, lonely journey. The service stations. The fast-food restaurants. The agonizing hours behind the steering wheel, listening to songs that reminded him of happier times. And of course there were the people he'd met, friendly locals he tried to avoid, but whose persistence had forced at least half-hearted conversations.

The story he'd invented was a relocation to Tucson, to live with a fictitious brother — a story he'd repeated so many times, he'd almost come to believe it. If only it were true . . .

Wayne glanced at the rolling terrain gliding past the automobile on all sides, at the golden sunset, at the first tumbleweed that bounced across the pavement in front of him. The land was strange — dry and scrubby — unlike any he'd ever seen. He caught a quick glimpse of a coyote, and though fascinated by the mangy creature, realized for the first time how far away from home he was, and how much this alien countryside differed from Alabama. He missed the trees, the lakes, the streams, his friends, his loved ones.

How would he, Wayne Alton Crocker, rate as a fugitive? Not very well, he supposed. Where would he end up? He had no specific destination in mind, and had chosen California only because it was in the opposite direction from what he'd mentioned to Nancy. But cops were smart. They'd find him soon.

Under the cover of darkness, he found an unimproved road that cut a path through a cluster of dusty sagebrush. Wayne parked the car and stepped outside to stretch his legs and relieve himself. The air was brisk and cold, the sky perfectly clear. Little by little, stars appeared, more than any he'd ever seen. The moon rose from behind a distant mountain and his thoughts turned to Nancy. How was she doing? If she looked to the sky at this very moment, she'd see the same lunar glow, the same stars, the same heavenly view they'd both seen through the bedroom window. But what would she be thinking?

Resigned to another sleepless night, Wayne slid back onto the front seat in desperate need of rest, however slight. The smell of blood had almost faded from the freshly scrubbed floormat. If only he could dream. Relax and revitalize himself. But Wayne knew that if by some chance he did fall asleep, there'd only be nightmares.

Back home in Alabama, Wayne's mother slept alone in her own bed. James Crocker was sleeping over at his brother's house in Vincent, reluctantly departing only after Edith called the police when he refused to stop banging on the front door.

At the wake of their departed son, Preacher and Maybelle Mason received their friends into their home. Young Nat comforted his bereaved parents and conducted himself in a manner mature beyond his years, reading scriptures to the mourners and leading prayer after prayer, to the amazement of all present.

Sheriff Arnold planned an early retirement and held a lengthy discussion with his wife as to whether they'd stay in Shelby County or relocate.

Nancy Barnett held a happy reunion with friends and relatives who drove great distances to sit by her side and wish her well. In the midst of the celebration, Liz Farrell and Jesse Granger slipped away for a quiet evening in a nearby restaurant.

And at the end of a narrow drive off Selton Road in rural Alabama, a tiny mobile home stood dark and empty.

18

Thursday
Day Seven

Wayne sighed deeply and stared ahead through the filthy windshield. He'd hoped to reach California by nightfall, but instead, had been delayed by a broken fan belt outside Carlsbad, New Mexico. To his good fortune, a friendly Indian happened by and offered him a ride into town. There, after hours of waiting at a run-down service station, he found a mechanic who was willing to drive him back to his car in an ancient wrecker and install a new belt.

Throughout the wait, Wayne worried that a passing policeman might notice the abandoned vehicle with an Alabama tag, and call for a license check. Even as he returned to the car with the sullen mechanic, he feared that federal agents might be hidden, ready to spring into action at his appearance. But the repair went smoothly, costing only a few dollars, so he continued ahead.

It was at the end of this long, weary day that Wayne found himself at the Cactus Motel in Arizona, where he listened to the sounds of lovemaking in the next room and longed for a way out of this ugly mess. And as he tossed and turned through still another sleepless night, Wayne realized it was the lack of *knowing* that haunted him so. Finally, he resolved to call home in the morning. The voice of his mother would be comforting, and he would try his best to explain.

Still, he feared that her phone might be tapped, that he might give away his location.

But, then again — what did it matter?

19

Friday
Day Eight

Despite both physical and mental exhaustion, Wayne awakened early, determined to call his mother. In the bathroom mirror, he saw a lonely, weary man unfit for life on the road. For a brief instant he again considered going to the police, but finally decided his mother's words might bring him renewed strength. And hope.

She would understand.

Mothers *always* understand.

Outside the motel office stood a telephone booth. With a pocketful of loose change, he walked across the dusty parking lot, the arid desert wind whipping clouds of sand and dust from the shoulder of the nearby highway. He felt a tingle of nerves return to his skin, the familiar swelling of his tongue and tightening of his chest. But he would go through with it this time.

290

As he waited for the connection, Wayne checked his watch. 7:15 A.M. Was the local time in Alabama one, or two, hours later? He couldn't remember, but regardless, Mom would be in bed, awaiting his call.

The seconds dragged by. Again he felt an urge to surrender. It would be so easy to hang up. But just as he was about to drop the receiver, the ring on the other end of the line buzzed into his ear. It rang only twice, then stopped with the sleepy but anticipatory sound of his mother's voice.

"Hello?"

"M-M-Mom?" he forced the word — the single most difficult word he'd uttered in his entire life.

"*Wayne!*" she answered excitedly. "Where *are* you?"

"Mom, I—"

"I've been looking *all over* for you. I had no idea where you might be!"

Wayne listened intently to the tone of her voice. He could detect no shame. No guilt or embarrassment or regret. Just happiness upon hearing from her son.

"Why did you leave?" she continued. "You scared me to death! If you had problems, you could've talked to me."

Her voice droned on and on, but Wayne focused on those all-important words. She had specifically asked — *why did you leave?* And that meant *she didn't know!* Her tone, her words — everything indicated that *she didn't know!*

But could it be a trick? A plan devised by the police to lure him home? It was possible, of course. But his mother would never willingly participate in such a scheme. She would never set a trap for her own son.

And if his mother didn't know, could it be that the police didn't know, either?

"Mom," he interrupted. "Is everything . . . all right . . . at home?"

"Well," she answered with a brief pause. Here it comes, Wayne thought. He braced himself, clutching the receiver tightly as she continued, "You know that your father was hurt, but don't worry, he's all right and, well — I probably shouldn't tell you something like this over the phone — but, Wayne, I've left your father."

Wayne hesitated, and swallowed hard.

"Wayne," she started again. "I hope you'll understand. It's something I should have done years ago and — well, we'll talk about it later." She sniffled once, twice, then continued, "But look at me, rambling on at a time like this. Son, I've been worried sick about you. Where have you been? Where *are* you?"

He couldn't speak. He honestly couldn't utter a sound. Nancy, he thought, you brave, beautiful lady. You believed in me. *I blew it, and in the end, you still protected me.*

Tears poured from Wayne's eyes as he broke into uncontrollable laughter. The relief was sudden and immense, a happiness he hadn't experienced since childhood when he awakened on Christmas Day to a fresh supply of toys. But this was the greatest gift of all — the gift of freedom, from a wonderful and courageous young woman who, in the end, cared enough to dodge countless questions and embarrassment on his behalf.

Finally Wayne calmed himself enough to speak. "Mom," he said with a deep breath and a joyful, cheek-stretching smile. "I can't wait to see you.

We'll straighten Dad out — don't you worry. *I'm comin' home.*"

EPILOGUE

January 1972
Six Years Later

Delivering mail could be a bitch sometimes, but at least it paid the bills and helped keep him in shape. And though he knew he'd never be rich, Wayne Crocker realized that a government job was secure and could finance a comfortable standard of living for himself and his family.

He scrubbed his feet on the front porch welcome mat and stepped inside his Pell City home. "Daddy's home!" he yelled. As usual, little Andy came screaming from the den, arms open wide, awaiting a hug from his dad.

"How's it goin', scout?" Wayne asked as he scooped the four-year-old up into his arms.

"Mommy made a mess!" Andy proclaimed, an innocent look of urgency in his eyes. "She's trying to clean it up in the kitchen before you get home."

Wayne laughed. "Well, she's a little too late, don't you think? Since I'm already home?" He planted a wet smack on the child's cheek. "Uh-oh," Wayne said. "Bet she's in a bad mood."

"Yeah!" Andy grinned.

"I'll tell you what, son. I guess we should dodge her awhile till she cools down."

Wayne walked into the livingroom where flames were crackling in the fireplace. She had obviously been busy, Wayne thought, setting himself on the sofa, if she's already straightened up and built a fire.

"Daddy?" Andy said, waving a thin book in his Dad's face. "Will you read this to me? P-L-E-A-S-E?"

Wayne pulled away. "Why, sure I will — if you'll get it out of my nose!"

Andy giggled again and scooted closer to see the pages between his Daddy's hands. "Read the train story, read the train story!"

Glancing past the illustration of a colorful engine, Wayne saw the day's mail scattered over the coffee table. There was a MasterCharge bill, a Sears catalog — and a letter.

"Daddy? Read *now!*" the child nagged impatiently.

Wayne reached for the envelope and turned it over in his hands. It was postmarked Columbus, Georgia and the return address read "Mrs. Nancy Stipley".

Wayne raised his head, focusing his attention on the fireplace. A fever had settled over his skin unlike any he'd experienced since that fateful November and despite the warmth, he shuddered from the memory. How often he'd wondered what happened to her. She had been included in his prayers for months, even years, and he had come to perceive his brief time with her as a major turning point in his life. So she had remarried — that much he could tell from the envelope alone. And she probably had kids by now, too.

She was a fine woman, and had made some Georgia Cracker a very lucky man.

"Wayne? Why didn't you tell me you were home?" Elaine said as she bent down to kiss her husband; her shoulder length brown hair hung in her face as their lips met. Her recently confirmed pregnancy was just beginning to show.

"Oh, hi, honey," Wayne drawled, tasting gingerbread on her lips.

"And before you have any dinner, Mr. Crocker," she said in a playful tone, "I want to know who Nancy Stipley is."

Wayne tapped the envelope against his leg and smiled.

"An old girlfriend?" Elaine asked.

"Daddy? *Read!*" Andy urged.

"In a minute, son," Wayne answered. He motioned for Elaine to sit at his left and he held her tightly. "Not an old girlfriend," he said. "Just a friend."

Elaine smiled and ran her fingers through his hair. "Well, aren't you going to open it?"

He was thinking about the kind of person it would take to survive the ordeal that Nancy went through, about the strength she showed in covering up for him. And he remembered the urges he'd fought to try to contact her later, even once going so far as to drive to Columbus just to see her home and possibly catch a glimpse of her from a distance.

And after all the times he'd wondered about her over the years, it seemed strange now to hold all the answers inside a sealed envelope and yet feel a reluctance to learn the truth. How would life be if all the secrets of the universe were suddenly known? Wayne's world was small, but he and Nancy shared a secret no one else would ever know, and though he wished her well and would love more than anything to see her again to discuss their haunting relationship of only a few days, it seemed foolish now to reopen the past.

A tear dropped from Wayne's cheek as he examined the envelope's Selton address. The letter had been forwarded to him by his mother. He wondered if his Dad had ever told her anything before he died. James must have dismissed his suspicions, because he'd never confronted his son, even with his dying breath.

"Well?" Elaine nagged. "Are you going to open it?"

Wayne cleared his throat and stood, leaning forward to toss the letter into the fireplace. "No," he answered, watching flames lick the paper. "It's time to read the train book."

WE hope you have enjoyed this
KNIGHTSBRIDGE book.

WE love good books just as you do,
so you can be assured that the
KNIGHT ON THE HORSE
stands for good reading, every time.